PRAISE FOR THE NOVELS OF KARMA BROWN

"[A] meticulous study of unresolved guilt and buried secrets.... An admirably layered portrait of how love can bend and still not break, and how the pain of betrayal and lost innocence, once confronted, can slowly fade."

—*Publishers Weekly* on *In This Moment*

"Brown delivers an emotional punch in *The Choices We Make*. This is a good, old-fashioned tear-jerker of a book."

—*The Toronto Star*

"With effortless and beautiful writing, Karma Brown twists heartache and hope together in *The Choices We Make*, taking you on each character's complicated emotional journey and exploring how the worst-case scenario can still bring joy."

—Amy E. Reichert, author of *Luck, Love & Lemon Pie*

"A warmly compelling love story [and] deeply moving debut."

—*Booklist*

"[A] beautifully written story of love and loss... *Come Away with Me* had me smiling through my tears."

—Tracey Garvis Graves, *New York Times* bestselling author of *On the Island*

"Karma Brown is a talented new voice in women's fiction."

—Lori Nelson Spielman, bestselling author of *The Life List*

"Laughing one minute, then fiercely blinking back tears the next, we tore through this novel—so gripping that we were both excited and scared out of our minds to turn the page. Multilayered and completely consuming...[a] stunning page turner."

—Liz Fenton and Lisa Steinke, authors of *The Status of All Things*

"In *Come Away with Me*, one woman's journey through grief becomes the journey of a lifetime."

—Colleen Oakley, author of *Before I Go*

Also by Karma Brown

In This Moment
The Choices We Make
Come Away with Me

THE LIFE LUCY KNEW

KARMA BROWN

PARK
ROW
BOOKS

PARK
ROW
BOOKS

Recycling programs
for this product may
not exist in your area.

ISBN-13: 978-0-7783-1934-4

The Life Lucy Knew

For questions and comments about the quality of this book, please contact us at
CustomerService@Harlequin.com.

ParkRowBooks.com
BookClubbish.com

Printed in U.S.A.

For everyone who believes in true love but won't admit it because it sounds cheesy. And for Adam, who is always and forever the macaroni to my cheese.

THE
LIFE
LUCY
KNEW

"For in the end, it is all about memory, its sources and its magnitude, and, of course, its consequences."

—Elie Wiesel, *Night*

1

I have a complicated relationship with my memory.

Most of us, me included, believe our memories are fairly accurate. That events happened the way we remembered them, like a video camera capturing a scene: hit the play button and you'll see the same images, the same order of events, unfold before your eyes. The quality as good as it was the first time the scene was captured.

But apparently that isn't at all how it works.

Like the bike I got when I turned eight, with the rainbow handlebar tassels I'd been coveting, and the tinny bell I insisted on ringing incessantly as I set out on a ride. I remembered waking the morning of my birthday and seeing it at the end of my bed, shiny and begging for me to ride it. But when I later recounted this memory as an adult at a family dinner, my mom told me that while, yes, I did get such a bike for my birthday, it was never in my bedroom. "How would we have sneaked it in there? And how on earth would you have carried it down the stairs, Lucy?" my mom had said, laughing. "It was in the living room, half-hidden by that ficus. Remember that plant? It lived forever..."

Yet no matter how I tried to place that bike behind the mangy ficus tree my mom routinely propped up with bamboo sticks and that lived past when I left home, I could only ever see it at the foot of my bed. The giant yellow bow glittering with the morning light coming through my thin curtains, its white rubber tires pristine, the paint glossy and chip free, the handlebar streamers sparkling rainbows.

At some point my brain chose a different setting for my eighth birthday gift, and every time I had remembered that event since, it solidified the image to the point where I argued with my mom that night about the recollection. She must have remembered it wrong; her brain more aged than mine, her memory less elastic. But when Dad and my older sister, Alexis, reinforced Mom's version—my sister and I shared a room, so surely she would have remembered a clunky bike at the end of my bed—I was forced to admit I had gotten it wrong. And just like that I began to doubt myself, and the memory. How *did* I get the bike, nearly as big as I was, down the stairs? That would have been a major feat, like my mom had said. Soon enough I had to admit maybe the bike had never been where I remembered it, even if the memory felt as real to me as any other.

"Honest lying" is what the therapist I have been seeing, Dr. Amanda Kay, called it. The perfect oxymoron if I had ever heard one—how can it be "honest" if I am lying?

Apparently this re-creating of the past happens all the time, to everyone, Dr. Kay explained during our first visit. In fact, each time we recall something, we aren't actually remembering the original experience; we're remembering a memory of it. Our memories are fickle things, changing imperceptibly the very next time we recall them. They are not intact the way we imagine them to be but simply a construct of the real thing. Then a construct of the construct. And on and on it goes.

"It's like putting a new layer of wallpaper over an existing one," Dr. Kay had explained. "Multiple layers later, all you can see is the pink pastel roses on the top and not the blue and white stripes from a few years back, but the stripes are still there. Even if now you'd swear on your life that blue is actually purple, the white stripes gray. Our memory is not as reliable as we like to believe."

"So we're creating a knockoff version of an event and then remembering the knockoff as the real thing?"

"Precisely," Dr. Kay had replied. "There's no way to guarantee accuracy in our memories. Our brains pick and choose moments from our past and stitch them together to create something that suits us best at the time."

I'd stared at her, the reality of my situation settling into me like an unpleasant virus. "So how can we trust the things we remember, the way we remember them?" I had asked.

"Because generally they're close enough." She had smiled then, the way she would at moments like these in our future sessions when she knew I was close to shutting down. Moments when I felt like I might never again be sure which memories I could count on and which ones were lying to me. "For the most part we get the highlight reels right and the extraneous details aren't as important."

Except when you wake up in a hospital bed believing you're living a different life than the one you actually have, it tends to be the details that matter most.

Like I said, I have a complicated relationship with my memory.

2

I woke to find my coworker Matt Newman beside my hospital bed. Crying, which confused me immensely. *What are you doing here?* I wanted to ask him, but my lips were numb, my tongue thick. The room was bright and unfamiliar, and my body tired in a way I'd felt only once before when I caught a bad flu that had sent me to bed for nearly two weeks.

My parents were on the other side of the bed and, unlike Matt, weren't crying but had forced, too-big smiles on their faces. "Relax, take it easy, you're in the hospital, sweetie," Mom was saying, while Dad bobbed his head up and down, like he couldn't agree more with what she was saying.

"Hey. Hey there, Lucy," Matt said, holding my hand, his thumb rubbing my skin. "Welcome back. You're okay. You're okay." It was as though he was trying to convince himself more than anyone.

"Where am I?" My voice was rough, like I'd swallowed a roll of sandpaper. I tried to clear my throat, then sucked greedily at the drinking straw Mom brought to my lips. The cool water felt amazing as it went down.

"You're in the hospital, love. Mount Sinai," Mom said, glancing at Dad with a nervous look as she put the cup of water back on the nightstand. "But you're going to be fine."

Matt, now leaning over me, whispered again how glad he was I was okay. *Am I okay?* I wanted to ask, because I certainly didn't feel it. But before I could get the question out, Matt shifted even closer and kissed me on the lips. On the lips!

"What are you doing?" I croaked. I would have pulled back and away from him if I could have, but there was nowhere to go, and besides, I barely had the energy to keep my eyes open. I had meant, *Why are you kissing me?* But Matt seemed confused by my question, even though I felt it should have been obvious why I was asking. What was Matt Newman, my friend from work—my "work husband" as I had taken to calling him— doing kissing me on the lips?

"Did something happen at the office?" *Maybe I got hurt at work and Matt brought me to the hospital?* But that didn't explain his tears. Or the kiss. Oh, God…*maybe I'm dying.* I had never seen Matt so emotional before, so it had to be something pretty terrible even if I couldn't remember what had happened.

"No, sweetheart. Remember? You hit your head. But you're okay now. Just fine," Dad said, smiling and bobbing and smiling and bobbing.

I couldn't remember hitting my head. I put a hand to my scalp and felt around sloppily, my fingers not finding any obvious sign of injury. I looked from Matt to Dad to Mom, then scanned the small room, full of balloons (so many balloons) and bouquets of flowers, a row of greeting cards lining the windowsill.

"How long have I been here?" I asked, still feeling confused, like my brain had been removed and replaced with pillow stuffing. And even though I had barely moved, had done nothing more than lift my arm to my head, my heart thumped like I'd climbed fifteen flights of stairs. Sweat formed under my armpits and I recognized the feeling—my body was in survival mode— but still I struggled to assign context.

"A little while" was all Mom said, which I knew based on the singsong quality of her tone meant "quite a while." Something bad must have happened. And then, in a sudden flash, it occurred to me what—who—was missing.

Daniel. Where's Daniel?

"Were we in an accident?" Daniel drove faster than I liked and had a tendency to change lanes without signaling. Maybe it had been quite serious—the accident—and things were direr than they were letting on. Daniel might be hurt (or worse!) and they weren't telling me yet because of my own fragile condition. I let out a sob and tried to sit up, needing to get out of this bed to find him, but my body didn't respond the way I expected and I crumpled to my side.

Matt, still close by after the kiss, quickly put a firm hand underneath my shoulder blades as I lurched, the other hand a vise grip around my upper arm to prevent me from slipping from the bed. Sharp pains stabbed through my head, piercing holes into my thoughts. With a groan I leaned heavily into him and let him lower me back to the bed as Dad said, "There, there, Lucy. Stay put, love."

I was full-on sobbing now, my vision blurry with tears. "Please tell me. What happened?"

"There was no accident, Lucy," Mom said, pulling a tissue out of the cuff of her sweater and dabbing at my eyes. Brushing my hair away from my face with gentle hands. "I promise you. A slip on some sidewalk ice. You hit your head when you fell."

"So he's okay," I choked out, closing my eyes as a burst of relief filled me.

"Who's okay?" Matt asked, sounding nearly as confused as I felt.

"Daniel," I managed, keeping my eyes closed to avoid the swaying of the room. I must have hit my head hard. "He's not hurt, right?"

The room went silent. Long enough that I forced my eyes open to see what was happening. Dad's smile faltered as he glanced at Matt, who had taken a couple of steps back from the bed and looked ill. Shocked, his face drained of color.

"Who, honey?" Mom asked as she stood over me, her hands still smoothing my hair, wiping at the corners of my eyes. Smiling, though her lips quivered slightly.

A flash of irritation moved through me. I was tired and having to repeat myself was hard work. Why couldn't she answer the question? "Daniel, Mom. My husband. Where is he?" My tone was harsh and my mom recoiled slightly. I should have felt bad about that, but my bewilderment whitewashed everything else.

Her mouth opened and closed and she looked at Dad, whose smile had now been replaced by a frown. My heart started thumping again. *Fight or flight.*

"Where's Daniel?" Now I shouted it. Everyone seemed shocked, especially Matt, who looked like I'd slapped him across the face with my words.

"I d–don't… Lucy, what do you…" Mom stammered.

Dad's fingers came up to pinch his lips as he watched me with worried eyes.

"Excuse me," Matt said, then bolted from the room. I heard the sounds of someone being sick outside my door.

"Is Matt okay?" I asked, momentarily distracted as I craned my head to the side to look through the open doorway and into the hall. But I couldn't see Matt and the movement made my head feel as though it was being drilled into. Mom kissed my forehead and said, "Shh, shh, shh."

Dad's too-big smile was back on as he stood behind her. "I'll go check on him," he said, walking quickly out of the room.

"Mom, what the hell is going on? Where is Daniel?" Why wasn't he the one here in my hospital room, kissing me on the lips and telling me everything was going to be okay?

"We can talk about that later," Mom said, shushing me some more. *Later? Why not now?* But before I could get another question out—my mind moving too slowly, like pushing molasses through a fine sieve on a cold winter's day—a nurse came in. Mom shifted out of the way, crossed her arms over her chest and said, "She's fairly, uh, confused right now." She sounded panicky, but my mother wasn't prone to panic and that was when I started to think I might be in real trouble here.

Thump. Thump. Thump. Thump. It was as though my body knew the truth but the connection to my mind was broken. I was missing something but had no idea what it was or how to figure it out.

"Oh, that's to be expected," the nurse replied, wrapping a blood pressure cuff around my upper arm and smiling at me. The cuff felt tight and her hands cold. My insides were jittery and I was shaking, hard. "Are you cold, Lucy?" she asked, her voice quite loud. The way you talk to a toddler, or a senior citizen with a hearing aid.

"Yes," I replied, teeth chattering to prove it.

"I'll get you a warm blanket in a minute." She glanced at Mom, now seated with furrowed brow in the plastic chair by the bed. "Why don't you go get something from the cafeteria, Mrs. Sparks? I've got a few things to do here, so Lucy won't be alone."

Mom pressed her lips together, seemed to hesitate but then nodded. "I could use a cup of tea," she said. Then she stood and bent over me, resting a hand on my cheek. "I'll be back in a jiffy and Dad's right outside."

Once Mom left, I focused on the nurse. "Has my husband been here?" She was reading the blood pressure monitor and her eyes briefly flicked to mine before going back to the monitor.

"I'm not sure, hon. Try to relax, okay? Your pressure's a bit high. Deep breath. There you go."

Relax? How could I relax when no one would tell me where Daniel was?

"I'm not feeling very well," I said, my words clipped because of my chattering teeth. Anxiety crested through my body in waves and my heart continued its wild thumping.

"You keep taking deep breaths. Can you do that for me?" The nurse smiled again—wholly relaxed—then walked over to the whiteboard on the wall and wrote a few notations. It was then I saw my name at the top of the board. *Lucy Sparks.*

Sparks? It had been over a year since I was Lucy Sparks… "Do you know where my rings are?" My finger was bare and my hand looked lonely without them.

The nurse moved back over to the bed to retrieve the blood pressure cart and her Easter-egg-purple scrubs filled my vision. "Everything you had on when they brought you in was given to your mom and dad." She pulled up the sheet and smoothed it down on one side. "Okay, hon, let me grab you that warm blanket and—"

"Please," I whispered, clutching at her arm with desperate fingers and pulling her toward me. My breathing wasn't right—too quick, unfortunately timed to my racing heart. I tried to infuse as much urgency into my tone as I could despite the breathlessness. "Please. I need to know where my husband is."

"I'm sorry, Lucy." She put her cool hand over mine, shook her head and gave me a sympathetic look. "I don't know anything about your husband."

3

I was indignant when they first told me the truth about Matt.

"That's impossible," I said, because it was. I was married, and married women didn't have boyfriends. So Matt Newman could not be who they said he was.

"It's the truth," Alex said without preamble. I'd stared at her and she repeated herself.

This first foray into my new normal happened the day after I'd woken up. A day after those very confusing moments when I tried to piece together why Matt was crying by my bedside instead of Daniel. Why the whiteboard in my room and my hospital bracelet read *Lucy Sparks*, my maiden name. Why no one seemed to know where Daniel London—my husband—was. Or understand why I was asking about him.

"Stop it, Alex," I said, waiting for her to admit she was messing with me, which was certainly offside considering the situation but not out of the realm of normal for our sisterly relationship. "Why are you lying to me? And where are my rings? Mom, please give them back. The nurse said you have them."

"There are no rings, love." Mom's voice was barely a whisper. She'd done some crying before she came back into my room, telltale red splotches under her eyes and on her neck that hadn't yet had time to fade. "There are no rings." My dad stood quietly beside my mom, nodding and solemn.

Alex said it again, stone-faced, the bravest of the bunch. "Daniel is not your husband, and Matt *is* your boyfriend, Luce. You've been living together for two years, in a condo in Leslieville—which I think you pay way too much rent for, PS."

"This is crazy." I lay back against my pillow. My breathing was erratic, my heart pounding hard enough an alarm beeped on the monitor attached to me. Everyone looked at the screen, then back at me with concern. "How can I be with Matt? I'm married. To Daniel." If I kept saying it, maybe it would turn out to be true.

The plastic bracelet itched my skin, and I tugged at it with my other hand. Seeing the name *Sparks* so clearly typed across it made me nauseated. I had to be dreaming. But when I pinched the skin on my wrist—hard—it hurt and felt all too real. "Daniel is my husband. We got married a year ago! You were all there."

"No, honey. We weren't." Mom grabbed my shaking hand and squeezed softly. "You have never been married. To Daniel, or anyone."

And then I'd lost my breath—it left me in a long wheeze and I had a hard time getting it back, even with the nasal cannula streaming pure oxygen up my nose. This wasn't a joke, or a dream. They were not lying to me.

Later my parents brought proof. Photo albums with pictures of Matt and me together—wearing matching ugly Christmas sweaters for my best friend Jenny's annual holiday party; on a boat in Mexico during some beach vacation, head to toe in scuba gear; holding up plastic cups of beer at a hockey game.

But Matt can't be my boyfriend, I'd whispered again. And then once more in case I was too quiet the first time. Matt and I worked at Jameson Porter, a Toronto-based consulting company with impressive clients and a better-than-most corporate culture. It was full of young, highly motivated types looking to climb ladders quickly, and I'd been there for nearly four years. Matt was a business consultant, while I worked in communications, as the director managing the firm's many press releases, industry reports and memos. We often grabbed lunch when Matt wasn't traveling and joined our coworkers frequently for after-hours drinks at nearby watering holes.

"That's the Matt I remember." I squeezed my eyes shut and clutched the photo album to my chest. It made me feel sick to look at the pictures.

"Well, that Matt? Your work friend Matt? He's also *your* Matt," Alex said.

"But…but what about Daniel?" A crushing sense of loss crashed into me. "What happened with Daniel?"

And why could I remember him sliding a wedding band over my finger? Dancing to Harry Connick Jr.'s "Recipe for Love" for our first song as husband and wife. His hand on mine as we cut into our wedding cake—vanilla with lemon curd. What about the memory of him tripping, and us collapsing in a fit of laughter, as he attempted to carry me over the threshold of our Leslieville condo? How did I have all these memories of us together when apparently none of them had ever happened?

No one could explain it. They weren't even sure where to start, except to acknowledge that obviously something was very (very) wrong inside my head.

"Honey, you and Daniel were engaged. But then you broke it off, oh, about four years ago now," Mom said. "Is that right, Hugh?" Dad confirmed it was. Alex nodded. They looked as distraught to be giving me this history lesson of my life as I was to be receiving it.

"Four years ago?" They all nodded again.

Defeated, I pressed my fingers to my eyes to try to stop the tears. I'd never been more scared, and even with my family gathered tightly around me, I'd also never felt more alone.

"It's called 'confabulated memory disorder,'" my neurologist, Dr. Alvin Mulder, said, his white-coated arms crossed over my chart, which he held tight against his body like a shield. "It's not uncommon in head injury cases."

Does "not uncommon" mean "somewhat common"? I wondered as I took in his words. *Or does it mean "rather unusual, but not exactly rare"?* Not that it mattered. The answer wouldn't change anything, couldn't fix anything.

After I had asked where Daniel was, causing Matt to throw up with shock and Mom and Dad to insist on more tests, everyone realized things weren't quite right with my memory. Obviously. But it wasn't only amnesia we were dealing with; it was something altogether scarier. Dr. Mulder confirmed while my physical injury had mostly healed, it appeared there were some "deficits." *And these deficits may be long-term,* he added, which caused Mom to slap a hand to her chest, her mouth open in a perfectly round circle. "How long-term is long-term?" she asked.

"Well, permanent might be a better way to think about it," Dr. Mulder said, and I felt a jolt inside me.

"Permanent?" Mom echoed, her hand now on her neck, her fingers rubbing the skin there with apprehension. "I see."

I didn't see at all. All I had done was hit my head on some ice. And now I might be stuck with this mismatched memory permanently?

"I prefer the term *false memories* to *confabulations*," Dr. Theodore Talcott, the hospital psychiatrist on my case, said. I glanced at him, careful not to turn my head too fast and set off a pounding headache, and he gave me a kind smile behind a trim, graying beard. "Your brain wasn't creating new memories when you were in the coma and our brains don't care for empty spaces, so it filled in the blanks."

He tucked his hands into his pockets, rocked back on his heels, now made eye contact with my parents. "And sometimes, like in Lucy's case, these gaps in the memory get filled with a combination of new and old information—which is why some of what you're remembering is accurate, while other things are not."

"Like her marriage," Mom said, still working away at the skin on her neck, now red and angry looking. "Dr. Talcott, you should know she's still having a very hard time believing it isn't real."

"Mom, *please*." I hated that she brought it up with the doctors again, even though it was clinically relevant. That she was talking to them as though I wasn't in the room, like grown-ups discussing their child's invisible friend in her presence. Voices a little too upbeat and encouraging, yet laced with trepidation.

"Please, call me Ted," Dr. Talcott said. My mom nodded, though I knew she would do no such thing because this was a case when formality mattered. "Ted" would most certainly not have the answers we needed, but "Dr. Talcott" just might.

"The thing with false memories that is so fascinating—so fascinating—is how real they seem to the patient experiencing them," Dr. Talcott continued, excitement filling his voice. He'd admitted to us earlier I was only his second false-memory patient—the first an elderly man who'd had a stroke and woken up believing he had won an Olympic gold medal in pole-vaulting at the 1948 London games. However, according to this man's wife, while he had been a pole-vaulter that year, he had failed to qualify for the Olympic team. "False-memory patients can recount incredibly detailed descriptions of the event they've invented. It's fascinating."

Mom scowled at his mention of this being "fascinating" three times in one breath. Because to us this was anything but—it was terrifying. *Devastating*, even. Especially when the doctors said they had no way of knowing if the hidden memories would reveal themselves, and if these false ones would eventually disappear when my brain reset.

"So what can we do?" Dad asked. "About these false memories? Is there some sort of treatment? Or medication? Whatever she needs." He rested a hand on my shoulder. "Anything she needs."

Dr. Mulder shrugged his shoulders, my chart still stuck to his chest. "Brain injuries aren't like broken bones. They don't heal with predictable patterns, and unfortunately there's little medically we can do." Dad smiled at me and rubbed my shoulder. I didn't smile back.

"Based on how things look right now, there's a good chance you'll have some postconcussive symptoms, like headaches and mild dizziness, and those we can treat with medication. Though we expect those symptoms will alleviate with time," Dr. Mulder said. "But as for the confabulation—as I said, there's no magic pill, so to speak. Which is why Dr. Talcott is here. This condition is better treated with psychotherapy."

"So, therapy is the answer here?" Dad asked.

"Yes," Dr. Mulder replied.

Therapist Ted nodded, adding, "There's great evidence therapy can help patients in these cases. But it's a long process. As you can imagine, trying to reintegrate into a life that isn't familiar can be a challenge." He leaned on the rail at the end of the bed, and I noticed a wedding band on his finger. Shiny. I wondered if he was recently married, which made me think about Daniel. And Matt. I blinked hard and swallowed against the nausea that accompanied my pounding head. "However, the sooner you're able to get back to your life, your routines, Lucy, the better."

I didn't want to do therapy, nor was I interested in this "long process." I wanted to see Daniel, to have him comfort me and tell me everything was going to be okay. I wanted to apologize for missing our first wedding anniversary. And I desperately wanted—needed—everyone to stop looking at me like they expected more, like I was letting them down with every screwed-up memory I recounted.

But most of all I wanted to remember. To know the truth the way everyone else in my life seemed to. It was so easy for them to correct me, to gently explain the memories that felt so real were not, in fact, real at all. It was simple for them to be hopeful, because they weren't inside my head where things were a jumbled mess.

If only getting things back to normal was as easy as going to a lost-and-found box, like we'd had in elementary school. A spot I could retrieve my memories like I might have a misplaced hat, or pair of sneakers, or my favorite pencil case. But it wasn't going to be that easy, because according to the only two people in the room who had experience with this sort of thing, what had been lost might never be found.

4

One week later I was finally out of the hospital and desperate to get home. My parents had wanted me to stay with them initially, but I had balked at the idea, imagining the sort of hovering they would do if I moved back into my old bedroom. But even Therapist Ted had thought that sounded like a wise idea.

"This next while may feel like you're speeding down a highway without the safety of your seat belt," he'd said during his last visit as I was getting ready to be discharged. "Being in a familiar place, with the people you remember best, is likely a good transition strategy."

"Our place *will be* familiar," Matt had interjected before I could respond. But even with his confident (if not a bit hostile) tone, he looked worried as he said it. And fair enough. My memory was fuzzy, to put it mildly. There was a lot I didn't remember and we were all on edge because of it.

Eventually my parents conceded, though they insisted on staying in our guest room for a while—at least until they were satisfied I wasn't going to fall apart without them.

I do know this place, I thought with relief as we approached the front steps to the low-rise brick building in Leslieville, a short distance from Toronto's downtown core. I could picture the buzzer pad that opened the front door, had no issue recalling the code. Once I walked into the building, I knew I had to go up a set of stairs, and then one more before reaching 2B, where I lived. When tested in the hospital on the wheres and whats of my current life, I had remembered the apartment and its location without trouble, had correctly described the high ceilings and exposed brick and great windows facing east so you could see the sun rise. But what I still didn't remember? That Matt and I had lived in this place, together, for the past two years.

Climbing the last flight of stairs, my dad stayed close behind me, holding my elbow, his other hand pressed firmly to my lower back. As I unlocked my condo's front door and walked through, my hand shaking with anticipation, I turned instinctually to drop my key into the silver dish on the hallway console. It was a small win, but an important one. I knew where I lived and where my key went, so I must belong here.

"Dad, I'm okay," I said, because he still had his hand on my back. I was embarrassed by all the attention, like I was a kid again versus a twenty-eight-year-old who hadn't needed her dad to help her do anything for more than a decade.

Still, I understood why my parents fussed. Why Matt's eyes continued to dart my way, like he was waiting for me to collapse, or to break into a million pieces right there on our hardwood floor. Be forced to admit I'd forgotten yet another critical truth about my life.

"Of course you are, honey," my dad responded, rubbing my back in tight little circles. I glanced over my shoulder at him and smiled, hoping it would help him relax. Mom busied herself with taking our coats and hanging them in our front closet, then announced she was going to put the kettle on. My mother felt a good cup of tea was the answer to nearly every situation, even this one.

"Here, let me take that for you," Matt said, his face pinched and full of hurt I knew I was responsible for. He reached for my overnight bag, looking so tired—dark circles under his eyes, his lips dry and cracking when he tried to smile. I didn't know *this*

Matt, who stood in front of me in jeans and a sweatshirt, unlike the tailored suits I usually saw him in. The Matt Newman I had worked with for the past few years, who always seemed well rested, confident and ready to tackle whatever problem was thrown his way, was not *this* Matt Newman, who needed a haircut, looked like he might cry at any moment. Too thin for his frame, his jeans a bit baggy on his hips, like he hadn't eaten a proper meal in weeks.

"Thanks," I said, letting him take the bag I had insisted on carrying myself ("there's nothing wrong with my arms"). I threw him a quick smile before he turned to walk into the bedroom. Though staying with my parents didn't seem the right option, I hadn't properly thought through what it would be like to come back here with Matt and the heavy weight of expectation.

As a result I was nervous around him, unsure about how to act and what to say and, quite specifically, where to sleep. My memory and my reality were at odds, in a battle it wasn't yet clear could be won. Because despite the proclamations from my family and Matt—along with the undeniable photographic evidence on the walls, the "his and hers" sides of the closet, the clues sprinkled throughout the condo—that this was *our* place, my memory still told a different story.

And while I did remember I was in a relationship, that I was in love, I didn't remember it being with Matt.

5

When I came out of the bedroom the next morning, Matt was already up. He sat on the couch reading a book, pillows and blankets folded beside him. I set the photo albums I'd taken to bed with me on the coffee table and gave Matt yet another forced smile. I had been doing that a lot in the past twenty-four hours.

My initial relief at remembering the condo had quickly given way to a series of awkward moments with Matt, culminating in a bizarre good-night incident when I went to bed. He had leaned in to give me a kiss on the cheek and I'd tried to give him a hug at the same time, which resulted in him kissing my nostril and us squishing uncomfortably into one another. We'd laughed, but it did little to cover how out of sync things were.

"Morning." He smiled back, still looking as tired as he had the night before. "How did you sleep?"

"Pretty well," I said, though the last time I'd glanced at the alarm clock it was after three in the morning.

"Glad to hear it." He set the book down on his lap and I glanced guiltily at the stack of blankets beside him. While I couldn't imagine sharing a bed with Matt, I suspected he couldn't imagine not sharing one with me.

When I first lay down on our bed, I chose the left side. For one, that was where I always slept, and two, there was a small stack of folded T-shirts near the pillow on the right side. Then my head hit the pillow and the scent of Matt (a soap and citrus smell that was distinctly *him*) wafted into my nose. It took me a few minutes to realize I was on his pillow, on his side of the bed. *But…but…*the left side of the bed was mine, the right Daniel's! However, it seemed Matt and I had the opposite arrangement, and I cried as I switched the pillows, though I stayed on the left side.

"I put the T-shirts you left out in the dresser. Hope that's okay." Being up half the night meant I had time to not only put Matt's shirts away but also reorganize my clothes in the other half of the dresser. I also learned Matt rolled his socks and boxers, and kept his side of the closet much tidier than mine. "I didn't want them to get wrinkled."

That was an excuse—the T-shirts had zero wrinkle risk, the cotton so soft it seemed a crease would never be able to hold its shape. No, I had put the shirts away because they reminded me of the boyfriend I couldn't remember who was sleeping on the couch right outside the bedroom door. *Out of sight, out of mind.*

Matt gave me a look I had a hard time deciphering. "Sorry. I probably should have left them. I thought—" I began.

He waved away the apology. "Totally fine. I, um… Actually, I had left them out for you." He dog-eared the novel in his hands—folding over the bottom corner of the page—and smiled, but it did little to hide his pained expression. His fingers strummed the book's cover in a relentless rhythm as he seemed to struggle with what to say next, finally shrugging before landing on, "You like to sleep in my T-shirts."

"Oh." A blush crept up my neck as I imagined Matt carefully choosing the shirts in anticipation of my homecoming, placing them just so on *my* side of the bed.

"It's nothing. Don't worry about it." Matt smiled again, more convincingly this time, and stretched his arms high over his head. His T-shirt rose above his belly button, showcasing a toned stomach, and I averted my eyes. How could I explain it felt like cheating, being here with Matt, glancing at his bare stomach this early in the morning? None of this made any sense. A wave of vertigo hit me and I held tightly on to the back of a chair, hoping Matt wouldn't notice. *Why did I think this was a good idea, coming back here?* I should have stayed with my parents.

"I turned the coffee on. Want a cup?" he asked, after what felt like an impossibly long and uncomfortable silence.

"Yes, definitely. But I can get it."

"No, no, you sit." He stood quickly, still in nursemaid mode, and I told him to relax.

"It's just coffee, Matt. I've got it."

"You're sure? Okay, thanks." He settled back onto the couch, turning on the television as though to prove everything was *just fine*. This was a perfectly normal morning for us.

I was relieved to find the mugs, as I remembered, lined up on one of the kitchen shelves. The faint sound of a newscaster's voice made its way into our galley kitchen, even though Matt kept the volume low so as not to wake my parents. Matt was thoughtful. That I remembered well.

I glanced at the calendar tacked on the fridge while the coffee finished brewing. It was March already—it was still shocking to think I'd spent nearly all of February in a coma. So much time lost. Scanning the days, I saw Matt had a dentist appointment in two weeks and there was a thirtieth birthday party for someone named Jake (*Jake from work?*) at the end of the month. The rest of the days were blank, except for every Monday and Friday where someone—Matt, I assumed—had written in *Lucy: Dr. Kay*. Dr. Amanda Kay was the outpatient psychologist who was going to help me deal with the side effects of my head injury, with my "new normal." I flipped ahead a few months, saw the many standing appointments and sighed wearily.

The coffeemaker beeped and I poured the hot liquid into the mugs, adding cream and a half teaspoon of sugar to both. It was only as I walked back into the living room that it occurred to me I wasn't sure how Matt took his coffee.

Paralyzed by this realization, I stood still, the mugs clutched in my hands. I must have made Matt plenty of morning coffees over the past two years. But my memory failed to kick in, and when Matt shifted his gaze from the television to my statue-still stance, I gave up and asked, "How do you take your coffee?"

The wince was nearly imperceptible, but I caught it. "However you made it is fine," he said. His eyes locked on mine as if hoping to convey this was the truth. But while I understood what he was trying to do, should have been grateful for it, the gesture made me angry.

"No, it isn't *fine*," I snapped. "Please tell me."

He paused. "Black."

I stared into the coffees, both of which were beige thanks to the pour of cream. "Right." I turned back toward the kitchen and he was up a second later and following me.

"Honestly, I'm fine with however you made it. Lucy, wait." He took the mugs with cream and sugar out of my hands and set them on the countertop. "It's okay," he said softly, pulling me to his chest. "This is all part of it. It's okay."

It should have been comforting, but our closeness felt unnatural. Matt was much taller than me (taller than Daniel) and we didn't fit together easily. I wondered where I used to put my head when he hugged me—against his sternum, maybe? Because that was about where my cheek rested now. With Daniel it was between his neck and shoulder, right under his chin. "Don't be upset," Matt said again.

"I'm not upset." I pressed my face into the soft fabric of his shirt, overcome by the hints of lemon and cedar and the warmth of him as I tried, unsuccessfully, to hide my crying. I didn't remember being so emotional before my accident, but this head injury had left me with unruly and unpredictable mood swings. The doctors told me the moodiness would probably get better, but it might not, too. That had been their answer to everything. *Your memory might resolve…or it might not. Your headaches will likely improve…but there's a chance they won't. Your brain is astonishing, will rewire as needed…but you may be left with a few holes, perhaps long-term.* No one wanted to promise anything, which meant I also couldn't count on anything. I was stuck waiting to see what happened along with everyone else.

I pulled back, stared into the face that was so familiar and yet not at all in this context. "I need to know these things, Matt. If I'm going to… I need to know—" I took a deep breath. "The truth. Even about how you take your coffee. It matters, okay?"

"Okay, Lucy." He ran a thumb under my eyes before lifting the thin fabric of his shirt with his hand and using it to gently dry my cheeks. I was pretty sure he wanted to kiss me, his gaze lingering on my lips. My heart beat fast and the vertigo was back, making my socked feet unsteady under me, as though I was standing on a floating dock. *Do I…want him to kiss me?*

"You all right?" he asked, holding me tightly.

"Yes." I wasn't, and we both knew it, but he accepted this without argument. A moment later we separated, though I wasn't sure who took a step back first. We leaned against the countertop, side by side, and Matt reached over for our coffees, handing me mine.

He grimaced after he swallowed his first sip, then laughed. "This is terrible." I laughed, too, glad for the distraction.

"Here, let's start over." I took his mug and set it into the sink, pouring him a new coffee.

He smiled as he took it, leaning back again, though he didn't drink it right away. *He did say black, right?* As I was about to clarify, he asked, "Did Daniel take his coffee with cream and sugar?"

Does, I almost said. But I swallowed the word back. *Lie*, I thought. *Say you don't know, can't remember how Daniel takes his coffee, or anything else about your life with him. Don't hurt Matt more than he's already been hurt.*

But I didn't want to lie about something I knew for sure; because that list was shorter than the list of things I didn't know.

I turned to look at him, but his eyes stayed downcast. "Yes."

He nodded, staring straight ahead. "I need to go in for a meeting, so I'm going to shower," he said, pushing off the counter's edge. "Thanks again for this." Matt held up the mug, but then rather than taking it with him, he set it in the sink, untouched beside the first mug.

"Sure," I murmured a few seconds later, too late because he'd already left the room. I stayed in the kitchen because I wasn't sure where else to go, thinking about Daniel and missing him enough there was a physical ache in my chest. I wondered where he was this morning—drinking his coffee with cream and sugar, completely unaware I believed he was my husband.

6

"Where's Matt?" Mom asked as she emerged from the guest room, fastening one earring and then the other. She had a Ziploc of tea bags tucked under her arm.

"Getting ready for work." I busied myself with stirring more sugar into a second cup of coffee, nodded toward the Ziploc bag now in her hands. "I have tea, you know." But then I stopped stirring. *Did I have tea?* I had no idea actually.

"Oh, it's fine. This is always in my purse," she said. "How are you this morning, Lucy love?"

"Good. Better." *Except I made coffee the way Daniel takes it and I forgot I liked sleeping in Matt's T-shirts and there's no way I'm fooling anyone, especially myself.*

"Good!" Mom handed me the tea and took two bobby pins out of her pocket, putting them in her mouth and pulling and twisting a front section of her long, silver-blond hair before fastening it with the pins. "Dad has a meeting with the Realtor this morning, so it's you and me, kiddo. I thought we could have a girls' day."

"A Realtor?" I asked, my voice ratcheting up. "Why? Are you and dad selling the house?" While I hadn't lived at home in nearly a decade, that house safely held my history and the thought of them selling it made me anxious.

Mom waved her hand around, her bangle bracelets jangling. "Of course not," she said. "Just keeping our options open. So, what do you think about meeting Alexis for a late lunch?"

"Sure. Maybe," I replied, though my plan was to stay put here at home until my memory fixed itself. "I'm a bit tired, though."

Concern flitted across her face and she frowned. "Of course you are, sweetie. This has been quite a…um, *transition*."

Dad came out of the bedroom, fastening the Rolex watch he wore daily that Mom had gifted him for his fiftieth birthday. Now nearing sixty, Dad looked a decade younger and still taught political science at the University of Toronto. He hated being asked when he planned to retire, like many of my parents' friends had, because he claimed to have no intention of ever quitting teaching. "Those kids keep me young," he would say, referring to his university students. "Retiring is the fast track to the grave."

"I'm going to spend the day at the house," he said to Mom and me. "Fix that leaky faucet in the master bathroom and touch up the paint in the front hall before tonight's class." *Those certainly sounded like tasks one did to get a house ready to sell…*

"Good. Yes," Mom said. "I'll stay here with Lucy."

"You don't have to, Mom. Stop fretting, okay? You're wrinkling with all that frowning."

Mom ran her fingers across her forehead as if trying to smooth the worry away, then smiled and patted my cheek. "Sweetheart, I am your mother and it's my job to worry. And these things?" She pressed a finger to the space between her eyebrows and rubbed vigorously. "These are my well-earned love lines."

"Barbara, have you eaten anything yet?" Dad asked, glancing at Mom's insulin pump monitor clipped to the front of her leggings.

"I'm fine, Hugh," Mom replied, annoyance coloring her tone. Dad held up a hand in surrender and I caught his eye, both of us thinking Mom's blood sugar was probably low. She got snappy when it dropped.

But Mom recovered quickly, her smile bright and irritation seemingly gone as she took the tea back from me. "I'm going to put the kettle on and call Alexis, find out about lunch. Sound good?"

"Maybe breakfast first, Mom?"

"Oh, not you, too," she muttered good-naturedly. "Fine. Breakfast. I'll make my famous pancakes and bacon." Then she saw the look on my face, which was probably a confusing mix of longing and disgust. "Oh, right, you're not eating bacon."

Along with the strangeness of forgetting Matt my boyfriend and remembering Daniel my husband, I also woke from the coma believing I was a vegetarian, among other small and apparently out-of-character changes. So even though bacon sounded appealing, a louder voice inside my head shouted I did not eat animals. Even ones disguised as delicious, crispy breakfast food.

"Okay, how about oatmeal? Does Matt like steel-cut?"

Another thing I had no idea about. I shrugged, feeling all at once useless like I had earlier with the coffee fiasco.

"I'm sure he does," she said, her tone soothing. "Back in a jiffy."

I sat beside Dad on the couch and he set a hand on my knee, patting it a couple of times. "So how are you feeling this morning, kiddo?" His graying, bushy eyebrows rose with the question. The skin on his arms seemed darker than normal, especially for the time of year. He and Mom weren't the snowbird types—they liked the cold, and Dad often said shoveling kept his core and arms as strong as when he was thirty years younger.

"Good. Better." My now-standard response. I gestured to his arms, bared from the biceps down because of his short-sleeved golf shirt. "Hey, why are you so tanned?"

He looked at his arms, holding them out. "Am I?"

"Your arms are for sure," I said. "Were you guys away somewhere?"

"No," he replied. "Lots of walking outside lately. Plenty of good vitamin D sunshine this winter."

I nodded and was about to ask the obvious—how one's arms got tanned in minus-twenty-degree weather when coats were a requirement—when a pot clanged loudly from the kitchen, followed by a long string of curse words. "Mom okay today?"

"She's fine," he said. "You know how she gets when her sugar drops." But then he looked pained, realizing his blunder.

"I know," I said, nudging him with my shoulder. "I remember, Dad."

He smiled, relieved. "She'll be better after that oatmeal."

"So, Mom says you're meeting a Realtor this morning. What about?"

He opened his mouth, then closed it and shook his head. "Nothing for you to worry about, pumpkin."

Telling someone not to worry about something was a great way to ensure she would do just that. "Dad, what's going on?"

"Your mother and I are considering a few changes."

"What sort of changes?" I asked.

Dad patted at my knee again. "There's a house a few streets over your mother has had her eye on. So we thought we'd see what we could get for our place. The market is excellent right now. Quite excellent."

"That's it? You might move a few streets over? Why don't you repaint the house or update the kitchen instead?"

Dad slapped his palms against his thighs as he stood. "All good ideas, sweet pea," he replied. "I'd best get going. Tell your mom I'll call her after the meeting." He leaned over to kiss my cheek, told me not to bother getting up.

"Go easy on yourself and remember what the doctor said. This is going to be a long process. Rome wasn't built in a day."

"I know." I smiled at the pithy remark he was so fond of. "I'll take it easy. Promise."

As he left and the front door clicked shut behind him, I felt a vibration from inside my sweatshirt pocket. Thanks to the lingering effects from the concussion, I was supposed to be "screen free" but had so far been noncompliant. Like many in my generation, living without my phone felt akin to going through life blindfolded.

The vibration signaled a text from my sister: all caps and begging me to take away our mother's phone. Obviously Mom had called Alex about lunch, my sister picking up only because she thought it might be about me, and was now holding her hostage with rambling chitchat. Our mother was not good at taking cues someone wanted off the phone.

One might think Mom and Alexis would get along brilliantly, both of them free-spirited and artistically minded—Mom had been a high school art teacher, who now dabbled with acrylic classes out of her home studio. But there had been plenty of explosive arguments between them over the years, the similarities not enough to dispel the oil and water quality of their relationship. I quickly texted Alex back, Be nice, and then clicked through to my email.

A few Welcome home! Hope you're doing great. We miss you! emails from my team at Jameson Porter, and one from Brooke Ingram, my second in command and closest work friend (outside of Matt). She had sent me a card in the hospital that read "At least it's not syphilis. Get well soon," which had made me laugh hard enough to cry and told you everything you needed to know about Brooke. Today's email was a running checklist of outstanding communications projects, which I'd asked her to send daily to keep me in the loop for when I went back to work.

Of course, like everyone outside of the doctors, my family, Matt and my best friend, Jenny, Brooke didn't know about my memory lapses. Matt and I had agreed to keep it quiet, hoping things might reset themselves soon and it would be a nonissue.

Knowing I probably had only minutes until the oatmeal was ready and Mom—or Matt—busted me for being on my phone, I clicked on the Facebook icon. Twenty-six unread messages. I didn't have time to deal with the messages or my bloated timeline, nor was I interested to see all those picture-perfect posts when my life felt like anything but.

Taking a deep breath, I glanced nervously toward the kitchen and then the bedroom before typing into the search box. I had almost done this a dozen times already but had so far held back because I knew it wouldn't help things. But today...well, the urge was too strong to ignore this time.

A handful of names filled my screen, and I scanned the first few until I saw him. *Daniel London.*

The picture was tiny, but I recognized him immediately. My finger hovered over the "add friend" button, but then the bedroom door opened and I jumped, my phone dropping between the couch cushions. I scrambled to pick it up again, quickly closing Daniel's Facebook page, which illuminated my screen.

"Everything okay?" Matt asked. *Black.* The thought popped into my mind. *Matt takes his coffee black. Try to remember.*

"Yes, yes," I replied, feeling as though I had Mexican jumping beans inside my belly. "Alex texted. Mom's making us oatmeal. Steel-cut."

"Sorry I have to leave. I love oatmeal," he said as he tightened his tie. I had the urge to write these things down: *black coffee, likes oatmeal.* "Going to say bye to your mom."

"Matt?" I rose quickly onto my knees and grasped the back of the couch with both hands so I was facing him. He was only a foot away and close enough I could touch him if I wanted to.

"Yeah?"

Looking into his face, which carried the hope that I might say something revolutionary (like, *I remember you now! I remember us!*), I had the feeling he wanted to reach for me but wasn't going to, because he wasn't sure what I wanted.

I paused, regretting the urgency with which I had said his name. I was quite aware anything I said now would be insufficient, but I pressed on regardless. "Thanks for sleeping here. On the couch, I mean. Last night." It was anticlimactic, and Matt was unsurprisingly deflated by my words.

"No problem," he finally said before heading into the kitchen. I watched him go, then sank back down onto the couch.

No problem. I wished it were that simple.

7

"You look better," Jenny said. She held up a white plastic bag, heavy with take-out food containers. "Lunch, as promised."

The smell of whatever was in the bag wafted past me, and my stomach grumbled. I pulled her inside and set the bag on the kitchen table. "You're a lifesaver."

Feigning a last-minute headache relieved me of lunch with Mom and Alex, but the second I was alone I wished everyone would come back. It was too quiet and the silence meant I could ruminate on my situation without interruption. Thank goodness for Jenny and her bossy insistence she was coming over whether I wanted her to or not.

"What silverware do we need?" I asked.

"Way ahead of you." Jenny opened her purse and pulled out two sets, rolled tightly in napkins. "I got you the chili. *Beef* chili."

"Thanks." I sighed. "I know I'm not actually a vegetarian, but I feel like I'm *supposed* to be."

Jenny reached across the table to rub my arm before unrolling our silverware and flattening out the napkins.

"It was that documentary on Netflix, or that's how I remember it. About how carnivores are ruining the planet. What's it called?" I snapped my fingers, trying to bring the name to mind. "Something about knives…"

"Forks Over Knives," Jenny said, prying the lid off her take-out container and stirring the golden orange soup.

"Yeah, *Forks Over Knives*. I can still picture all those tortured animals—God, even the chickens made me sad—but still, I want to eat meat." I cringed, slapped a hand to my forehead.

"Look," Jenny said, licking a drip of her soup from her thumb, "you're a good and kind person who loves animals, even chickens, and it's *okay* that you still want to eat them. You're just a bit mixed-up. *I'm* the vegetarian."

I rubbed my fingers deep into my temples. "Yes. You told me that." It was Jenny who, after watching *Forks Over Knives*, had done a one-eighty two years ago—going from Friday night wings and a beef brisket sandwich obsession to stocking her fridge with vegan butter and cashew cheese overnight. I sighed. "I'm like a memory thief."

"Luce, pace yourself. It could be like this for a while, right? And in the meantime," she began, passing me a soft white dinner roll and a pat of melting butter, "my plan is to be like a battery pack for your memory. I'll give you a boost whenever you need. We'll get you sorted."

"I think I need to make a list." Testing my memory, I tried to recall where I kept the notepads and pens (*hallway console drawer*) and was encouraged to find them exactly where I remembered. With a deep breath I grabbed both and went back to the kitchen table, uncapping a pen. "I need to write down what I remember and then figure out whether it's real or not."

Jenny tugged the pad and pen out from under my hands and moved them over to her side of the table. "You know how I love lists," she said. "But let's eat first. Then we'll work on it until we go cross-eyed. Deal?"

"Deal," I replied, opening my lunch container and digging into my very meaty, guilt-inducing chili.

"Okay, where should we start?" Jenny asked. She had the notepad and pen on her lap but had yet to write anything down.

"I have no idea." I was exhausted. A headache threatened and I felt too full from the chili, even though I'd eaten only half of it.

"Maybe with the stuff you know for sure?"

"Okay. Fine." I sighed.

She raised an eyebrow, tapped the pen a few times against the blank page. "Tell me, without thinking too hard about it. What are you feeling about everything, right this second? One word."

"Weird," I replied. "It's weird. Being here with Matt. Without...Daniel."

"Weird," she said, writing the word down in capped letters. Underlining it with a bold stroke of pen. "Yeah, that's one word for it." She grimaced, but in a comical, exaggerated way that made me laugh. I instantly felt better. It was easy with Jenny and I needed easy right now.

"So, I have to ask." She clicked the end of the pen repeatedly. "Have you and Matt, well, since you've been home...you know?" She wiggled her eyebrows.

"No! God, Jenny, I just got home. I still can't even—" The words caught in my throat. "Matt is my friend. I don't... I can't think about him like that."

"Matt is your boyfriend," she said, enunciating the syllables. She spoke more gently now. "He's a good guy, Luce. Better than good actually." She underlined the word *weird* again, and as I watched her, another word popped into my mind. *Afraid.* Abruptly I started crying.

"Oh, no. Lucy. I'm sorry, hon. I didn't think." Jenny shook her head, grabbed my hands, pulled me from the chair where I was sitting and tucked me in beside her on the couch. I rested my head on her shoulder and cried harder. "This is messed up."

"Yes, it is." My voice cracked and I wiped at my damp face, my hands coming away with streaks of the mascara I'd carefully applied before she arrived, trying to look like I had my shit together.

"I know Matt is supposed to be my boyfriend. Obviously."

I gestured around the room, where photos of us sat on top of bookshelves and on walls. His constant presence in this place I still couldn't picture him in.

"But I don't remember him that way. And the memories of… Daniel." I practically whispered his name. "They're vivid, Jenny. They feel so real to me I can't believe they're not. I remember everything—the engagement, living here together, getting married. Everyone has to think I'm crazy."

"Stop it. No one thinks you're crazy."

"Well, *I think* I might be a bit crazy," I said, my eyes widening. "How did all this happen from hitting my head? How can I remember marrying Daniel when we supposedly broke up years ago?"

"Have you gotten in touch yet? With Daniel?"

I shook my head and thought back to my earlier Facebook search, which I'd abandoned after Matt came into the living room. "Besides, even if I did, what would I say? 'Hey, Daniel,'" I began, pretending to type on my phone. "'Hope things are good with you, wherever you are and whatever you're doing, and, oh, *hey*. I remember our wedding day even though I'm apparently the only one who does. All the best!'" I let out a harsh laugh, and Jenny smiled gently.

"I can help if you want," she said. "We're Facebook friends. He's gone back to school." I was instantly jealous, Jenny knowing things about Daniel I didn't. "Grad school." She paused then and took a breath, her face clouding over briefly. "He's actually pretty lame on social."

"What was that look about?"

"What look?" she replied.

"Is there something you're not telling me?" I narrowed my eyes. "Jenny, you promised me you wouldn't keep things—"

"No. There's nothing." She sighed and then looked at me directly. Softened her voice. "But, Luce, you're with Matt, right? And Daniel is—"

"Not my husband," I mumbled, picking a piece of lint off my black sweater.

"Not your husband," Jenny repeated.

"What happened with us?" I was asking myself as much as Jenny. But she seemed to think I was searching for an answer from her.

"You never talked about it, after you broke up," she said with a shrug. "Just moved out, went back home with your parents for a bit. You wouldn't give any details and I didn't pry. Figured you'd tell me when you wanted to.

"And then six months later I started hearing about this cute strategy consultant with great hair who did triathlons and was obsessed with hockey and made you smile when you said his name, and you never mentioned Daniel again."

"Until I woke up a few weeks ago, wondering why he wasn't at the hospital and where my wedding ring was." I gave a wry smile.

"Hey, I have something for you." Jenny got up and reached into her purse. She handed me a gold-toned plastic bag. I looked inside, pulled out a black-and-gray-striped tie and a receipt. I stared at the tie, not understanding, before looking back at her.

"You bought this when we were out shopping the day of your accident." I glanced back at the tie, fingered the silky fabric. "I know you don't remember, but you bought it…for your anniversary."

I turned the tie over and read the label, but it carried no meaning. "A tie?" My memory chugged as it tried to slide the right pieces in the right slots. "I bought a tie?"

Jenny laughed. "I told you it was lame. I mean, a tie for an anniversary gift? But you said he would get it. It was an inside joke and you were very pleased with yourself."

"I bought this for my anniversary. With…" I nearly said

"Daniel," before reminding myself that, no, there was no anniversary with Daniel.

"It was for Matt," she said, confirming the truth once again. "For your three-year anniversary."

8

I had the notebook with my memory list on the table, a slew of highlighters fanned out on the coffee table. The pink highlighter (the color I'd chosen to signify fabricated memories) was uncapped, the nonmarker end in my mouth as I scanned the list.

"Did we watch *Forks and Knives?*" I asked Matt, who was sitting on one of the living room chairs, catching up on work. It was Saturday morning, and almost three weeks since I'd come home from the hospital. My parents were back sleeping at their own place, my mother finally convinced I wasn't on the verge of a breakdown and could cook for myself. And while things with Matt weren't as awkward now, they were far from back on track. Most days it felt like we were merely roommates.

It didn't help that I would twirl my wedding ring that wasn't there, particularly when I was nervous or anxious—a gesture Matt caught more than once, looking wounded when he did. I had also made his coffee wrong twice since that first day, but he claimed he didn't mind the sugar so much.

Sometimes I imagined I was living parallel lives, the knock on my head making it possible to see both timelines simultaneously. Or perhaps it was an elaborate setup, coordinated for reasons too fantastical to believe. I had mentioned as much to

Dr. Kay at my appointment the day before, trying to lighten the mood. She had smiled when I'd said, "Maybe I'm a CIA operative who had memories implanted during a mission gone wrong?" before replying, "Well, that would make things easier to accept, wouldn't it? So how are things going at home this week, Lucy?"

Damn, she was skilled at not allowing me to dodge my complicated feelings, to avoid talking about the things that kept me up at night and preoccupied during the day. I would much rather have discussed the theory, however implausible, that I was a rogue special agent versus accepting all this happened because a store didn't throw salt on the ice outside their front door, and I had made a poor footwear choice—heeled booties versus sensible winter boots. All of which led to me slipping—so dramatically both my feet left the ground before I landed, hard, on the back of my head and knocked myself out.

"*Forks* Over *Knives?*" Matt asked, eyes still on his laptop as he finished typing. He was back from his dentist appointment—the one I'd noticed on the calendar that first morning I was home—and his mouth was frozen from having a cavity filled, so he sounded like he had a lisp. "The documentary? On Netflix?"

"Yes," I replied, nibbling on the end of the highlighter. "Did we watch it?"

He nodded. "We did."

I drew a thick pink line over *Forks and Knives* on my list with the highlighter, crossing out the *and*, writing *over* in its place with pen. "Did I mention wanting to become a vegetarian after that?"

Matt smiled, but his frozen mouth only half rose with the movement on the left side, making him look like he was smirking. "You did."

"So what happened? How did I go from that place to two servings of pot roast at Christmas dinner?" It was so bizarre, not remembering such basic details of my life. Relying on someone else to fill in the blanks, trusting him to give me the truth. Because of course he could have told me anything and I'd have to believe him, which was unsettling at best and terrifying at worst. But as my anxiety intensified I reminded myself to take a deep breath and to remember Matt loved me. He didn't want to hurt me and certainly wouldn't lie to me.

"You declared yourself on a 'meat break' and then two days later you told me you missed bacon too much."

"I missed bacon? That was all it took?" I shook my head. "Wow, I'm glad to hear I stand by my convictions."

Matt laughed and then winced as he put his hand to his cheek. "You love bacon, Lucy."

I *did* love bacon. Even as I thought it, I knew it was true, despite the memory of my turn to vegetarianism still feeling real. I could as easily be convinced my diet was meat free.

"Definitely *not* a vegetarian," I murmured, highlighting the word *vegetarian* in pink. The whole vegetarian thing wasn't new information, but I put it on the list for the satisfaction of crossing it off, even though seeing yet another pink line made me uneasy. "But at least I know I didn't make the whole thing up. I mean, I did try not to eat meat and we did watch the documentary."

Matt nodded, still amused. "Do you want to watch it again?"

"Definitely not," I said. Matt smiled and then went back to his laptop. He squinted at the screen in concentration. "Hey, where are your glasses?" Matt always wore glasses to work, but it had only just occurred to me I hadn't seen him wear them since I'd been home.

"Contacts," he replied. "I hate them, but they're better than always losing my glasses."

"Oh," I said, wondering when he had made the switch. Missing the way he looked in his glasses—handsomely bookish.

He closed his laptop, gestured to the notepad. "So what else is on today's list?"

I had divided up the main list in chunks of five or so memories, which had been an exhausting task. My brain bruise had fully healed, but my mind was still "lethargic," according to my doctors, and would be for a while. They had suggested not pushing things too much, offered gentle warnings that my "softer" memories could potentially lose some of their defined edges if I did.

I read the items in my head, touched one with my finger. "Your parents."

"My parents? What about them?"

"They live in California, right?" Matt nodded. "I remember meeting them once. When they came to visit the office and took us out for lunch. We went to that Korean barbecue place, remember?" Again, Matt nodded. Of course he remembered. "It was fun. Your dad is supertall, and your mom hugged me after lunch."

"They just celebrated their thirtieth wedding anniversary," Matt added. Then he paused, and I said, "What?" and he finally added, "We threw them a big party. Do you remember?"

I didn't, so I shook my head, feeling frustrated—as well as mildly irritated with Matt because he obviously knew I didn't remember the party. I had just finished saying I met his parents only one time, at the office, so why bring it up?

"You and my sister, Evelyn—you remember Eve, right?" Again, reluctantly, I shook my head and the frustration swelled. "Anyway, doesn't matter." But his face certainly looked like it mattered a lot, that I didn't remember his sister. I wondered where she lived, if we were close. "The two of you organized everything. I was on a case in Montreal and had barely been home in weeks, so you took over." I wished I could crawl into his head so I could see it, too. "Eve lives in San Diego. She's a marine biologist. Here, I have a few photos on my phone." He clicked through the photo icon until he found what he was looking for and sat beside me at the table.

In the first photo we stood between his mom and dad and a tall, tanned woman with a blond bob who looked like Matt and whom I guessed was his sister. The five of us wore beaming smiles, and I was in a canary yellow A-line dress. I could tell I felt good in that dress by the way I held myself, and I wondered if it still hung in my closet, when I might have another occasion to wear it. There were flutes of champagne, which we reached out in cheers toward whoever had taken the picture. A dark sadness filled me and I tried to stay engaged as he flipped through a few more photos, but I was fading.

"Eve looks like you," I said, because I couldn't think of what else to say. Nothing about the photos felt familiar, which was surreal because if I had organized the party, if we had flown five hours for it, and had, as Matt was telling me now, taken a week's holiday to do some skiing at California's Heavenly Mountain Resort before coming home, why couldn't I remember any of it? Not a single thing tickled my memory.

Until I saw the photo of us dressed head to toe in ski garb, standing at the top of a mountain with the blue sky behind us and our poles raised in the air, grins from ear to ear on our cold-red faces, sparkling snow diamonds everywhere.

With a rush I remembered that photo being taken.

But…it was Daniel, not Matt, I remembered standing beside me. His newly grown beard keeping the bottom half of his face toasty warm, though I had complained about how much the coarse hairs prickled my chin. In my memory it was Daniel with the one arm around me, the other jutting his pole up to the bluebird sky. Daniel, who, after the ski patrol took this photo for us, turned his phone around and kissed me deeply while snapping a selfie. And as that memory landed into my mind, Matt flipped to the next photo and there it was. The kissing selfie. Except it was Matt kissing me in the picture, not Daniel. Matt's beard, which he no longer had, tickling my chin while we pressed our lips together.

Matt watched me carefully, kept the kissing selfie on his screen, waited for my reaction. An icy feeling filled me and the mild headache I'd been dealing with all day pounded with insistence. I pushed back from the table quickly, and the chair legs screeched as I did. Matt, clearly startled, stood up as well, his phone clattering to the tabletop. I stared at the photo and in a strange detached way noted how happy we looked. How right we seemed together, our lips fitting together so perfectly despite the bulkiness of our goggles and helmets and the inches he had on me. Then the screen faded, the picture gone.

"My head is killing me," I said, looking away from Matt's phone and glancing toward the bedroom. "I think I'm going to lie down for a bit."

"Sure, sure," he said, his face a mix of concern and confusion at my abruptness. "Do you need anything? Can I grab your pills for you? A glass of water?"

I shook my head, which made the pounding worse. "I think it's going to ease up. I just need some rest."

"Okay." Matt let out a breath, his hands jiggling on his hips in that nervous-energy way I recognized. It occurred to me I hadn't seen him take his bike out yet this week. I remembered he normally rode daily, always to and from work, and was usually training for some kind of race.

"Why don't you go for a ride?" I said. It was chilly outside, but the snow had melted and the slush had evaporated to only small puddles here and there.

"Maybe later," he said, but I knew that meant he wouldn't go. "I probably shouldn't have made you look at the photos. They said no screens for a while. Sorry, Lucy. I didn't... Sorry."

"It's fine," I said. "You didn't make me look at anything. I wanted to. And I don't think a couple of minutes is going to do much damage."

He nodded but didn't look convinced.

"I'm okay, Matt. Honestly. An hour or so to shut my eyes. Seriously, go for a ride. I bet you'll feel better, too."

With a glance at his bike, which hung from a hook on the brick wall in our entryway, he seemed to consider this. "Maybe I will. But I'll be here when you get up." He gave me his lopsided smile and for the first time since coming home I felt a rush of something more intimate toward him. It was a whisper of something, but it was there. Maybe it was the selfie, after all.

Even if I remembered standing beside a different man, I couldn't ignore the evidence: at some point, in my not-so-distant past, I had been in love with Matt Newman.

9

I doodled along the edges of the paper, making tiny swirls and intricate mazes of triangles. The paper itself was cheap. Thin and flimsy under the heaviness of my pen strokes. On it were a series of questions that should have been easy for me to answer. I continued doodling, my pen lazily making a tornado of swirls down the side, and glanced over the list again.

What's my favorite food?
Where did I go to university?
What was my major?
When is my birthday?
Who's the prime minister of Canada?
Who's the premier of Ontario?
Who's the president of the United States?
Where did I take my last vacation? Who with?
Where do I live?
Where do I work?
How long have I worked there?
Do I exercise?
Do I have any allergies?
Who was my childhood best friend?
Have I ever had a pet?
What are my current hobbies?

They were all questions taken from a sample list Dr. Kay had given me. "It's meant to spark your memory," she'd said when she'd handed me the papers. "Some of these seem like silly, incredibly simple things. But it will help your memory confidence, being able to get the answers right and with ease."

Memory confidence. This was a new term to me, but one Dr. Kay used often during our sessions. Our goal, as she explained it, was to help me build a framework for my memory. To create the landscape the way it existed today, and to work off that rather than trying to go back to how things were before I slipped on the ice.

"Lucy, we hope you get your memories back, but there are no guarantees things will get better than they are now. Your memory is a bit like a trickster at the moment, and we need to help you find a way to trust it again."

So I'd been writing down memories I knew were real, the way you add a completed to-do item on a list for the satisfaction of checking it off. Memories from my childhood were easiest and most concrete, like when only a year after I was gifted my beloved birthday bike with the rainbow tassels, it was stolen and I told my parents I had locked it up—though I hadn't. Or the time in ninth grade when I forged a doctor's note and skipped school, then got caught when the principal called my mom to check how I was feeling because I'd misspelled tonsillitis (*tonsellitus*) and she was onto me.

I've also been thinking a lot about this "honest lying" thing. I mean, I've told friends I loved their haircuts when I didn't, told bosses I made a dinner reservation for out-of-town clients when I didn't (I forgot, blamed it on the hostess) and exclaimed my delight over gifts I knew I would be regifting or returning. These are all times I lied, on purpose and with intent. But now my own memory lied to me and I was as gullible as I had been when Alex told me as a kid if I swallowed my gum it would expand until my stomach exploded.

"It may not feel like it," Dr. Kay said, bringing me back to the present. "But we're making progress. Great progress actually." She pointed to the list, my new cheat sheet, where I had been diligently filling out answers and adding questions.

Along with my memory confidence list, Dr. Kay and I spent a lot of time talking about Daniel, which I appreciated because he was a topic avoided in most other conversations I was having. My parents seemed to believe if they didn't mention him, or the fabricated marriage memory, it didn't exist, and after the coffee incident that first morning, Matt and I hadn't discussed Daniel at all. I understood why no one wanted to talk about it, of course, but it was hard on me not to acknowledge him.

So Dr. Kay's office was one place I could share—without worrying about how it all sounded—what I was feeling when it came to Daniel, which was a cornucopia of things. *Loss. Confusion. Love. Bewilderment. Abandonment. Desire. Guilt.* She never said much when I talked of Daniel, simply nodded encouragement to keep going, keep sharing, and on occasion would pepper the discussion with a few questions to keep things moving. To prevent me from shutting down and folding into myself, which many times I desperately wanted to do.

Depression was, according to Dr. Kay, an issue we needed to stay on top of. "It's not unusual for people suffering memory loss to also suffer depression," she said. "Accepting things as they are versus how you wish they could be is a challenge for anyone, but especially for those who are struggling with big holes in their recall."

I wondered if I might already be depressed. I was far from feeling happy about things, but having never experienced depression—or at least having never remembered experiencing it—I wasn't sure what we needed to keep an eye on exactly. Mentally, I added it to my set of questions. *Ask Jenny or Alex if I've ever been depressed.* I figured if I had been, I would have confided in one of them.

"How are things on the relationship front?" Dr. Kay asked, and I looked up from the list and my doodles.

"Well, I'm working on accepting Daniel and I aren't actually married, if that's what you mean," I replied.

She smiled. I knew that wasn't what she had meant, but I didn't feel like talking about Matt right now. "How's that going?" she asked.

I shrugged. "Okay?" She waited for me to continue. I sighed. "I can still picture our wedding day so clearly. The dress. The flowers. The rings." I looked down at my bare left ring finger, tucked my hand under my thigh. "But I think I might be remembering my sister Alex's wedding."

"What makes you think that?" Dr. Kay asked.

"I was going through some photos my mom and dad brought over, and Alex's dress looks pretty similar to mine. Or the one I thought I wore. At a wedding I apparently didn't have."

The dresses—the one I remembered wearing when I married Daniel and the one Alex wore on her wedding day—were not similar; they were identical. Peach-colored satin, but so pale it looked almost off-white in the sunshine. Vintage-style, to the knee with a rhinestone belt and capped short sleeves. Remembering myself in that dress had been somewhat confusing, though, because it was a style I would never have imagined myself wearing. My perfect dress would have been more classic, based on my style: maybe a strapless A-line, with a modestly poufed skirt, in winter white.

So how could I explain the vintage peach satin dress I thought I wore, which *was* much more Alex's style? I couldn't. Until I saw the photos of her wedding. I had forgotten entirely she was—well, had been—married. She and this sound engineer, Paolo, from Brazil met at a music festival in New York State and he followed her back to Toronto under the guise of a few weeks' vacation. Apparently Alex sprang the city hall wedding on us two days before it happened, and she told me when recounting the story that Mom had been none too pleased, which should have surprised no one.

Our mother considered herself a forward-thinking parent:

one more interested in experiential learning over structured homework; one who cared little if grandbabies came before a wedding; and one who would have been as delighted for Alex to marry a woman as a man, which was entirely possible. My sister didn't subscribe to convention and since high school had been in plenty of relationships, gender irrelevant. My parents were happy when Alex was happy, so Mom couldn't understand why she hadn't told us about Paolo.

Alex and Paolo were married for less than a month before having the marriage annulled when Paolo went back to Brazil. As it turned out, his first wife was as surprised by this spontaneous wedding as my parents, and I, had been.

"And it wasn't only the dress. We both had cupcakes instead of wedding cakes. And her bouquet was...my bouquet," I told Dr. Kay. "She carried paper flowers. They were beautiful."

"How does it make you feel, knowing these facts don't belong to you?"

It was a strange way to put it, but she wasn't wrong. I had taken ownership over the details, had crafted an entire section of my past around them without ever realizing they weren't mine. How *did* it make me feel? Completely unhinged. Like I might never find my way back.

"It makes me feel like I'm insane," I said, being honest with Dr. Kay because I had no reason not to be. If she had a reaction to my use of the word *insane*, she didn't show it. "But don't they say crazy people don't know they're crazy? So maybe I'm okay?"

"You are okay," Dr. Kay said, leaning forward onto her crossed knees. I was somewhat reassured. She looked relaxed, not concerned in the slightest by my admission.

"Mostly it makes me feel alone, and yet entirely reliant on other people," I said. "I can't remember some things, other things I'm remembering completely wrong and some stuff I've made up altogether. Who can possibly relate to that?"

"How much of these memories with Daniel have you shared with Matt?"

At first I said nothing. Wasn't sure how to talk about Matt and Daniel in the same sentence without the hit of bitter guilt that came with it.

"You're allowed to mourn the loss of the marriage you re-member, Lucy. Your feelings are valid. I know you know this, but it's worth saying again—these fabricated memories will feel as real to you as any confirmed memory does." I nodded, looked down at my list, the words blurring as my eyes filled. "But that also doesn't mean what you have with Matt isn't real or important."

"I miss him. Daniel, I mean." I took a deep breath, fiddled with my watch. Saw our hour was almost up. "I have to keep reminding myself it didn't happen, because...it still *feels* so real."

Dr. Kay handed me the box of tissues and I took one. "Do you wish you could talk with him?" she asked.

"Daniel?" I said, wiping at my eyes. "All the time."

She paused for a moment, considering this. "Then why don't you try to contact him?"

"But...I thought that wasn't a good idea. I'm supposed to be focusing on my 'memory confidence' and talking with Daniel, seeing him..." There was a flutter in my belly at the thought. *Excitement.* "Isn't that going down a rabbit hole I should stay away from?"

"It's possible seeing him will help your brain reconcile the missing pieces," Dr. Kay said. "One of our goals in spending time together is to help you develop coping skills. And if you're able to talk with Daniel and understand firsthand he's not the person your memory wants you to believe, it may be easier to compartmentalize that particular issue."

While I liked the idea of remembering things as they were, I was somewhat panicked at the thought of no longer recollecting Daniel as my husband. I was unsure what to do with Dr. Kay's suggestion. On the one hand, getting permission to contact Daniel made me feel lighter than I had in weeks. *It is doctor recommended,* I could say, leaning heavily on this justification. *She thinks it might help*, I would add, and of course no one would question it then. They all wanted me to get better.

But on the other hand, what if I saw Daniel and all the memories I had of us together—being in love, being husband and wife—disappeared? Then I would be left without the safety that came with thoughts of Daniel. Because even if the memories were false, they were all I had.

"Apparently I haven't spoken to him in four years," I said. "Since we... Since I ended our engagement."

"You don't have to do this, Lucy," Dr. Kay said. "But I understand your desire to track down the truth about things. To not have to rely so heavily on your family and friends to fill in the missing pieces. I think that's a great instinct and you should see where it takes you."

"But what would I say to him? I mean, this all sounds so..."

"Crazy?" she said, and we laughed. I was shaking, the thought of seeing Daniel, of talking with him, causing adrenaline to course through me. "Reach out however's easiest for you, whether it be via email or phone, or even with someone else's help," Dr. Kay continued. "Just see what happens."

In my mind I was already writing the script of what I would say to him, how I would say it. As if reading my mind, Dr. Kay asked, "To finish up today, why don't you tell me what your expectations are for this meeting, if you decide to go through with it?"

Good question. "I honestly have no idea," I said. "There's a tiny, irrational part of me that wishes he'll tell me I am remembering things right. That this has all been one big misunderstanding." Dr. Kay smiled gently at me, though not in a pitying way. "And there's a big part of me that hopes I get the closure I need. That seeing him will wiggle something in my mind and I'll remember everything right and things will go back to normal."

"What is that for you? 'Normal.'"

I paused. Even if I was scared to shatter the connection I felt to Daniel, to accept we were not together and lose everything that came with that awareness, I realized I was more scared to stay in this wacky bubble where I couldn't trust my own mind.

"I think normal is what life looked like five minutes before I slipped on that ice."

10

"I have to tell you something," Jenny said, shaking cinnamon into her latte, her eyes on her mug. We were at my favorite café, Bobbette & Belle, only a few blocks from my place, indulging in a lunch of salted caramel macarons and raspberry scones with clotted cream, and milk-whipped coffees. Caffeine had proved to be an asset for helping with my concussion headaches, so the two shots of espresso in my latte practically felt medicinal.

I stopped slathering the clotted cream onto the warm scone and looked up at her as prickles of anxiety filled me. I had no idea what she was about to tell me and for a moment considered maybe it had nothing at all to do with me. How glorious that would be! To not be the center of attention. But then she said, "And I don't think you're going to be happy about it," and I knew for certain I was wrong—it had everything to do with me, after all.

"What's up?" I asked, trying to appear stress free as I continued layering the cream onto my scone. Relaxed, like whatever she had to tell me would be *just fine*. I took a bite and chewed, waiting.

"So, I know you're thinking of getting in touch with Daniel," she said, now stirring the cinnamon into the frothy milk.

She took a sip and the milk left a thin foamy mustache above her upper lip. "And I think that's great. Brave, even."

Hmm. Brave? "Okay. And?"

"*And* here's the thing," she said. But then she stopped and looked at me worriedly.

Now I was irritated. "What is it, Jenny? Spill it. You're making me nervous." And she was, my heart rate up and my palms sweaty.

"He's married, Lucy."

It was as though she'd sucker punched me. Even though no one had ever slammed their fist into my gut—as far as I could remember—this had to be what that felt like.

"Oh," I managed, trying to catch my breath. The first shock waves dissipated and then I felt stupid. Naive for not having considered such a scenario. Why wouldn't Daniel be married? We were approaching thirty; this was when people coupled off in a more permanent way. And we hadn't been together for over four years. *Of course* he would have met someone else and fallen in love.

Jenny was speaking fast now, clearly wanting to get it all out as quickly as possible. It made me dizzy, trying to hold on to all the details as they arrived rapid-fire from her. "He got married two years ago. I wanted to tell you. Said we *had* to tell you. But, well, it was *suggested* maybe you weren't quite ready to hear that."

I wondered, flickers of anger moving through me, who had made that suggestion.

"And honestly, we all thought things would have settled by now. That you would have, you know, remembered everything." She cringed at this last part, tried to say it quietly as though my memory lapses were less significant if discussed in hushed tones.

"I guess I shouldn't be surprised," I finally said, hating how high and squeaky my voice was. "To be honest, I'm an idiot for not considering that." *Do not cry, Lucy. Do not cry.* I dug my fingernails into my palm, relished the pain there because it shifted my focus from the pain elsewhere.

"No! Don't say that," Jenny said, grabbing my one hand still resting on the table. "How could you have known? I should have told you." Her mouth turned down in a scowl. "It wasn't right to keep it from you for this long. I'm sorry."

I let her hold my hand, pressed my other hand harder against my stomach as I tried to take a few deep breaths. "So, who did he marry?"

Is this what it feels like to be cheated on? A sense of sickness spread out from my belly, threatened to take over my whole body. It was quickly followed by the trifecta of doom, embarrassment and regret for any decisions that had led me to this place. Whatever I was experiencing in this moment, I never wanted to feel it again.

"Yeah, so, here's the other thing." Jenny gently squeezed my hand a few times. "He married Margot. Margot Hendricks. Well, I guess she's now Margot London. Unless she didn't take his name. She probably didn't take his name. She was kind of a dick about it at your engagement party. Remember?" Jenny looked stricken, her eyes scanning my face as she watched me take in the news. "I'm so sorry, Lucy. I know this has to be a massive shock."

My breath came out in a rush, along with my words. "He married Margot? *Our* Margot?"

"Yes," Jenny said with a sigh. "Our Margot is now his Margot."

I had met Margot Hendricks at university, in social studies class. Though we'd never been close the way Jenny and I were, she was someone I had looked up to. An outspoken feminist who didn't only give lip service but actually showed up at protests and marched and made her voice heard. She spoke three languages fluently, thanks to her Swedish mother and Spanish father, and talked of becoming a professor before one day joining the United Nations. Whip smart as she was, Margot Hendricks never made you feel like you were anything but equal to her, even though we all knew she was the brightest of our group. And most relevant to this particular conversation today in the

café, she never—in the four years we were at school together—
had a boyfriend or even a whiff of a relationship.

We had stayed in casual touch after graduation, when I went
to work and she started grad school, and she had come to Daniel's and my engagement party—but that was the last time I remembered seeing her.

"Were we still friends?" I asked Jenny. Margot seemed someone I would have stayed in touch with, even if only through
happy birthday posts and the occasional liking of a photo on
social media. At least until she married my ex-fiancé.

Jenny shook her head. "I don't think so."

"You don't think so?" I asked, frustrated by this noncommit-
tal answer. "Or no?"

"No. You are not friends. As far as I know." Jenny and I had
been best of friends since we were eighteen years old, and I
spoke to her nearly daily. She would know if Margot and I had
stayed in contact.

"Are you friends with her?" She shook her head slowly. "And
you still don't know why Daniel and I broke up?" *Was it because
of Margot?* I wondered.

Jenny looked surprised, her eyes widening—my tone clearly
suggesting I thought she might have omitted that truth, as well.
"I swear to you, Lucy, I don't know why."

I nodded. The headache was back and I needed to go home.
But I continued to push my brain, trying to grasp on to memories
of Margot. How had she ended up with Daniel? They had known
each other only casually, and only because he and I were dating.

What the hell had happened, to all of us, since then?

11

"You know, I've never had sex in the water," Lucy said to Daniel, shifting her body between his legs and leaning back against his chest, the hot water in the bathtub pushing up the sides, threatening to spill over the edge. There were pink rose petals floating on the surface of the water, the heady floral scent enveloping them, seeping into their pores. Two glasses of red wine, nearly empty, were on the tub's ledge. Daniel wrapped his arms around her, kissed the side of her face, her outstretched neck. She shivered and goose bumps prickled across her exposed arms.

"Really?" he murmured, still nibbling her neck. "How did I not know this?"

She shrugged against him. "You don't know everything about me," she said, smiling back at him. "I still have some secrets."

"I'm sure you do," Daniel said. "This revelation is giving me so many—" He stopped talking to take his mouth lower, onto the delicate skin of her collarbone. Lucy closed her eyes, felt the way his body changed under hers and wished they had more time.

In about an hour a room full of their closest friends and family would toast their engagement with champagne and far-too-pricy appetizers, and choosing this bath over quick showers had already guaranteed they were thirty minutes behind schedule. "So, so many ideas."

"Oh, yeah? Like what?" Her heart beat quickly. She knew they needed to get out of the bath and into party clothes, but she didn't want to. Not quite yet. Lucy moved one of Daniel's hands lower, until it sank under the water and settled between her legs. "Maybe something like this?"

"Exactly what I had in mind," Daniel murmured, moving his hand with precision, the gentle pressure and warm water a delicious combination. She sucked in a breath, opened her legs wider so they pressed against the sides of the bathtub, her left kneecap connecting hard with the overhanging faucet. Later, visible because of her above-the-knee cocktail dress, a crescent-shaped bruise would form on her knee, but the pain barely registered now because of what Daniel was doing to her. "I think this will get us in a more celebratory mood, don't you?"

She couldn't speak, was too focused on what was building between her thighs, throughout the rest of her body. As his fingers became more purposeful, she arched against him and moaned, no longer caring about the water that now splashed over the edge of the tub. Afterward, she lay breathless against him, eyes closed. "You were right," she murmured. "I definitely feel like celebrating now."

"Good," he said, his mouth close to her ear. "But if we're already late, why not a few minutes more? We could do something about your bucket list right now." He slapped his palm down on the water's surface gently, causing a few ripples. "We have water, and I'm sort of an expert."

"An expert?" Lucy laughed, twisted her neck so she could look at him. "Besides, I'm not sure I'd call it a bucket list item, and we don't have room in here for that."

He looked down at their naked bodies filling every spare inch of the bathtub. "I'm willing to give it a try if you are."

"Hmm, tempting, but I have a feeling we'll end up regretting that decision. The last thing we need tonight is a pulled muscle."

She kissed him, and though she was still in the afterglow of the orgasm, she was also beginning to feel the pressure of the ticking clock. "I'd say we have about three minutes before we have to shift into panic mode."

He groaned, laid his head back against the tub's ledge. "Do we have to go?" He sounded like a petulant middle schooler being told to hurry because the school bell was ringing soon.

Lucy sat up and turned to face him. "Yes, we have to go. If we didn't show, I'm not sure which mother would kill us first."

He laughed, deep from his belly, and then grabbed her in a hug from behind. "Definitely yours."

"You're probably right," she said. Lucy's parents were fairly laid-back, liked to refer to themselves as "free range"—and that had been mostly true during Lucy's childhood. She and Alex were allowed to play outside on the street even after it got dark, were expected to do their own laundry and make school lunches, and they never once complained about the state of Lucy and Alex's bedroom. But along with turning the lights off when you left a room, their mother was militant about lateness. Once, Alex had slept in the day they were driving to Boston to visit their cousins and wasn't in the car at the predetermined time— 7:00 a.m. sharp—and so their mother had put the car in Drive and left fifteen-year-old Alex at home, even as Lucy cried (she was only nine and couldn't imagine how Alex could survive the four days alone).

Lucy disentangled herself from Daniel and stood in the tub, shivering as she grabbed a towel. She plucked a few of the pink petals that clung to her wet skin, then patted her body dry before bending at the waist to wrap the towel around her hair. Daniel was right behind her, planted a kiss on the goose-bumped skin on her shoulder before grabbing his own towel and aggressively rubbing it against his arms and legs, like he was trying to exfoliate with it. "I will never understand why you use your towel for your hair when you're so clearly freezing," he said.

She was already applying body lotion, starting to warm up now that she was dry. "One of life's great mysteries."

He laughed and wrapped his arms around her body as they locked eyes in the mirror. Lucy gave him her most serious look. "Daniel, stop. We do not have time." She glanced at her phone on the vanity. *Mom was going to blow a gasket.* "We're already going to be late."

In a flash Daniel whipped off his towel and pulled her toward the bedroom, then tossed her, laughing, onto the bed. The towel fell off her head and the wet strands of hair stuck to her back and shoulders. "Seriously, we don't have time!" But her protests were lost in her laughter as Daniel jumped into bed beside her, snuggling both of them under the duvet.

"If we're already going to be late..." he said, grinning, his own damp hair stuck to his forehead in wet spikes.

Lucy thought once more of her mom's inevitable irritation, and of their friends who would be standing there waiting for them to arrive—the champagne perfectly chilled and ready to pop—then said with a sly grin, "What's another few minutes?"

They arrived at the Thompson Hotel, where the engagement party was being held, nearly an hour late. It was hard to say which mother was angrier, though after some discussion they decided they had been right with the earlier guess. While Daniel's mom was visibly displeased—telling because she was the stoic sort who rarely showed emotion—she did express relief they weren't hurt after they said their taxi driver was in a fender bender (which did not happen, but was completely plausible).

But Lucy's mother would have none of this excuse. She was onto them the minute her younger daughter opened her mouth—Lucy had never had much luck trying to feed her mother anything but the truth, so should have known better. But at least she didn't call them out on it in front of everyone. Merely narrowed her eyes before saying, "Well, how awful. *I'm so glad* it wasn't more serious." Dad hugged Lucy tightly, while

Daniel's father, a personal injury attorney, had a dozen questions
for his son about the accident and what happened. Luckily Daniel's mother shut that down quickly, reminding everyone they
were here for a party and the champagne had been waiting long
enough, and *Obviously everyone is fine, so let's get on with things.*

And despite lamenting the social gathering—Daniel was
raised on a regular diet of parties and events thrown by his
high-society parents and had developed a severe aversion to
anything requiring black tie—Daniel relaxed as soon as he got
a couple of drinks in him. They danced and sashayed among
friends, chatted politely with their parents' acquaintances and
extended families, and by midnight only a handful of die-hards
remained, including Lucy and Daniel, Jenny, Margot, Alexis and
her current beau, Allen, who was a performance artist (Lucy had
to laugh watching Mrs. London attempt to understand what it
was he did for a living).

Jenny, Margot, Alex and Lucy kicked off their shoes, then
stole a full bottle of top-shelf Scotch and a glass off the bar
and headed up to the rooftop, giggling drunkenly as they did.
Lucy poured the glass full to the top and it was passed down
the line while they leaned against the rooftop's ledge, enjoying
the warm night and the very expensive booze Daniel's parents
were paying for.

"So, Mrs. London," Jenny said, after a big sip from the com-
munal glass, "when's the first garden party?" The rest of them
broke into sloppy laughter, and Lucy snorted.

"Screw you, Jenny," she said, taking a sip straight from the
bottle. The Scotch warmed a path right to her belly. "There is
only one Mrs. London, and she's downstairs."

Margot raised a brow. "You're not taking his name?"

"Of course she isn't," Alex said, grabbing the bottle of Scotch
and taking a swig. She wiped her mouth with her arm and hiccuped. "We're Sparks girls. Forever and ever, right, Luce?" She
threw an arm around her little sister and kissed her on the side
of the head.

"I'm sort of surprised." Margot swirled the remaining finger of Scotch in the glass before tipping it back.

"You are?" Lucy asked, spinning out from under her sister's arm to look at Margot. "Why?" For whatever reason, even in her drunken state, Margot's opinion mattered a lot to Lucy.

Margot shrugged at Lucy's surprise. "You seem the type."

Lucy was immediately offended, despite believing there was nothing wrong with wanting to take your husband's name... even if she didn't want to. But Margot's words stung. *You seem the type?* Was that a diss or a compliment? Maybe she saw Lucy as confident enough in who she was for it not to matter if she gave up her maiden name.

Jenny murmured something about how she would for sure take her husband's name, because her last name hadn't been the easiest to live with.

Alex snort-laughed and said, "I don't know. 'Jenny Dickie' has a certain ring to it, don't you think?"

But Lucy decided she was too drunk to sort out what Margot meant, so better to come right out and ask. "The type?" she finally said, turning to Margot. "What does that even mean?"

Margot pushed off the wall, then came to stand right in front of her. "It means nothing. Don't get worked up, okay?" Then with only a few inches between them, she leaned in and gave Lucy a quick kiss, right on the lips. The move erased any response Lucy might have given, and she found herself slightly breathless. "I should have said *he's* the type," Margot added, smirking.

Daniel's the type? The type to what? Want his wife to take his family's name?

They had discussed it, the whole last name thing, after Daniel proposed. And while he admitted he would have preferred them to share a surname, he was fine with whatever she wanted to do. Lucy was about to announce all of this, felt the need to defend Daniel and her feminism, but by the time she pulled herself together, Margot was already walking back toward the stairs. "Come on, ladies. We're out of booze, and therefore possibilities, up here."

They stumbled behind her, Lucy touching her lips as she did, which were still slightly tacky from Margot's gloss. A few shots of tequila later Lucy had forgotten the conversation—and the three or so hours following it—entirely. Until the next day, when she and Jenny nursed hangovers with plates of waffles and rehashed Margot's comment. Lucy let Jenny reassure her she and Daniel were not "predictable" and Margot clearly had no idea what she was talking about.

"Maybe I will take his last name," Lucy said defiantly, cutting her waffle with more gusto than was required.

"Maybe you will." Jenny pursed her lips and pointed her fork Lucy's way, matching her tone.

"I can still be a feminist and take my husband's name."

"Damn right you can," Jenny said.

Lucy put down her fork. "Lucy London." She repeated it a few more times. "Not bad, right?"

"Not bad at all," Jenny said. "But I'm probably not the one to ask. *Jenny Dickie*, remember?"

They laughed so hard that Lucy, who had unfortunately just taken a bite of her breakfast, spit the piece of her waffle right into Jenny's face, which only made them laugh even harder. Then Lucy went home and told Daniel she was going to take his name, after all.

12

It was Saturday morning—the day after I learned about Daniel—and I had vowed to move on. Yes, I still felt married. But I wasn't and so refused to indulge any more in the fantasy because Matt deserved better. *I* deserved better.

When Jenny told me Daniel had married Margot, I initially felt like one does on a roller coaster when the safety bar slams into your chest on a particularly tight drop. It hurt, a lot, and took my breath away. By the time Jenny finally left my place, after I assured her I was okay and made her promise not to call Matt like she wanted to, I was bone tired and unable to keep up the pretense everything was fine. So I locked myself in the bedroom with a bottle of water and one of Matt's protein bars and refused to come out. It was juvenile and far too dramatic of a reaction, but I needed to be alone.

I scared Matt enough with my refusal to open the door that he called my parents to come over, and the three of them pleaded with me to let them in. Mom said she was making us a pot of tea, and would I come out to have a cup and chat? I'd shouted at her then, "I do not want a cup of tea, Mom! Stop it with all the goddamn tea, okay?" and then felt terrible when I heard her say to Dad she was going to go put the kettle on regardless, in a shaky voice I wasn't used to hearing from my mother.

They all thought I locked myself in the bedroom because I was upset about Daniel and Margot (Jenny had folded with guilt, told Matt what happened at Bobbette & Belle), and I *was* upset, but that wasn't all of it. I also felt betrayed by Matt, Jenny, my family, because they'd decided they knew better than me about what I could or could not handle. And in a way I was also embarrassed—mortified actually—to be the last one to know.

Eventually I calmed down and fell asleep. And the next morning I unlocked the door and joined the living again. My parents had gone back home at some point in the night and Matt was asleep on the couch, still in his work clothes with his phone lying on his chest. I tiptoed to the kitchen and started a pot of coffee, then sat on the coffee table across from him and shook his arm gently.

He stirred, cracked open an eye. Then he bolted upright, his hair a disheveled mess and his button-down shirt twisted and crumpled. "What time is it?"

"Early," I replied. "About seven."

He ran a hand through his hair and glanced at me. "You okay?"

I nodded, ready for the inevitable conversation where we'd apologize to one another (me for my theatrical reaction, him for not telling me what he knew about Daniel and Margot), and he would take responsibility for making sure I was okay and I would let him.

But instead he said, "That stunt last night? That was bullshit, Lucy." He wasn't concerned about making this easier for me; he was *mad*. Then he stood and stretched, yawning wide as he did. "I'm having a shower and then we're going out. Wear something warm."

We walked in silence to our car—a VW Golf with bike racks I had no memory of owning—and aside from him saying, "Running shoes," when I asked what I should wear on my feet, Matt didn't even attempt to engage me in conversation. I didn't try, either, unsettled by this dynamic between us and having no idea where we were going or what to expect once we got there. Eventually he would have to speak to me, but I wasn't sure what he would say when he did. I considered this might be the beginning of the end. I had pushed him too far, and the idea made me unexpectedly sad. I wasn't prepared to let go of Matt, even if it might be best for both of us. But what he wanted was out of my control, which was a sobering realization.

Lakeshore was busy as usual, but thanks to it being Saturday it wasn't long before we were turning into High Park, Toronto's giant green space smack in the middle of the city. Matt easily found a parking spot—it was only eight in the morning, and most people were still waking up—and then he turned off the car but didn't make a move to get out. So I waited, shored up my emotions in preparation for whatever came next.

Matt stared out the front windshield and I watched him. When it appeared he still wasn't ready to speak, I shifted my gaze, saw a woman jog by pushing a running stroller. Another couple with two tiny dogs and one big one, all in matching plaid coats, walked the path toward the off-leash park. The snow was entirely gone now, the grass a muted green-brown color that soon would be lush and vibrant with a little more rain and sunshine. I wondered if Matt could hear my rapid heartbeat, which was thunderous in my own ears.

"I know you don't remember this, but we used to come here a lot on the weekends," Matt said, and I jumped because I had been lulled into the silence. "We'd go for a run and then have breakfast at the café."

"I run?" That didn't sound like me.

He nodded. "You run. You've done three half-marathons. But you're a bit of a fair-weather runner, so you usually don't train through the winter." I glanced at my legs, encased in jeans, and tried to imagine them propelling me for that many kilometers.

"We were going to do the full in May actually, so you were putting in a lot of mileage before your accident."

A full marathon? That was, like, more than forty kilometers. "Are you sure I'm a runner?"

Matt laughed then and I relaxed somewhat. He didn't seem angry anymore. "I'm sure." He undid his seat belt and opened the car door. "Let's go."

"Where are we going?" I asked, getting out of the car. "Not a run, I hope."

"We're not going for a run." He locked the car, then took my hand and I let him. Curled my fingers around his, liking the way it felt. "Not today, anyway."

He led me across the road that encircled the center of the park, and we walked through a small parking lot and into the Grenadier Café. I took a deep breath of the smells of breakfast cooking in grease, and my stomach grumbled.

"I may not remember eating here, but I think my stomach certainly does."

Matt smiled, and a sensation of happiness spread through me. We sat at a table and took off our coats, then grabbed trays and lined up at the food counter.

"What do I usually get?" I asked, looking over the menu.

Matt paused for a moment. "Why don't you order what you're in the mood for?"

"I would like to get what I always get." I tried to keep the small burst of irritation out of my voice. He had brought me here for a reason, which I guessed was to help me make inroads to understanding our past. And right now, standing at the breakfast counter with Matt, all I wanted was to be that Lucy again.

"Pancakes. Side of tomatoes and potatoes. Double order of bacon," Matt said. "Oh, and coffee and grapefruit juice."

"Wow. Okay. That's a lot of food. Tomatoes and potatoes, eh?" He shrugged and we placed our orders (three scrambled eggs, Canadian bacon, hash browns, coffee for Matt), then took our number and drinks back to our table.

Over breakfast I grilled Matt about other things. What else did we used to do on weekends, aside from jog ridiculous distances? Where had we traveled together, and where did we want to go? Did I like to cook? What was our favorite take-out spot? How did I get into running? I wished I had my notebook with me, but I tried to hold on to all his answers so I could transcribe them later into my list. And if it was hard for Matt to have to tell me answers to questions I should have remembered easily, he didn't show it.

"I was training for a marathon and you said you were tired of being a 'running widow' on the weekends." Matt stacked some eggs and bacon onto a piece of buttered toast. "So you told me you wanted to give it a try, see if it could be something we did together."

"Huh," I said, sprinkling salt and pepper on the fried tomatoes. "And just like that, I was a runner?"

"Not quite," Matt said, laughing. "But you were a natural actually. It wasn't long until you were keeping pace and we were covering a lot of distance. It was nice. Training together."

"I'm sure it was," I murmured. *I'm so sorry I don't remember, Matt.*

He smiled and then pointed to my plate, which I felt like I hadn't made much of a dent in. "How's your breakfast?"

"Great," I replied, stretching back against my chair to try to find more space in my stomach. "But I'm full. I can't believe I used to eat all of this in one sitting."

"You did, but it was after a twenty-kilometer run, so you were on empty." He crushed his napkin and placed it on top of his nearly empty plate. "Ready for part two? I promise no running or food involved."

I groaned and rubbed my stomach. "It would not be pretty if you made me run right now." He laughed and took our trays back to the counter.

This time as we walked I took his hand, and our clasped fingers played lazily as we headed down a steep hill, enjoying

the sunshine as it warmed us up enough to force us to zip open
our coats. It was that strange time of year in Toronto where
you needed to change clothes three times in a day, as the temperature could drop or rise easily by ten degrees from morning to afternoon. We walked in a comfortable silence, smiling
and exchanging hellos and "Good morning" with other walk-
ers and joggers.

"Warm enough?" he asked as we got to the bottom of the
hill, veering to the right and following the path. Even though
Matt said we had come here often, my only memories of High
Park were from my university days. Jenny and I had joined an
Ultimate Frisbee team that practiced at the park—but my par-
ticipation in the sport didn't last long, despite the fun social side
where we'd drink pints postgames, as I hated the running and
was a terrible thrower.

"Yep." Though my body was heating up from the walk and
sun, the tips of my ears were still a bit chilly, but not cold enough
for the toque I had stuffed in my coat pocket.

Matt stopped in front of a path entrance that continued into
the belly of the park, and I read the sign: Welcome to the Zoo.

"Oh, the High Park Zoo!" I said, my voice lifting with enthusiasm. "I've always wanted to come here."

Matt cleared his throat, looked at me uneasily. My stomach
dropped and my prior burst of energy fizzled. "We've been here
a lot, haven't we?" I said.

"It was on our running route," he replied. "You always made
us stop at the capybara pen. Said you thought it was some sort
of mutant guinea pig experiment gone wrong but they were
still adorable."

I smiled and pulled on his hand, determined not to let all the
good feelings I was having be overshadowed. "Come on. Let's
go see if I still think that, okay?"

He resisted a moment, perhaps doubting the wisdom of this
field trip, but then seemed to relax as I felt the tension leave his
fingers and he fell into step beside me.

"You probably won't remember this," Matt began, and we both chuckled as I added, "What's new?"

"Touché," he continued, adding, "But Bonnie and Clyde escaped last spring and they were fugitives in the city for weeks."

"Who are Bonnie and Clyde?"

"That's what they nicknamed the capybara couple. They were quite the celebrities last year. And apparently absence does make the heart grow fonder, because now they're the proud parents of three little capybabies."

I snort-laughed. "Capybabies?"

He shrugged, offering a wide grin. "This city loves these damn rodents. Spent fifteen grand searching for them. Even the mayor's office Tweeted out a capybaby birth announcement last week."

"I wish I remembered all this. Or any of it," I said, sighing gently. Matt stopped suddenly, forcing me to stop, too. We faced one another, and he took my other hand in his.

"I'm so sorry this is happening to you, Lucy." So earnest, he was. He pulled me closer, but there was still a sliver of space between our bodies. I shivered and he noticed, rubbing his hands up and down my arms to get rid of the chill.

"Happening to *us*," I whispered. "I'm sorry, too, Matt. I wish I could get better. Get back to—"

I was about to say "normal," but then Matt was kissing me. And without hesitation I pressed my body against his. He tasted of salt and coffee and I kissed him back, eager to get as close to him as I could. To morph into past-Lucy, who ran twenty kilometers on a Saturday morning, ate pancakes and two servings of bacon and regularly kissed her boyfriend in front of the capybara pen at the High Park Zoo.

He pulled back enough to apologize for the spontaneous kiss, but I put a finger on his lips, asked him to be quiet. Then I kissed him and for a moment felt like maybe, one day, I could again be that girl I no longer remembered.

13

Matt was trying hard to sort out what to say. I could see his valiant attempt to control his face, the way he held his lips together so he looked mildly pensive but nothing more. The curious rise to his eyebrows—not so high it seemed questioning, but noticeable enough to prove he had thoughts about what I had said yet wasn't sure how to convey them.

I had, moments earlier, suggested he move back into our bedroom, and our bed.

Once Jenny told me about Daniel being married—and I recovered from the painful shock—and Matt took me to High Park, something shifted inside me when it came to us. It wasn't that I remembered loving him (I didn't… *Would I ever?*), but I understood he felt those things for me, while Daniel did not. The man I thought I had married loved another woman and, in fact, wasn't in my life in any capacity. I needed to give Matt and my memory a chance, something I couldn't do if I was stuck in this fabricated world with Daniel. Which was why I kissed him back at the zoo. Pretended we were merely a contented couple out for a Saturday stroll, our greatest worry being where we might brunch afterward.

That kiss and its intensity had wiggled something free inside me. Not a memory exactly, but a strong desire to do more of that because it felt good. Maybe even *right*. I wondered if a more intimate situation with Matt might jump-start my memory, like live cables attached to a dead battery. Perhaps I was even close to some sort of breakthrough, though I had to remind myself breakthroughs were a bit like winning lottery numbers: exciting to imagine, unlikely to ever happen.

"I…I'm not sure what to say," Matt finally said. "I mean, yes. Yes. But are you sure? Because you should be sure and you don't need to do this for—"

I stopped him. "I'm sure."

He nodded and then dropped his head so I could no longer see his face as he took a deep breath. I was nervous, not knowing what he was thinking or feeling. I understood Matt had a lot more to lose than I did in this scenario, which in some ways made my suggestion unfair. "Sorry," he said gruffly. *Oh, no. He's crying.* He sniffed a couple of times and then cleared his throat, getting himself under control as he raised his head back up.

"Luce, look. Nothing would make me happier than us being back to…sharing a room again. But there's no rush, okay?" He understood as well as I did I wasn't proposing us only sleeping in there, a nice wide gap in the bed between us as we did. And so he wasn't going to treat it lightly, which made me feel even more secure in the decision.

"I'm fine in the guest room for as long as necessary. I have no expectations of you, or of this. Today, at the zoo…it wasn't about this." His gaze held mine and in that moment any doubt that *this* was precisely what I wanted evaporated.

At first I felt buoyed by the realization, and then just plain sad. Matt was incredible and he was mine. He loved me, and I—until I forgot everything that seemed to matter most—loved him right back. What an unfair tragedy to have such an important, perfect thing erased from your mind. "I wouldn't have suggested it if it wasn't what I wanted."

He watched me for a moment longer. "I don't want you to get mad, but I have to ask."

"Okay…ask what?"

He took a deep breath. "Did you change your mind because of Daniel? Because he's married?"

Tell him no. I paused for a beat too long. "Maybe. I'm not sure exactly."

Matt nodded, probably expecting this answer, though likely wishing for it to have nothing at all to do with Daniel. I'm sure it made him sick to his stomach every time Daniel's name was mentioned.

"But I *know* it has more to do with you. And today," I added. "Is that okay?"

"It's more than okay," Matt said. "But I need you to understand something, Lucy. I love you. And like I said, there's no rush for any of this. I'm not going anywhere." He stepped closer to me, brushed a stray hair from my forehead, then rested his hands gently on my shoulders. "So if this is about Daniel more than it's about me, or us, it's fine. I can wait. And if you're never… ready…" He held his composure. "Well, I'll accept that."

I placed my hands on his hips and leaned against him, closing my eyes. He held me for a moment, settling his chin on the top of my head, and I turned my face so my cheek rested on his chest. *This must have been it*, I thought, comfortable and secure. *Our position.*

"Thank you for saying that," I said. "But I still want to try, okay?"

"Okay," he murmured, his lips on the crown of my head. "Would it be all right if I…if I kissed you again?" His voice was quiet, unsure despite what I had said. Like we were kids exploring the boundaries of our relationship, trying to see what else might be there.

I leaned slightly away from him so I could look into his face, but kept my arms wrapped around his waist. "Yes."

He smiled and pressed his lips to mine. I wish I could say this time there was a blinding flash of recognition and I remembered everything. But I didn't.

However, I did like the feel of him. The way his lips were gentle with mine until I responded, giving him permission to go deeper. And while it was true my mind couldn't recall my history with Matt, it seemed my body remembered and responded to him. It wasn't long before we stumbled into our bedroom, barely breaking apart for a breath—what we'd started at the park warming us up for what came next.

The sex was fantastic, if not a bit intense, and though it was the first time I could remember being intimate with Matt, it didn't feel entirely unfamiliar. Which was odd, yet reassuring. It seemed a part of me hadn't forgotten what Matt and I had, or how well we had worked together, once.

Yet as I lay naked beside him afterward, trying to hang on to the lingering, warm buzz of what we'd done, I had to fight the instinct I'd betrayed Daniel.

14

It was the end of March, almost two months since the day I slipped on the ice, and Matt and I were headed out for Jake's thirtieth birthday party. Matt had been asking me daily for the past week if I was sure I wanted to go (yes, or mostly yes), and then if I thought I *should* go. He seemed more anxious about it than I was, and while I wasn't looking forward to Jake's party exactly, I was tired of the four walls of our living room and my antisocial status.

Matt and I had been sleeping in the same bed now for the past two weeks, and things were progressing in the sense it had started to feel more natural to have him beside me all night. We'd had sex only a couple more times, and while it had been nice to share that closeness with someone—my body certainly craved the release—I couldn't shake the feeling I was being unfaithful. It hovered over me, settled like a sickness in my gut even when I tried to push it away and remind myself *I was* with Matt. Thinking about Daniel was actually the unfaithful act.

I told Dr. Kay I'd decided not to contact Daniel, and she listened carefully as I unleashed my frustrations in the safety of our session about everyone keeping the truth from me. After acknowledging my resentment, she said, "Everyone is trying to help you, Lucy. The best way they know how. And they won't always get it right."

What could I say? Of course they were trying. They loved me. I felt bad after what she said, for the stunt I pulled by locking myself in the room and making everyone worry. But Dr. Kay wouldn't let me get too self-pitying, either. "Own your feelings, Lucy. But don't try to control or suppress them. No one expects you to get it right all the time, either."

She asked what had set my mind about not contacting Daniel, and I admitted that while part of me still wanted to see him, a greater part of me wanted to let him go.

"What do you think you need, Lucy?"

"I don't think I need that anymore. To see Daniel, I mean. What I need is to convince my brain to accept the truth, because it's still hanging on to last year's news." I smiled, or at least I tried hard. "Do you know how impossible it is to try to get your brain to convince your, well, brain what it believes isn't true?"

"I'm guessing it's not easy," Dr. Kay said. "Not at all."

No, it isn't.

When Matt and I arrived, the party was already in full swing. If I thought I was prepared to be out at a bar, I was wrong. Between the sounds of celebratory voices, the band playing full tilt and so many bodies packed into the room, I could barely catch my breath. I focused on my belly, extending it with a deep breath, then letting it out with a low, controlled hiss. It helped somewhat, so I did it a few more times as Matt clutched my hand and led me toward the bar.

We stood in line and he leaned close. "You okay?"

"Stop asking me that," I snapped, then immediately regretted it when Matt dropped my hand, looking stung. My emotional pendulum swung from swift anger to remorse, and I swallowed hard as I forced the necessary apology to my lips. "Sorry. I'm okay. Thanks."

Matt nodded, then gave his body a little shake—rolling his

shoulders a couple of times and jumping up and down a few inches while we waited in line, as though he were getting ready for a race. It was what he did when he was nervous, needed to release energy so he could focus.

"Gin and soda?" Matt asked as we approached the bar.

"Please. Lots of lime."

He was leaning on the bar, about to give our drink order, but then he turned back to me. "You want lime?"

"In my gin and soda?" I replied. "Always." That was my go-to drink order, or at least I thought it had been. I frowned. "Isn't that what I drink?" He gave me one last curious look, then shrugged before leaning across the bar to give our drink order—beer for him, gin and soda for me, lots of lime.

I tried to relax but was struggling to find my bearings, the environment too loud and boisterous for my fragile brain and fickle emotions. Matt handed me my drink, asked again if I was okay. "Lucy? Do you want to leave?" Part of me did, but I also wanted to enjoy my drink and dance and have fun with friends on a Saturday night. I wanted to be past-Lucy for one night and figured maybe I could find her with enough gin and sodas—or maybe that would help me forget all of new-Lucy's problems.

"No, I want to stay." I smiled wide as though to prove I was okay. Everything was under control.

Matt shifted uneasily in front of me, his eyes darting around the room like he was expecting something to happen at any moment. He hadn't even taken a sip of his beer. "Look, Lucy, there's something I should have said before…before we got here. And I'm not sure—"

But before Matt could finish his thought, someone grabbed me in a hug from behind and my drink spilled with the sudden shift of my body. "Lucy!" the hugger shouted, spinning me around before embracing me again. It was Jake, the birthday boy. He held me at arm's length, gave a low whistle. I laughed at Jake's theatrics until I saw Matt's face. He did not look well

at all. But there wasn't a chance to ask him if *he* was okay, because Jake was hugging me again. This time I held my drink
away from our bodies so it didn't spill. "You look better than
ever. Are you sure you didn't make up this hospital stuff to hide
an extended vacation?"

"Yeah, hospitals are the new spas," I said. Finally Matt smiled,
then tucked me protectively into his side and kissed my temple.
Did I like that? Matt acting like I needed a shield? I tried to decide if it was sweet or cloying, voted for the latter and shifted
slightly away from the nook of his arm to clink glasses with
Jake. "Happy birthday," I said.

"Thank you," Jake replied, eyeing me closely. "So, how are
you really?" He held the neck of his beer bottle between his
thumb and forefinger, rested it on his hip casually as he waited
for me to answer.

"Good! Great!" I said. Matt squeezed my elbow gently, and
I smiled at him. But as much as I wanted to take care of myself, to prove I was *just fine*, I was feeling rattled because now I
realized this was how I would spend the evening: not drinking
and relaxing with friends, but answering their same concerned
and curious questions, over and over. "I'm doing well, thanks."

"Glad to hear it. So crazy, right?" He looked between Matt
and me and I saw Matt shake his head a little. But while I caught
it, Jake didn't seem to. "I've had a dozen concussions playing
hockey but never had anything like that happen. Crazy. I can't
imagine."

Matt stiffened beside me and I realized why he had been so
anxious leading up to tonight. Why he had given me so many
outs for the evening, and why he had tried to give Jake the sig-
nal to stop talking.

Jake knew. About my memory. Glancing around the room,
I felt like all eyes were on me. I spotted a handful of our colleagues in the crowd, was immediately self-conscious being on
display like this. *How many of them know?* My irritation from
earlier blossomed into full-fledged rage, and my head pounded

as though the only place for my anger to go was straight out the top of me.

"Amnesia would be a trippy thing." Jake gave a low whistle, took a sip of his beer.

"She doesn't have amnesia, Jake," Matt interjected. I glanced at him sharply, but he kept his eyes on Jake. "It's just a few—"

"It's called false-memory syndrome," I said, keeping my tone even despite the pounding through my skull, the simmering heat in my cheeks. I was *just fine*, thank you very much. "Actually, apparently they don't call it a syndrome anymore. So I guess it's false-memory…"

Now I turned to Matt. "What should we call it, do you think? Maybe 'Lucy hit her head and then made shit up' condition?" I laughed hard—forcing it out—and so did Jake, still not noticing the bands of tension between Matt and me. Matt looked down at his feet, not laughing with us.

"Atta girl," Jake said, clinking his bottle against my glass, which I raised in response and took a long sip. "You haven't lost your sense of humor. Glad to see it."

"Thanks. Me, too." I took another long sip of my drink as Matt whispered in my ear, "Maybe you should slow down?"

"Maybe," I said, then drained my glass.

"So, any idea when you might be back to work?" Jake continued. "We miss you. Especially this guy." He clapped Matt on the shoulder. "He mopes around the office. Seriously, it's freakin' sad. Lucy, get back to us soon, okay?"

I glanced at Matt, who stayed silent.

"I will. Shouldn't be long now," I said.

"Oh, yeah? That's great news."

"Mmm-hmm," I said, now desperate to escape. It was exhausting playing "just-fine"-Lucy—my skin crawled, my stomach rolled, my head pounded with the effort of pretending to be okay when I wasn't. "Every day a little better."

Jake nodded, sipped his beer. "Fantastic," he said. A couple of guys I didn't recognize (*Did I know them? Did we work together, and I'd forgotten?*) came up and pulled Jake away for shots at the other end of the bar. He offered one last "You look great, Lucy. Thanks for coming tonight," over his shoulder as he went and Matt and I stayed in place, saying nothing.

There was a long moment of silence, then, "Lucy, I'm sorry. I tried… I didn't mean to—"

I held up my hand, and Matt abruptly stopped talking. "I thought we'd agreed to say nothing to anyone at work." My hands shook as I set my empty glass on top of the bar. "Why did you tell Jake? It's no one else's business."

"At some point it's going to be their business, Lucy!" He was practically yelling. In part because he was upset and frustrated—high-strung with the stress of the past few weeks—and in part to be heard over the bar's loudness. "What did you want me to say when he asked? What?"

"How about nothing?" My voice rose to match his. "Or that I'm still dealing with the postconcussion stuff. Which is the truth, by the way."

"You don't know what it's been like," he said, his voice pleading. "I didn't plan on saying anything about the memory thing."

I had to get out of there because I didn't want to hear any more excuses about how Matt had once again made a decision for me, kept something from me. I also couldn't seem to catch my breath and needed to get outside into the fresh air, but Matt was right behind me and grabbed hold of my arm, begging me to let him explain. We were now in a quieter corner down by the washrooms, so I leaned back against the wall and crossed my arms over my chest, which heaved with the effort of trying to take in a full breath.

Matt rubbed at his face, looked worried as I gasped for air and asked if I wanted to sit down. I shook my head and focused on slowing my breathing. "What, Matt? What happened?" My voice was strained, thready with my erratic breathing and how pissed off I was.

He sighed and pressed a palm to his forehead, but kept his eyes on mine. "When Jenny texted about what happened at lunch and that she was worried about you—like, 911-level worried—I was on a conference call with a client. Jenny was panicking, so then I started panicking. It's been hard…not having you there, at work." But I knew what lived between those words. *It's been hard you not remembering me, and us.* "I bolted from the conference room to call Jenny, and then Jake came to make sure I was okay and asked me what was wrong and it…it slipped out. I'm so sorry, Lucy."

Slipped out? Even though I felt awful for everything I had put him through, I'd had it. Enough with people who supposedly had my best interests in mind making unilateral decisions that directly affected me, behind my back and without my consent.

"I need to go home," I said, unable to argue about it anymore. I was drained, and dizzy from the gin. And before Matt could say anything in response, like, *Okay, let's go home*, I added, "Alone."

"Lucy, come on. This isn't like you," Matt replied, his words sharp, his cheeks flushed with frustration. He nearly immediately realized his mistake—reminding me I was not the same person as before—and cringed, then took my hand in both of his. Begging me through his touch to stay, to calm down and to forgive him. His tone softened as he said, "There's no way I'm letting you leave by yourself."

"Good thing it isn't your choice, then," I replied. "Please let me go, Matt. Now." I pulled my hand out of his, took a few steps back and promptly ran into the wall. A sob choked me and I ran toward the front entrance of the bar. The tears were already streaming down my face as I stumbled outside onto the street. Still struggling to take in a full breath, I hastily wiped my tearstained face and looked around for a cab, until I noticed one idling by the curb and strode toward it. Another car pulled up behind the taxi and three guys spilled out, but I gave them little notice as I focused on not having a complete breakdown on the sidewalk. I was opening the taxi's door when I heard, "Lucy?"

I turned, and there stood Daniel London.

15

He looked different, his hair longer and scruffier than he used to wear it when we were together—the way I still remembered it. I wouldn't say he looked older exactly, but there was something about him that felt unfamiliar now.

"No way. Lucy Sparks." Daniel's face broke into a slow smile as I stared at him, unsure what to do next. My knees started shaking and I was grateful for the taxi's open door, which I used to prop myself up. Daniel pointed to his two companions, then back to me. "Dave, Greg, this is Lucy." He paused, still smiling. "An old friend."

I barely glanced at the other two but managed to say it was nice to meet them. "Hey, guys, I'll catch up with you inside," Daniel said to his friends. Then we were alone and all was quiet, until the taxi driver asked me if I wanted him to wait.

"Yes," I said through the open window, still trying to catch my breath. *How long can a person hyperventilate before they pass out?* "Please wait." He started the meter and I turned my attention back to Daniel. It was dark, but we were near a streetlight, so I could now see better how his face had changed: crinkles at the corners of his eyes, a little extra weight had softened his jawline, a soul patch under his bottom lip. But the smile was the same, and it slayed me to see it.

"It's been a long time," Daniel said. He tucked his chin inside the collar of his coat, rubbed his hands together to warm them. I was in too much shock to even feel the cold.

"H–has it?" I stammered, then corrected myself. "It has. But it doesn't feel like it, to be honest." *Keep it together, Lucy.* "I can't believe it's you. Daniel London."

"In the flesh," he replied, grinning. Then he leaned in to hug me, and it caught me off guard. The embrace was awkward, as was the struggle to right ourselves after it. "It's been, what... four or five years?"

"Something like that."

"So how are you?" he asked, leaning against the taxi beside me. "You look great."

"Thanks," I said. "I'm good. Doing well. How about you?"

Why did we break up? What the hell happened to us, Daniel? I tried to quiet my mind, to give little credence to the strange luck that brought us together tonight. To ignore the screaming questions about why I wasn't Mrs. Lucy London. But Daniel, standing so close to me now, was extremely distracting and I was struggling to concentrate. He was stockier than Matt, shorter, too, and because of that our eyes were nearly level when he turned toward me, which was disarming.

"I'm back at school, grad school actually," Daniel said. "Turns out the law wasn't my thing. Dad is less than thrilled, but hey, I'm used to disappointing that man." He shrugged like it didn't matter, but he looked upset. I remembered how hard Daniel's father used to be on him. The assumption he would become a lawyer, join the family firm, follow confidently in his father's well-heeled footsteps. It was a constant source of frustration for Daniel when we were dating, the expectations his highbrow parents had set out for him.

"That's great," I said. "For you. Less so for your dad, I guess." I wondered if I should let the driver go, catch another cab later. I wanted to talk to Daniel all night.

"So how about you?" he asked, nudging my arm with his.

A shock rang through me, which I mostly hid by shoving my hands into my coat pockets. "What have you been up to?"

There was an intense moment of disappointment that came with his question, because it confirmed what I knew to be true but had been struggling to believe—Daniel London had no idea what I'd been up to because Daniel London was not my husband. After a short pause to collect myself I filled him in on work, using only as many words as needed. I didn't trust myself not to blurt out what was really going on. But if my discomfort and angst showed, Daniel didn't seem to pick up on it.

"Jameson Porter is a great firm," he said. "Have a buddy from high school who works there. That's actually why I'm here tonight. It's his birthday."

"Jake Anderson?" I said. "That's why we're—I'm here. For Jake's party."

"Really? Small world, isn't it?"

"It is," I murmured. I fought to maintain my composure; all this small talk wasn't helping. "I guess I should get going."

"Ah, too bad you're on your way out. It would have been great to have a drink."

"Yeah, I know. But I have this…other thing to get to tonight," I said. "It was great to see you, Daniel." He had no idea how great. Or how confusing.

"You, too, Lucy." He leaned over and gave me a kiss on the cheek and it was all I could do not to turn and kiss him back. His lips were cool and his facial hair felt strange on my skin, but everything else about him felt right. *Familiar.* I pulled back, though it took everything in me to do so, and smiled to hide the tornado of emotions. Daniel reached around me and opened the taxi's door wider, and then he stepped to the side so I could get in.

"Thanks," I said, glad to finally be sitting. My legs were like wet noodles.

He shut the door and rested his hands on the window well and it was then I saw it—his wedding band, glittering gold under the streetlight. My stomach lurched, tickling my gag reflex and bringing the drink I'd guzzled dangerously close to coming back up. *God, please let me not throw up in this cab in front of Daniel.*

"Listen, do you want to get a coffee sometime?" I asked. I had planned to say goodbye and not look back, but I wasn't ready to have things end so abruptly. "So we can catch up?"

He paused for a beat, a curious look on his face. "Didn't we already do that?"

My stomach dropped, and if I could have crawled under the taxi's front seat, I would have. I wished I could reach into the space between us and grab my words and shove them back inside my mouth.

"Totally kidding," he said, smiling that smile I knew so well. The one I'd fallen for all those years ago. "Coffee would be great."

I plastered a wobbly smile on my face, my insides tingling at the prospect of spending more time with Daniel. Then Matt's face popped into my mind and I considered how he would feel about this exchange. If roles were reversed—and knowing how I felt about Daniel—I definitely wouldn't be happy about it. I silently berated myself for being so weak, for not doing what I knew was the right thing and staying away from Daniel London. It was a fluke we'd run into each other and I should never have turned it into something more.

Sadness settled over me, because Daniel was right here— somehow, *right here*—but he wasn't mine to want, or to miss. Nor should I be planning a seemingly innocent catch-up coffee with him, because I knew it was much more than that. And Matt—the good man I'd run out on in the bar—was mine, but unfortunately he wasn't the one I desperately wanted to be with right now.

I trembled as I imagined what might have happened if I hadn't left the bar when I did. If Matt had been beside me when I ran into Daniel. I wasn't sure I could have hidden what seeing Daniel had done to me, unraveling me like a sweater pull, leaving me vulnerable and exposed.

Daniel reached into his back pocket and pulled out his phone. "What's your number?" he asked, and I gave it to him without hesitation. "Okay, well, I better get in there. And you need to go to your thing," he said. "But it was great running into you, Lucy."

"You, too, Daniel." *You have no idea how great.* "Have fun tonight."

He tapped on the edge of the window well with both hands and waved as the driver pulled away. I let out a long breath, put a hand over my mouth and focused on not vomiting all over the cab's interior.

"You okay back there?" the driver asked, eyeing me suspiciously in the rearview mirror. "There's an extra fee if you get sick, so tell me before you do so I can pull over."

I took my hand away. "I'm fine," I said, and he nodded, turning the music up.

While I hadn't planned any of this, I knew it had been a mistake to give Daniel my number. It would be best for everyone if he deleted it later tonight, when he got home and into bed with Margot and realized reconnecting with your ex for a friendly coffee was never a smart idea. And yet...as the cold wind whipped through the taxi's open window I whispered a small prayer Daniel wouldn't delete my number but would call me for that coffee instead.

16

I didn't tell anyone about Daniel, convincing myself it was because it didn't matter; seeing him changed nothing. I'd also decided I wouldn't have coffee with him, even if he called. Which wasn't likely. We had run into each other outside a bar—it was bound to happen at some point, wasn't it?—and it had been the polite way to end our conversation. That was all it was, nothing more. This ran in a loop in my head for two days, and I had nearly convinced myself Daniel London would stay in the past, where he belonged. And then he called.

It was Monday and Matt had been apologizing nonstop since Sunday morning. He arrived home less than an hour after I did the night of Jake's party, and though it was dark, I could see his silhouette framed in our bedroom doorway. I knew he was debating where to sleep. I wondered what it had been like when we'd fought before, which we inevitably had at least a few times through our relationship, and what happened next. It was bizarre not to remember these intimate rhythms between us.

I let Matt stand there in the doorway a moment longer, then sat up and turned down the duvet on his side. "Come to bed," I said.

He stayed where he was. "I'm sorry, Lucy."

"I know." I patted his side of the bed and rolled back over, tucking the duvet around me. "Let's go to sleep."

We didn't talk about what happened, our argument at the bar or the fact he'd let it slip to Jake about my memory. But he continued to apologize, at unexpected times: like after I asked him if he wanted grilled cheese or a turkey sandwich for lunch on Sunday; or when I was brushing my teeth before bed; and Monday morning as he stood at the front door, helmet on and messenger bag slung over his suited shoulder, ready to go to the office. And with each apology I felt worse about giving Daniel my number. I was with Matt, because at some point in my past I still couldn't remember I had *chosen* Matt.

He finally left for work, thankfully taking his incessant apologies with him. Glad to have the house to myself, I pulled out the memory confidence list I'd been neglecting. I had an appointment with Dr. Kay in the afternoon and so couldn't put off my "homework" any longer.

What's my favorite food? *Bacon, chocolate croissants, pancakes*
*note: eat more vegetables
Where did I go to university? *University of Toronto*
What was my major? *Psychology and English, double major*
When is my birthday? *November 10*
Who's the prime minister of Canada? *Justin Trudeau*
Who's the premier of Ontario? *Kathleen Wynne*
Who's the president of the United States? *Donald Trump*
Where did I take my last vacation? Who with? *California, Matt*
Where do I live? *Toronto (Leslieville)*
Where do I work? *Jameson Porter Consulting, communications director*
How long have I worked there? *Four years*
Do I exercise? *I'm a runner!*
Do I have any allergies? *Not sure—ask Mom and Dad*
Who was my childhood best friend? *Nancy McPherson*

Have I ever had a pet? *Yes, as a kid. Rabbit—Marshmallow*
What are my current hobbies? *Ask Matt and Jenny*
Favorite restaurant? *Ask Matt or Jenny*
Did I watch *Forks ~~and~~ Over Knives*? *Yes*
Am I a vegetarian? *No (because, bacon) *Jenny is vegetarian*
Favorite TV show?

I had no idea what my favorite show was. I remembered watching *Mad Men* with Daniel and *Breaking Bad* with Jenny, but I couldn't recall how either of those shows ended (were they still running?) or what shows Matt and I had watched together. I was still on the no-screens protocol, but a quick Netflix history check couldn't be a big deal...

I turned on the television as my phone rang. Glancing at the screen, I saw an unknown, though local, number. For all the hoping I'd done over the past few weeks and the fact I'd given him my number a couple of days earlier, it actually didn't occur to me it might be Daniel.

But it was, and he was wondering, *Was I free for coffee?* He had some time between classes and would love to see me. "To catch up," he added. I thought back to his *Didn't we already do that?* comment and cringed. But—perhaps too enthusiastically—I said I'd be happy to meet him, and he suggested Moonbean Coffee Company in Kensington Market, close to campus.

I arrived at Moonbean early and ordered a giant latte in a bowl before finding a table by the window, under the navy blue ceiling. Daniel arrived right on time, and my heart lurched when I saw him walk through the front door. There were still parts of him that felt alien—the facial hair, the fine lines across his forehead and fanning out from his eyes, the slightly unkempt look to his longer hair—but overall he was still the same Daniel.

This was a huge mistake.

Because no matter how hard I'd been working to let him go, to focus on my life with Matt, Daniel was comforting to me in a deeply significant way. I was scared by the weight of my longing when I saw him walk through Moonbean's door, and the desire to have him recognize me in the same way.

My face must have displayed this convoluted mix of emotions, because the smile dropped from his face and he quickly sat across from me before even ordering anything at the counter. "Hey, are you okay?" he asked, removing his gloves and unzipping his coat without taking his eyes off me. I was mortified when I started crying.

Daniel took my hands in his and I stared at his ring, the tears dripping down my nose and onto the tabletop. "Lucy, what the hell's the matter? Hey. Hey, what's wrong?"

I shook my head, tried to speak but couldn't. Oh, how I wanted to run out of there. Either that or to reverse time so I could avoid this scene entirely. But there was nowhere to flee. And besides, this was Daniel; he *knew* me. I would be okay with him, even with my mess of a life on full display.

He let go of one of my hands and passed me a napkin from the table. I took a deep breath, getting ahold of myself. "I'm so sorry. This is... Well, embarrassing doesn't quite cover it." I gave him a weak smile, wondered how blotchy my face was.

He smiled, squeezed my hand. "I'll try not to take it too personally."

"Can I get you a coffee? Something to eat?" I asked, rising from my chair, wanting to put some distance between my outburst and whatever came next.

Daniel rose, too. "I'll get it. Want anything else?"

"I'm fine with the latte, thanks," I said, then looked out the window as he went to the counter to order. It had started to rain, and people hurried by under umbrellas, walking around small puddles gathering on the sidewalks.

"So, are you going to tell me what's going on or should we make small talk for a while until you're ready?" Daniel asked, settling back into his chair with his coffee and omelet sandwich.

"Honestly, I don't even know where to start. Things are a bit screwed up at the moment."

"I'm getting that. How about at the beginning?" Daniel replied, stirring two sugar packs into his cream-heavy coffee. He tapped the spoon twice on the edge of his mug (*a memory flash, Daniel always doing this after stirring his coffee*) and waited for me to tell him why I'd burst into tears.

And so I did. About the slip and fall, the coma and head injury, about how when I woke up in the hospital my memory wasn't what it used to be.

"Shit, Lucy, that's intense. But I'm glad you're okay. Or mostly okay," he said. He hadn't yet touched his sandwich, which had to be cold by now. "What exactly does 'spotty' mean?"

"Your lunch is getting cold," I said, searching for a distraction. Unloading the events of the past two months was cathartic, but it also left me feeling split wide-open and close to tears again.

"Is it amnesia?" he asked, his forehead wrinkling with the question.

"Sort of," I said. I suppose I could have left it at that. But then I decided I had come this far, and as Dr. Kay was fond of saying, I needed to "be true to the experience." Skirting the realities of the situation wouldn't help me. And if I was being honest, I was curious to see what his reaction would be.

"I've forgotten some stuff entirely, from the past few years in particular. Like the actual accident, for one." I didn't mention it extended far beyond the day of my fall. Or about Matt. That was too big of a parcel to unload right now.

"But I also have these, uh, *false* memories."

"False memories?"

"I have a few memories that aren't real, but they feel super-real to me."

"Wow," he said, leaning forward, sandwich hanging from his hand. "All from hitting your head?" I nodded, sipped my lukewarm latte. "Like what sort of memories?"

"Well, I remember switching to vegetarianism. But apparently it never happened."

"You? A vegetarian?" Daniel laughed.

"I know, right?" I sighed, ran my finger around the lip of my latte bowl, a small amount of the foam transferring to my finger. "Apparently brains don't like blank spaces. So when I was in the coma and not making new memories, my brain decided to stitch some things together and voilà. Customized, fake memories." I shook my head, realizing how strange it all sounded once I said it out loud. "I told you, it's screwed up."

Daniel nodded. "You're not kidding. How have you been dealing with everything?"

I shrugged. "I'm not? I mean, I'm trying. I haven't been cleared to go back to work yet, and I'm still screen free. It's a postconcussion thing," I explained. "But I am seeing a therapist—right after this actually—who's helping me with my 'memory confidence.'" I put air quotes around the last two words. "Here's hoping that helps."

"I hope so," Daniel said.

"Me, too."

"How's your family doing?" he asked. "With the memory stuff?"

"It's been tough on them obviously, but they've been there for me. However, I was beginning to think my mom might move into our place permanently. Force me to drink tea 24/7. You know how she is with her tea."

"I do remember that," Daniel said, laughing again. He had drunk many cups of tea with my mom while we were together, even though he hated the taste of it. "So, 'our place'…you live with someone?" He watched me without reproach, innocently interested.

"I do. Matt. He's been great, amazing actually." I flushed, felt terrible for being here with Daniel even though it was only a coffee. Because I knew Matt wouldn't want me here. And he would be hurt by how much I was sharing with Daniel, whom

I had opened up to more in the span of thirty minutes than I had in weeks with Matt. That didn't say good things.

"I'm glad to hear it."

"Thanks," I replied, smiling as best I could. Then I thought about Margot, the other part of this equation, and my heart sped up. I felt hot and flustered, and before I could stop myself, I blurted out, "I heard you and Margot got married."

"We did," Daniel said, leaning back in his chair. "Two years ago, tomorrow actually."

"Happy almost-anniversary." I hoped I sounded genuine. "And please say hi to her for me."

"Thanks. I will." Daniel looked at his plate, fiddled with his fork and cleared his throat. He chewed the edge of his lip the way he used to when he had something to say he knew I probably didn't want to hear, and I regretted bringing up Margot. But I still had so many questions only he could answer. *What happened with us, Daniel? And how in the hell did you and Margot end up together?* He'd once commented he wouldn't be surprised if she never married—far too independent to compromise for a relationship. *So how are you with her, and not me?*

However, asking those questions would mean admitting exactly what I remembered, and what I didn't. Not to mention being wildly inappropriate for a quick visit with a guy I hadn't talked to in years, and who owed me no such answers.

"Where are you living now?" he asked a moment later, thankfully changing the subject into less emotional territory.

"In Leslieville. What about you?"

"Not too far from you actually. A block south of Danforth. Right across from Withrow Park."

"Nice spot." Withrow Park had a big tobogganing hill, packed with sleds and gaggles of kids most winter weekends. It was the perfect neighborhood to settle and start a family and I tried not to think about him and Margot one day holding hands as they watched their kids sled that hill.

"We love it. We've been slowly renovating our place, which

is not something I ever thought I would do. But I'm practically a master tile layer now." He smiled, and I returned it despite how disconcerting I was finding our conversation. It was ridiculous to think I still knew *this* Daniel—of course I didn't. It had been years, and he was married and a whole different person now. For example, the Daniel I knew had plenty of skills, but home improvements would never had made the list (I had been the light bulb changer and toilet fixer and picture hanger in our relationship).

It would have been interesting to consider him like this, if I could have extricated myself from the emotional side of things. Doing his master's in education, swapping suits for jeans, rolling up his sleeves to lay tile and replace hardwood flooring and mud drywall. I wondered how I would have adapted to these changes, if we had stayed together. And, as quickly, wondered if I seemed different to him, as well.

"What else has been keeping you busy these days? Still writing?" Daniel asked.

"I write a lot of press releases and client memos, if that counts."

"It does. But I more meant your other stuff. The book stuff."

"Books, like novels?" I had no recollection of ever writing anything other than essays in university and a few short stories I had tried to get published postgraduation, without success.

Daniel nodded. "You always had this notebook with you, full of first lines for novels you wanted to write one day."

"Did I?" I shook my head. "I don't remember." Where had that notebook gone? I made a mental note to put it on my list of questions needing answers.

"I'm sure your press releases are impossible to put down." He winked and I laughed.

"Oh, and apparently I'm a runner now," I said. "I've done three half-marathons, if you can believe it."

He whistled. "Impressive. And I won't lie, it is a bit hard to believe." We both laughed, hard, because Daniel-era Lucy hadn't known the first thing about running. "Remember that time we tried jogging up the Casa Loma steps? I still feel bad about what happened to you."

"I *do* remember actually." I winced at the recollection of my tumble down those stone stairs, rubbed my fingers absentmindedly into the wrist I'd broken in the fall. I'd had to wear a cast for eight weeks. "It was not my finest moment."

"Nah, you were a trouper," he said. "I was impressed you didn't pass out when they started the ring cutter." *Right.* My engagement ring had been cut off my rapidly swelling hand in the emergency room. I looked to my finger, remembering how gorgeous it had been and how much I had loved wearing it. Felt gloomy it was no longer there.

"I guess somewhere along the way I finally figured out how to run without tripping." I was encouraged our memories lined up, at least on this event. Glad we had this coffee date if for no other reason because it reinforced I hadn't completely rewritten the past. "But hang on…" I was remembering something about that run and my broken wrist, and the timing of it. "That was only a week before our, um, party." I tried not to squirm, having brought up our engagement. But there was a question I needed answered right now. Daniel nodded, confirming I had the timeline right. "Did I have a cast for the party? Because of my wrist?"

"You did."

"Black fiberglass. I remember." It came out in a whisper, my mind preoccupied by another critical detail: the rose petal bath with Daniel, which had made us late for our engagement party. There was no way I would have been in the bath, doing what we were doing, with a cast.

I was confused, the memory clashing with his confirmation of events. Had that bath happened at a different time? Were we late to another event, and somehow I had mashed the two things together? Or had I made it up entirely? "Um, were we late for the party?" I asked Daniel. "Like, piss-our-mothers-off late?"

He frowned, reaching back in his own memory. "I don't think

so. I met you there, because you were at your parents' place and came with them."

"We didn't go together?"

"Nope. Your mom was helping you with your hair, because of the cast." Daniel glanced at his phone, some sort of notification appearing on his screen with a gentle buzz. He looked up again and said something else, but it was as though I went underwater—I could see he was talking but couldn't hear the words.

I tried to listen, especially because he seemed to be repeating himself. But my brain was busy attempting to reconcile my memory with reality, and as I pushed—forcing my mind to bend, to adapt—it felt as though the floor beneath me tilted. I jerked the way you do when you're nearly asleep and have the sensation of falling and Daniel put a firm hand on my upper arm.

"Lucy!" Daniel looked as worried as I felt. He kept his hand on my arm. "You all right?"

"Yeah. I get these headaches. Sometimes they make me a bit dizzy," I said. I waved away his concern, though I was fairly certain if I stood up now I would hit the floor. "Concussion leftovers. I'm okay."

"You sure?"

I nodded. The floor was solid and stationary again under my feet.

"Good." He let out a breath, relaxed his hand on my arm. "Not about the side effect, but about being okay." Daniel glanced at his phone again, picked it up. "Hey, I'm sorry to eat and run, but I have to make a call before class," he said, smiling apologetically.

"Of course." I followed his lead, put on my toque and coat. "I'm sorry I didn't get a chance to ask how things are going with you and your master's. Maybe next time." I smiled, wrapped my scarf around my neck.

He stood and put on his coat, zipping it right up to his chin. "I would love that." Then he hugged me, and I leaned into him. Was nearly overcome again, his body so recognizable against mine. I wanted to grab hold and never let go. "Same time next week?" he asked.

"Same time next week," I said, reluctantly stepping out of his embrace. I had to wonder if he wanted to see me again, or was simply being kind with my whole admittance of the head injury thing. Maybe I'd end up canceling next week. We could be friends, and the memory of him as anything more would fade, lose its clear edges the way memories tend to do. Or maybe (*just maybe*) I would tell him the truth.

Regardless, it was clear after our coffee a problem remained, one I didn't know how to easily solve: I still loved Daniel.

17

"How are things going with Matt?" Mom held up a gauzy white top that looked like at least a dozen other tops she had hanging in her closet. She glanced at the price tag, clucked her tongue and carried on. Even though she could have easily spent the money, she had these rules about the price of things. A top had to be less than forty dollars, unless it was cashmere and then she made an exception, on occasion. Pants and skirts were given a little more leeway for whatever reason, up to sixty, and shoes could go up to a hundred, but they had to be leather and "sturdy." I once bought a pair of ballet flats for over two hundred dollars—they were worth it, the most comfortable shoes I ever owned—and Mom brought it up every time I wore them. "Two hundred dollars," she would exclaim. "For a glorified slipper!"

Today we were hunting for a new top for her, appropriate for a fancy dinner out. This was our fourth stop and no luck so far. I hated having nothing better to do, but I didn't—aside from an appointment later in the afternoon with my neurologist, Dr. Mulder, where I would hopefully be given the green light to get back to screens and, ideally, work.

"Things are fine, Mom." I didn't want to talk about Matt, because talking about him led me straight to thinking about Daniel. And I wasn't in a good place to unravel what was going on with Daniel, or rather, how I was feeling about him. I mean, there was *nothing* going on with Daniel, but try explaining that to my discombobulated memory, my grief-struck heart.

So I focused us back on the task at hand—shopping. I pulled a deep purple silk shirt off a rack and held it up. "What about this one? It looks nice with your hair." She took it from me and held it against herself, frowning as she sashayed in front of the store's full-length mirror.

"Not bad," she said. Then she turned over the price tag. "Oh, good grief. No." I glanced at the tag—one hundred and ten—and put it back on the rack. "But it is pretty. You're on the right track, love."

"Why do you even need a new top?" I asked, following her as she weaved between the racks of clothes. It occurred to me she was creating busywork for us—an excuse to get me out of the house, to make me feel needed. Her praise for my fashion sense was the giveaway. Mom thought I wore too much black, not enough jewelry, and wished I would abolish my beloved ponytails forever. "Dad doesn't care about stuff like this."

She paused for a moment, a gold-hued cardigan in her hands, then shook her head. "You're right. This is silly. How about some lunch? We have—" she tugged the arm of her coat up to look at her watch "—an hour before your appointment. Okay?"

"Sure," I said, though I wasn't hungry. And I had a feeling Mom would be circling back to things I didn't feel like talking about. Sure enough, as soon as we sat down with bowls of soup and a plate of salted rosemary focaccia in front of us, she started up again. We sat side by side at a bar table, watching winter-wear-bundled people walk by the window as we ate.

"Any questions you have for me from your list?" she asked, dipping a strip of bread into her lentil soup.

I swallowed a spoonful of my own soup, shook my head and broke off a piece of bread. "Don't think so."

"Lucy, what's going on with you?" Mom put her spoon down, turned toward me and wrapped both her hands around my arm nearest to her. I had been about to dip back into my soup but was now pinned, my spoon sticking up out of my hand.

I looked over at her. "Nothing is going on with me. What do you mean?" Except *everything* was going on with me. My memory was still a mess. I'd had coffee with Daniel. I hadn't told Matt about it. "Could I have my arm back now?"

She sighed deeply but released my arm so I could get back to my soup, even though my already-weak appetite had waned. "I'm worried about you, sweetheart," she said. "Dad, too. What did Dr. Kay say, about how things are *progressing*?"

"Dr. Kay thinks I'm doing very well," I replied. "She thinks I'm making *excellent progress*." I stuffed some bread in my mouth to give myself a break from answering anything further, and Mom nodded.

"Okay, good. I'm glad to hear it, because if things aren't working out with her, your dad and I are happy to help you find someone else. Someone better suited to your particular situation. To your *goals*." She dipped her spoon back into her soup, and now I watched her.

"Mom, you know I may never fully recover my memory, right? I may be stuck with these strange half-baked memories forever."

"Mmm-hmm," she said, but she didn't look at me. Stared into her bowl as though the answer to everything could be found there.

"Mom. *Mom*." I waited until she looked at me, and then I saw it. How scared she was for me. And that scared me. Now I put my hand on her arm and squeezed reassuringly. "It's going to be fine. I am okay. Yes, I'm confused and upset and I feel like I can't trust my own mind some days, but I am okay." It was important she believed this, even if I had a hard time selling it to myself.

I pulled out the memory list from my purse. I was using a small notebook, and I turned to the page where my pen marked the most recent question I'd written down.

What happened with Margot? I laid the notebook on the empty space between us and pointed to the question. She read it, looked back to me.

"Okay, so I know Margot and Daniel are married." A piece of rosemary bread was caught in my throat and I took a big sip of water to get it down. "But did I know they were together? Before my accident? And were we still friends, Margot and I?"

Mom glanced back at the list and seemed to be stalling. "Please tell me, Mom, if you know something. I hate how you guys are always coddling me about this stuff."

"We are not coddling you," she said, annoyed at the suggestion. "We care about you and are trying to help."

"Fine, then tell me. Did I know about Margot and Daniel?"

"Yes," Mom said. "You told me they were dating, but you were already with Matt and, quite honestly, you seemed fine with everything." She wiped her fingers with a napkin. "As for whether you were still friends with Margot back then, I'm not sure. I do know I didn't hear much about her after you and Daniel broke up."

I nodded and swallowed hard. Felt nervous about the next question. "Do you know why Daniel and I broke up?"

Mom shook her head, placed her hand over mine. "I don't, love. You never told us. Came home one day with your overnight bag and said it was over." She pushed her used napkin deep into her empty teacup, swiveled so she fully faced me. "I thought you two would get back together, quite honestly. Told your dad it was probably prewedding jitters. But you were very clear it was over for good. We canceled the wedding venue a few days later, and you know what? I never once saw you cry about it."

I felt incredibly disappointed, having pinned all my hope on Mom and what she might know about my breakup. I had hoped to avoid asking Daniel, but it seemed no one else in my life had the faintest idea about what went down between us.

"It's so strange, isn't it, how your mind decided to ignore all that? How it zipped things together and gave you and Daniel a happy ending. Our brains truly are amazing." *Amazing.* That was one word for it, though not the one I would use at the moment. She checked her watch, sprang into action. "Are you finished?" She glanced at my soup and I nodded, though it was three-quarters full. "We should get going." She put on her coat, buttoning it quickly. "I thought we might walk, if you're up to it."

As I gathered my stuff, I thought about what she'd said. It *was* strange and disturbing, and for the hundredth time since coming out of the coma, I wished my mind had chosen another aspect of my life to confabulate. I also wished I had worn my more practical boots, versus the heeled ones I chose that wintry day, completely inappropriate for the weather but a much better match to my outfit. Or that the store had known about the leaky awning, the pool of water that had gathered outside the door and frozen solid overnight into a slick, clear patch of ice that looked like wet sidewalk pavement. That I hadn't chosen to buy that tie in that store that day for an anniversary I had no memory of.

So many things could have happened differently, though I supposed it also could have been much worse. The doctors did say I was lucky to come out relatively unscathed—at least medically speaking. But that was of little comfort these days as I navigated this disordered world of mine, gingerly putting one foot in front of the other as though I was walking the edge of a cliff, blindfolded.

18

At my appointment I was cleared to go back to work in the next week, which was a huge relief. As suggested by Dr. Mulder when I was discharged from the hospital, I had been keeping a symptom log for the past few weeks. He was pleased to see the headaches had tapered off and the dizziness seemed a thing of the past.

"How's the memory doing?" Dr. Mulder asked.

I paused, and Mom—who had insisted on coming into the appointment with me—took over. "She's been working very hard."

Working very hard? I had a fairly impressive memory list going, had kept all my appointments with Dr. Kay and was determined to find my way back to preaccident-Lucy. But when it came to what I actually remembered, I was not much further ahead than I had been the day I woke up from the coma. The same holes existed, and some of what I did remember from the past few years was fictional. However, Dr. Mulder seemed satisfied by Mom's answer. "Good. Keep up with the therapy." He flipped through the pages in my chart. "Who are you seeing again?"

"Dr. Kay," I said.

"Amanda Kay? Great. She's fantastic. Well, Lucy, I think everything is looking great. How are you feeling about things?"

Mom shifted in her chair to look at me, but I kept my gaze on

Dr. Mulder. "Pretty good," I replied, then quickly added, "I'm managing." It felt like the most truthful answer I could give. I may not have been thriving, but I was managing.

"You've faced some unique challenges, Lucy, and it seems you're handling it all very well," Dr. Mulder said, giving me a warm smile.

"Thanks," I said, because I wasn't sure what else to say. "So, does all this mean screens are okay now?"

"Screens are fine," Dr. Mulder said, continuing to smile like an indulgent grandparent. Probably thinking about how us twentysomethings were addicted to our devices—the unbalanced priorities of today's youth. Then he gave me a more serious look. "Unless you see an uptick in headaches or any dizziness. Keep the log going for a few more weeks, especially as you start back to work, and be cognizant about how you're feeling."

He shook my hand, then Mom's. "All the best, Lucy. I'm thrilled to see how well you're doing."

Mom called Dad as soon as we were out, to let him know how the appointment went. I wanted to remind her the headaches and dizziness had been the least intrusive side effects—the ones we had expected to dissipate, unlike my memory issues. But she was so delighted to be delivering good news I stayed quiet, smiled and nodded as she prattled on first to Dad and then to me as we made our way back to my apartment.

I thought Matt would be relieved I could go back to work, but he was mostly concerned.

"You're sure he said you're ready? It's going to be a lot of time on the computer, Lucy." He frowned, used a spatula to transfer the pesto sauce he'd made from the food processor to a bowl. He dipped his finger into the forest green mixture and tasted it before adding another teaspoon of salt. The kitchen smelled amazing, the garlic and crushed basil leaves filling the small space. I leaned against the counter nearby and marveled at his culinary skills. Daniel had been a terrible cook, and I wasn't much better. I remembered Jenny suggesting we get a good handle on delivery options near our apartment so we didn't have to subsist on toast and canned tomato soup after we were married.

"Work was pretty stressful before you, uh, had to take leave," he added.

"What do you mean?" I asked, curious as to what he knew that I didn't. He had mentioned earlier we'd stopped sharing the ins and outs of our daily work grinds once we started dating. Something about trying to find separation so we'd stay sane. "Like church and state," he had said, smiling. "We leave the office at the office."

But now he shrugged. "You were putting in long hours and dealing with some stuff with your team."

I frowned, not remembering anything particularly stressful about the office other than the usual deadlines and workload. But I also had zero recollection that Matt was not only my "work husband" but also my real-life boyfriend. So it was entirely possible things had been utterly falling apart at work before my accident, and I didn't remember.

"Well, I'm sure I can handle it. And Brooke's been amazing at keeping things running smoothly," I said. "Plus, the dizziness is gone and the headaches are so much better." Matt still looked unconvinced. "Matt, I've been home for over a month. I'm tired of being trapped here and the doctor said I'm good to go. It's time to get back."

He nodded, tapped the spatula against the edge of the bowl to clean it of the pesto and then started the pasta water. It seemed he had more to say but was holding his tongue and I decided not to push him on it.

"Give me a job," I said, rolling up my sleeves.

"Here. You can grate this." He handed me a wedge of Parmesan cheese and the grater. "We need about half a cup."

I went to work on the cheese while he tossed some sliced chicken breast into the bubbling olive oil in the frying pan. "Okay, full-disclosure time," Matt said, pushing the chicken around the searing hot pan with a wooden spoon. He lowered the heat, turned toward me. "I *am* worried about the headaches, and the screen time."

I nodded. I got it. Dr. Mulder and Therapist Ted had been very strict initially about the importance of resting my brain, and it was hard to shift gears. To believe, without some sort of test or scan to prove it, I was okay and my brain had in fact healed. Especially because while the concussion symptoms had abated, my memory was still a disaster. I was better in some ways, worse in others.

"But I'm most concerned about, well, the memory stuff."

I tapped the wedge of cheese against the grater, releasing the shredded pieces stuck to the inside of the stainless steel pyramid. "What about it specifically?" I asked, keeping my tone even. I wondered where this conversation was headed.

Matt set the pasta noodles in boiling water. "When I told Jake about what was going on, I didn't mention the part about you not remembering the office."

"I *do* remember the office, or at least the people in it," I said. "And my job." I was beginning to adjust to this routine—where people worried and I tried to justify why they shouldn't. "Where should I put the cheese?"

"Right there is good. We'll sprinkle it on after." He went back to stirring the pasta, the chicken. "But what if you can't remember the work, once you're there? It seems like you're expecting to sit at your desk and get right back to it. And I'm worried for you it won't be like that. Even if you remember everyone's names, you may not remember other important things."

To be honest, I was also slightly worried about this. My work and Jameson Porter seemed to have survived from getting caught up in my false memories (if we took Matt out of the equation), but it was true I likely wouldn't know for sure until I immersed myself back into it.

"I appreciate the concern. Honestly, I do," I said. "But I re-member the work, and our coworkers. I nailed the list." Matt had added the names of our colleagues and some of the big clients at the firm to my memory confidence list and I'd had no problem recollecting any of it.

"That you did," Matt said with a smile, draining the noodles. He started to assemble dinner while I got out plates and silverware. "Want a drink tonight?"

"Sure," I said, reopening the cupboard door for wineglasses. Matt pulled the cork out of the bottle and poured the red wine, handing me one of the filled glasses. "Look, I know it might be a bumpy reentry. But what's the alternative? I'm good at what I do, Dr. Mulder said I'm okay to go back and, to be totally honest, I'm starting to hate our apartment." I sprinkled grated cheese on top of our plates of pesto pasta with my wineglass-free hand—the chicken strips looking deliciously crispy and also, for a brief moment again, guilt-inducing. I knew I was an enthusiastic carnivore, but I sometimes still felt like a vegetarian.

"I know how hard this has been, Lucy," he said, carrying our dinner plates to the table. "And I don't want to make anything worse for you." The corners of his mouth turned down—classic consultant "fixer" Matt, when faced with a problem he wasn't sure how to solve. I hated being responsible for that look.

"Okay, enough of this worry and angst. I get plenty from my parents." I picked up my wineglass, held it high. "Let's talk about something fun. Something happy, okay?"

"Cheers to that," Matt said, clinking my glass. We tucked into the pasta, which was delicious. I was suddenly starving.

"Tell me how we ended up together," I said. Matt looked at me sharply, midbite, like I'd said something I shouldn't have. "What? I don't remember, and I would like to."

"I just thought…" Matt started. "I thought you wanted to talk about something that had nothing to do with all this." He gestured in a wide circle between us, and I laughed.

"But that's fairly tricky, isn't it?"

Matt grinned. "Yeah, I guess it is."

I swirled a few long noodles onto my fork. "Okay, so tell me how we went from friends to *here*."

"It was Halloween, and I didn't have a costume…"

19

Lucy leaned against the entryway of Matt's "office"—a cubicle, like every consultant at Jameson Porter had because they traveled so often closed-door offices were a waste of both space and resources—and waited for him to notice her. Which he finally did a few moments later.

"Oh, hey," he said, his eyes back on his computer screen a second later. He swore under his breath and leaned forward, adjusting his glasses as he stared intently at whatever was up on the screen. Lucy smiled. Matt wore glasses only when he was working on the computer, but she'd mentioned more than once he should wear them all the time—they suited him.

Uncrossing her arms and pushing off the frame of the cubicle, Lucy walked into the small space and went to sit down in the chair in front of Matt's desk until she realized her dress wouldn't allow it. So she stayed standing. "How's it going?"

"It's not." He sighed, leaned back and clasped his hands on the back of his head. He closed his eyes as he stretched his back into a deep arch against his chair. "The Rooneys are at it again." Matt had been working on a strategy plan with the Rooney family and their large auto parts business for close to a year, and the infighting between the four kids and their founder father, Donald—who refused to let go of the reins, despite his inability to be nimble with the changing landscape of the industry—had been a source of constant frustration and setbacks. "I'm set to go back out Monday, but I'm not sure it can wait."

It was Friday, and Matt had been in the office for only two days this week. He'd been spending nearly every Monday through Wednesday in Winnipeg at the Rooneys' head office and plant, trying to help them implement their growth plan. The constant travel was normal for the firm's consultants, and Matt rarely complained about the harrowing schedule—necessary to secure a partnership position in a couple of years—but the endless back and forth made Lucy glad she was in communications. The only time she had to travel was for the annual Jameson Porter retreat.

"Which 'F' is it?" Lucy asked, watching Matt tug the ends of his hair, back to worriedly scanning his email. Project problems within the office were described by one of two F's—Fixable or Fatal (Jameson Porter took its internal cultural lingo nearly as seriously as the work itself)—and Lucy hoped for Matt's sake the Rooney strategy could be stamped Fixable.

"Probably Fatal, but there's a chance to turn it around if I can convince the siblings to oust Daddy Rooney. Three of the four are on board, but the fourth is digging his heels in." He sucked in a breath, puffed out his cheeks, looked irritated. Matt had invested much time and energy into the Rooneys. If things went belly-up now, he would be devastated. "I don't want to have to bring Jeremy in." He cursed under his breath. Jeremy Darby was a partner and Matt's mentor, though he was fairly hands-off—something Matt appreciated and didn't want to change.

"Maybe I can help? Write a memo?" Part of Lucy's job at Jameson Porter was drafting reports for the clients on behalf of the consultants, to aid with communication and to keep things moving forward with the project. "I can do it right now if you want."

"I may need to take you up on that," he said. Then he pulled off his glasses and glanced away from his screen, finally giving Lucy a good look. "Whoa. What's happening here? What's up with your hair?" he asked, gesturing to the left side of Lucy's head, where she'd used nearly an entire bottle of gel to make her shoulder-length hair stick out straight to the side, like it was windblown.

Lucy laughed. "Glad you finally noticed." She pointed to the skirt of her black dress, which was also sticking out to the same side and angle as her hair. She raised her eyebrows, pointed to her outstretched hair and skirt again. "Get it?"

He stared at her blankly, clearly getting nothing.

She popped outside the cubicle, grabbed the umbrella she'd left leaning on the wall—it was broken and opened inside out, the way she wanted it to—and held it up. It had actually taken quite a bit of work to get it to stay, and she'd sliced her finger trying to bend the metal prongs, she explained to Matt. Another few seconds passed, Matt's face still blank.

"It's my Halloween costume!" Lucy said. "Gone with the Wind. Get it?" She held the umbrella up again, but off to the side this time, and tried her best to take a stance that made it look like there was a strong gust of wind blowing her from right to left.

Matt laughed, loud and booming. "You're amazing," he said, sliding his glasses on top of his head, where they nestled in his short, wavy hair. She took a bow. Then his smiled faltered. "It's the Halloween party." He looked around his cubicle, sparse aside from the mess of papers on his desk, a few half-empty coffee mugs, his messenger bag in one corner and his bike leaning against the opposite wall with his helmet dangling from one of the handlebars. "I forgot my costume at home. Shit!"

One of their colleagues, Jake, and his roommate were hosting a party for a bunch of people from work. Things had started at 8:00 p.m., and it was already nearly eighty-thirty, which was why she'd come to track Matt down. He had his phone on Do Not Disturb and they were supposed to be heading over to the party together.

"What was your costume again?" Lucy asked, trying to remember if he'd told her already—her mind a bit sludgy, thanks to the few pulls she'd already had off the large bottle of rum Brooke kept at the back of her filing cabinet.

"It's lame, but best I could come up with because, as you know, I suck at this sort of thing." She nodded. Matt was brilliant at business strategy but less so with anything creative. They'd been friends long enough for her to know this. "I was going as a serial killer. But like 'cereal'—the stuff you eat—versus, you know." He shrugged. "I had all these mini cereal boxes on string I could hang over my shoulders, with fake plastic knives sticking out of them."

Lucy nodded, smiled. "Got it." He admitted there would probably be at least five other "cereal killers" at the party tonight, but it had been all he could think of. "Okay, I have an idea. I'll be right back."

She was back five minutes later with one of the wire hangers from the dry cleaning she hadn't yet taken home, and the bottle of extreme-hold hair gel she'd used to secure her hair for her costume.

"Just finishing up," he said, typing without taking his eyes off his screen. While Lucy waited for him, she started to unwind the metal hanger, being careful not to reopen the cut on her finger. "And…done." He turned everything off and slid his phone into his suit jacket pocket as he stood. He glanced at the wire hanger, the bottle of hair gel she'd placed on the edge of his desk. "So, what's your idea?"

Lucy held up the partially unwound hanger and smiled.

"I still don't get it," he said, looking from her to the hanger and back.

Rolling her eyes, Lucy continued to unravel the hanger. "This," she said, struggling a little to straighten a particularly gnarly bend, "is for your tie."

He glanced down at the black-and-gray-striped tie lying flat to his chest. He lifted it off his shirt, waggled the end. "For my tie?"

She stepped closer to him, tripped as the wire hanger in her dress caught on the edge of the chair and nearly took a header into his desk. "Easy there," he said, chuckling as he grabbed on to her, steadying her. "Did you already start the party?"

"Shh," she said, putting a finger to her lips. "Brooke may or may not have a bottle of rum in her office, and I may—or may not—have helped her make a dent in it." Then she noticed he was still holding on to her arm and didn't seem like he was going to let go, which caused Lucy to blush and focus harder on the hanger.

The truth was Lucy had a bit of a thing for Matt…though this fact seemed to be lost on him. Besides working together they were also good friends—and their friendship had moved beyond Jameson Porter, past workday lunches and watercooler visits. She'd cheered him on as he crossed his most recent marathon's finish line, and when Lucy was sick with the flu, he brought her soup and the first season of *Game of Thrones*, which she had yet to watch because she was so ill she fell asleep with her head in his lap that night.

Over the past year they'd gotten to know each other pretty well, and Matt counted Lucy among his closest friends. And Lucy had admitted to Jenny nearly six months earlier she was smitten—Matt was reliable and trustworthy and kind and handsome, in a nerdy way she loved. And he was altogether different from her ex Daniel (in both personality and looks), which made him even more appealing. But Matt, for as much as he obviously cared for her, had so far kept Lucy firmly in the friend zone.

"Take off your tie," Lucy said, unfurling the last of the wire hanger kinks. He did, handed it to her. She folded and bent and twisted the wire, positioning it at the widest end of the tie. "So, how much do you love this tie?"

He shrugged. "Not much."

She started pushing the wire up and through the inside of the tie. "Good. Me, neither."

Matt laughed. "Noted."

"Here, hold this end," Lucy said, handing him the skinniest

part. She pushed the wire in more firmly and it popped through the fabric at the front. "Oops," she said, cringing. "Sorry about that. I guess I owe you a tie."

"Good. You can get me a nicer one."

"And…going to try to bend it around this part here…" Lucy tweaked the wire through the fabric until it bent enough to come down the other side, making sure the part he would tie around his neck was wire free. "There. Done." She recoiled the wire a bit inside the end of the tie so nothing was sticking out, then told him to put it back on. He did with a little difficulty, and after some adjustments Lucy took the wire-filled end of the tie and bent it in a few waves, making sure it stuck out to the same side as her hair and skirt. "Now, a little gel here…" With goo-slathered fingers she worked the gel into his dark hair, pulling the longer bits the best she could—his hair was fairly short and the waves seemed impervious to the gel—out to the same side as the tie, then stepped back.

He took the same stance she had taken earlier, like a huge gust was blowing him over, and Lucy clapped her hands together. "Perfect. We can be Gone with the Wind together."

"Now I won't embarrass myself at the party with my lame costume."

"Well, I can't prevent you from embarrassing yourself," she said. "Because we have some drinking to do, and who knows what's going to happen after that." *True, true*, he said. "But at least we'll do it together. Ready to head out?"

He glanced around the office, nodded. "I'll leave my bike," he said. "I have a feeling I won't be in the best shape to ride home."

"Definitely wise," Lucy said, pushing him toward the bank of elevators down the hall from the offices. "Now let's get out of here. You have some catching up to do."

They laughed and then the elevator doors opened, and in their haste to get in, they got caught against the slowly opening doors, his tie and her skirt preventing a graceful entrance. They untangled themselves and he gently nudged her forward first into the elevator, his hands on her hips and her smiling at his touch.

As predicted there was much drinking, and it would turn out to be the night that changed everything between them. Matt and Lucy won "most original costume," which meant a bottle of tequila they decided to open and share right then and there. He walked her home—well, they stumbled to her place, their costumes disheveled, the wire in both his tie and her skirt long gone, discarded in Jake's bedroom, where they'd sneaked a few secret kisses, the thrill of it leaving both of them breathless, wanting more.

It was hard to detail exactly what happened next, the evening hazy with alcohol and desire. But when they woke up the next morning, Lucy was lying beside Matt, gently snoring in a way he still found adorable, her gelled-hair still sticking out to the side—though it had wilted significantly—and naked aside from his boring black-and-gray tie, which she wore loosely around her neck.

20

The tie. It made sense now, why I had bought Matt that uninspired, black-and-gray tie for our anniversary.

"That was it," Matt said, and my thoughts snapped back to him. "The moment you put the gel in my hair, I realized I didn't want to be only friends anymore. And it seemed you felt the same."

"It was the gel?" I asked, laughing a little. The story had been sweet and funny and romantic, but it felt like someone else's story. Or like a great scene in a movie we'd watched. I was sad not to recall it, desperately wanted to remember things the way Matt described them.

"I still use that gel sometimes," he said, smiling. "Good memories." His face was hopeful, and I realized he was waiting for me to agree. *Maybe she'll remember it now…maybe she'll remember me now…*

I stared at my half-eaten pasta cooling on my plate, unsure what to say. I didn't remember any of it and I felt terrible about that. So many times in these past weeks I longed to mourn what I'd lost, but was unable to because I was constantly confronted by what everyone else had lost, too. And even though it wasn't my fault—I would have given anything for things to be different—it broke my heart, every time.

"We didn't officially start dating until a few months later, though," Matt added.

I looked up from my plate, surprised. "We didn't? Why not?"

He shrugged, then grinned. "I was an idiot."

I waited for him to elaborate.

"We were such great friends and I didn't want to screw that up," he said. He looked sad again, likely thinking about how everything got screwed up anyway. "But I came to my senses right around Valentine's Day, when Jake asked you out."

"Wait, Jake asked me out? *Jake* Jake?" I asked. "What did I say?" It was so bizarre to have no memory of any of this, yet to know it had all happened.

"No, of course," he replied. "You said you were waiting for me to come around."

The longing to remember such a happy time in my life ran deep. "Please tell me Valentine's Day isn't our anniversary," I said, cocking one eyebrow.

"Come on, do you think I'm that lame?" he asked. Then he laughed at the look on my face. "Right. I told you about the cereal killer costume. No, our anniversary is February 15. I figured twenty-four hours was enough of a buffer."

I laughed, too, and then had an idea of something I could do for Matt. Something small but, I hoped, significant.

"So, I know it's still over a week away, but where should we do lunch your first day back?" Matt asked, trying to keep the mood light. Trying to make things easier for both of us. "Are you done?" He was half standing, his fingers on the edge of my plate. I nodded and he took it and stacked it on top of his plate. "Maybe sushi? Burritos?"

"No," I said. He paused, hands full of our dirty dishes.

"Okay, no to burritos and sushi. What about that falafel place—"

"No, I'm not done."

Matt looked confused, glanced at my plate in his hands. "With your pasta?"

I held up a finger—a "give me a minute" request—and got up from the table and headed for the bedroom. If he said anything else, I didn't hear him, because I was already rummaging around in the closet.

Matt was soon at the bedroom door, the dishes gone from his hands, a curious look on his face. "What are you doing, Lucy?"

"Looking for something."

He paused, his voice measured as he asked, "Anything I can help with?"

"Don't worry, this isn't a memory lapse thing." I stuck my head farther into the depths of the closet, reached toward the back and, moving a few items aside, pulled out a shoebox. I set the box on the bed and opened the lid, lifting out the gold-hued plastic bag. "I'm sorry it isn't wrapped," I said, handing it to Matt.

He took the bag from me but didn't open it. He seemed nervous, unsure what to do. "What's this?"

"It was your anniversary present," I replied, sitting down on the bed. I kept my voice even, a swirl of emotions moving through me. I could only imagine how it felt for Matt to hear me refer to our anniversary. I pushed past the lump in my throat. "I bought it when I was shopping with Jenny. The day I slipped, and, well…you know the rest. So, here."

He pressed his lips together, his face solemn. Then he opened and looked inside the bag. At first I thought he was going to cry and I steeled myself for it. But then his face broke into a grin and he pulled the tie out of the bag. Black-and-gray stripes, decidedly boring.

Exactly like the one I'd ruined for his Halloween costume.

"I didn't remember, about the tie," I said quickly, because I didn't want him to get his hopes up. "When Jenny gave it to me, I couldn't figure out what it meant. But now I know."

"It's perfect. Exactly the right gift," Matt said, grinning as he tied it around his neck. "How does it look?"

He was dressed in a long-sleeved T-shirt and jeans, and so

he looked ridiculous with the tie on, but I smiled. "It classes things up for sure." Matt laughed and sat beside me on the bed, putting an arm around my shoulders. He kissed my temple as I leaned into him.

"We're going to get through this, Lucy. You and me, together."

I took the long end of his tie and held it out to the side, the way he'd described the costume. "Was it like this?" I asked.

"Pretty much," he said. "And it was awesome."

He kissed me then, and it was nice. Warm, comforting and starting to feel more normal every time.

21

I convinced myself there was no need to tell Matt I was going to meet Daniel again. I had decided it would be the last time and so told myself mentioning the meet up would only assign it more importance than it deserved. Matt had enough to worry about these days and I didn't want to pile on anything else. But the real reason I didn't tell Matt was because I knew it would hurt him. How could it not?

So, with all that swirling through my mind, I said nothing—again. Actually, worse, this time I flat-out lied. I told Matt I was meeting Jenny, because he asked if I wanted to go out for lunch and I needed an excuse. I felt rotten about the lie all morning and waffled between calling Daniel to cancel and telling Matt plans had changed and I could meet him for lunch, after all.

But as time ticked on I didn't cancel on Daniel or admit the truth to Matt. Instead, I dressed carefully, straightened my hair and even spritzed on some perfume. And as I was getting my coat out of the front hall closet I caught a glimpse of myself in the mirror and immediately went back to the bedroom, put my hair in a ponytail and wet a washcloth to rub off the perfume. This was not some sort of romantic reunion, where I put my best face forward and hoped Daniel was intrigued enough to want to see me again. He was married, and not to me. It couldn't be simpler than that.

Moonbean Coffee was busy when I arrived, but I managed to snag the same table as last time, near the window. I ordered a latte and tried to unwind the tangle of nerves in my stomach. I hadn't realized how anxious I was to see Daniel again—maybe because I knew there was a chance I'd end up telling him everything, and I wasn't sure where that would lead. Or where I hoped it might lead. Which instantly revved up my guilt, wrapped the anxiety ribbons tighter around my chest, because I couldn't think about Daniel without also thinking of Matt.

I was also edgy about going back to work. I probably wasn't ready—Matt was right—but I was impatient for things to normalize, and going to the office felt like a normal thing to do. So I would fumble my way through it and hope for the best. And anything seemed better than spending another week in our apartment, restless as I waited for something to happen, to change.

Five minutes passed, then fifteen. I checked my phone repeatedly, ordered another latte and a muffin. Waited some more. An hour later my coffee was half-drunk and cold, the muffin partially eaten, and Daniel still wasn't there. And with a cold wave of humiliation I realized what had happened—Daniel wasn't coming. He had forgotten all about me.

Now I understood when he said, "Same time next week?" he *was* merely being polite, and I had been a fool to assume it was a firm date. Maybe he had every intention to have coffee with me again, but as the week went on he forgot about it as the pressures and responsibilities of his own life flooded in. I thought back to our conversation at this very table, one week earlier. Had we agreed to this? Yes, I was sure we had.

But then a terrifying thought: What if my brain made up the whole thing? What if I had gone to sleep one night and my mind crafted this memory, like it had all the other ones of Daniel while

I was in the coma? With shaking hands I tapped my phone on and went back through my calls.

Daniel London. Last Monday, and we'd talked according to my phone's log for five minutes and forty-five seconds. I resisted the urge to ask the barista if she recognized me, and could only hope the coffee date with Daniel had in fact happened the way I remembered.

With a sigh and a few belly breaths, the shaking in my body subsided slightly. I felt confident the memories of running into Daniel at the bar and having coffee last week were real, but as for today's meeting, who knew what the truth was. The flare of anger was swift, and I jammed my phone into my purse before standing up and hastily pulling on my coat. I hated this, all of it. I wished I could start over somewhere else, like someone in the witness protection program. I could create an entirely new identity, not dependent on anyone or anything that came before. Change my name, tell believable stories of a past I didn't need to be corrected on. Because I wasn't the same person I used to be, and it scared me to realize I didn't know myself anymore.

While I waited for my appointment with Dr. Kay, I pulled out my notebook, opened it to a blank page and wrote the date, taking a few moments to capture my morning routine (*laundry for work, review of my questions and answers for my appointment with Dr. Kay, meeting Daniel at Moonbean—he didn't show*). I had decided on my brisk walk to her office I would do this every day, morning and evening, to make it easier to track my memory and make sure I wasn't forgetting anything critical. The fresh air had also done me good. I wasn't as agitated as I had been in the coffee shop—agitation, I knew, could be a side effect from my head injury, but more likely it was a symptom of how out of control I felt about my life.

Dr. Kay's office smelled like cinnamon and clementines and then I noticed the candle burning on the edge of her desk. Some sort of seasonal Bath & Body Works candle, probably a gift from a client over the holidays. The scent reminded me of Christmas Eve from when I was a kid, when my mom would make mulled wine to take in large flasks for our traditional caroling through our north Toronto neighborhood. I took a deep breath through my nose and settled into one of two chairs by the window.

"How are you, Lucy?" Dr. Kay asked, shutting the door behind her and setting the timer before joining me by the window.

"Good. I'm fine." It came out automatically, because that's what you say when people ask you how you are. But then I reminded myself Dr. Kay did want to know how I was, especially if I wasn't fine. "Actually, scratch that. I'm okay but not great."

She nodded, crossed one leg over her other knee, causing her dress pants to rise up slightly at the ankles. She was wearing pink socks with snowmen on them, which made me smile. I gestured to her socks. "I see you're hanging on to the holiday spirit. Christmas-scented candles and snowmen socks in April. Nice."

"It's more about what's clean in my drawer in the morning," she said, laughing. "I get a lot of holiday-themed gifts, as you can imagine. But I'm fairly partial to that candle. And these socks." She leaned forward, looked at her ankles. "They're cozy and happy, don't you think?"

"I do," I said, shifting my coat on the arm of the chair so it wasn't hanging over my lap.

"You could hang that up," Dr. Kay said.

"It's fine here."

"*Fine*. There's that word again," she said, smiling gently at me. "So, tell me. What's going on?"

"I saw Daniel. We talked." If she was surprised by my confession, she didn't show it. "I mean, it wasn't planned or anything. I ran into him outside a bar after a birthday party."

She nodded. "And how was it, seeing him?"

I let out another long breath, through my nose. "Weird. Confusing. But also nice." I went to twist my wedding band, my stomach dropping at the sight of my bare ring finger. *When would this sink in?*

"Tell me about the 'nice' part."

It seemed an odd question because the answer should have been obvious. It was nice to see him because I missed him. But then I reminded myself part of accepting what was happening to me meant saying stuff out loud, to give it a different perspective. "Clarity leads to clarity," Dr. Kay was fond of saying, and even though it seemed nonsensical, it resonated.

"I still feel things for him I know I shouldn't, but it was *nice* because seeing him made me feel relaxed. Like I wouldn't have to explain myself to him, and that was a relief."

"Because you feel like he knows you so well?"

I nodded. "Exactly. It sounds ridiculous, because in reality we don't know each other at all anymore. We haven't talked in years. But still. It was comforting to run into him." I paused for a moment. "Especially because things had blown up with Matt at the party."

"What happened with Matt?"

I had been all set to talk more about Daniel. To tell her about meeting him for coffee, and how I'd confided in him about what was going on—or at least about most of it—and he'd suggested we meet again the next week. I wanted to discuss it more, get her opinion and feedback. Hoped she might say yes, I should see Daniel as often as I wanted to because it could only help my brain as it tried to fill in the blanks and reshape the out-of-place bits. So when she asked about Matt, I was momentarily quieted, as I tried to come up with a segue back to Daniel.

"Lucy? Is it okay if we talk about Matt?"

"Yeah, sure. I...I was going to... Absolutely," I stammered. "What was the question?"

"What did you two fight about?"

"Oh, that. He told someone at work what was going on. With my memory," I replied. "We had agreed to keep it between us."

"I see," Dr. Kay said. "How did you feel learning that?"

"Well, based on the fact I walked out on him, not great," I said with a small chuckle. "Sometimes my emotions are like giant tidal waves, totally out of control. I didn't handle things as well as I could have." I cleared my throat, picked a piece of lint off my sweater. "I know it's hard for him, too."

"That's pretty understanding," she said. "You know, Lucy, it's okay to be angry with Matt. He broke your trust, and right now trust is pretty critical for you."

I considered what she said. She was right—I needed to be able to trust people in my life, now more than ever. But I also had to find ways to keep moving forward. "Being angry is exhausting," I said. "And I'm already so worn down—trying to remember what's true and what I've made up—I need things to be okay with Matt."

"And are things 'okay' with Matt?"

I paused, opened my mouth to answer, then closed it again. I thought about Jake's party, our spontaneous "date" in High Park, the Halloween story Matt recounted, the anniversary gift tie, which had led to a very satisfying evening. "Better? I don't know how to explain it." I shook my head. "We've been... Well, we're sort of back to the way things were before. In the, uh, bedroom." I blushed, embarrassed more by my inability to come right out and say we were sleeping in the same room, doing things couples do.

"I still don't remember any part of our life before my accident. Sometimes I even forget he's not only my friend," I said. "But I'm having these...feelings for Matt. Feelings you don't have about your friends."

"What do you think those feelings mean?" Dr. Kay asked.

"I'm not sure," I replied without having to think about it. "Not yet, anyway."

Dr. Kay shifted in her seat and watched me closely. "Lucy, as we've discussed, you know there's a chance these changes in your memory will be permanent. And if that's the case, you will be a different person going forward than you used to be.

Which is okay! This is a transition, perhaps even more so for those around you because they remember past-Lucy."

I could tell whatever she had to say next was important by the way she leaned forward, clasping her hands and settling them on her bent knees as she observed me. "You have the right to change your present if it doesn't fit with the future you envision. We know it doesn't line up with the past you remember, and the future is a big question mark at this point, isn't it?"

I nodded, bit my lip because I was trying to keep the tears at bay. I understood what she was saying and it made perfect sense. Sometimes, as I lay in the dark with Matt sleeping soundly beside me, I fretted about never finding my way back to him. To us. And then shame would worm through me because I knew I would be able to move on; I would be okay without Matt. Though I was beginning to understand it wasn't as easy as one might think to leave behind a past you didn't remember.

But what would that do to him, if I up and left? Declared *his* Lucy dead—gone the day she slipped and fell, obliterated as her brain shifted across the midline with impact, leaving deep bruises where so many of her critical memories were stored. No, I couldn't leave him. Even if staying meant letting go of Daniel, for whom I had feelings that were comparatively easy to articulate.

I loved Daniel, but I owed Matt the chance to know if our past could catch up to my present.

"Lucy?" I brought my attention back to Dr. Kay. "It's okay to imagine a different future than the one seemingly laid out in front of you right now. You are not held to anything, or anyone. You are responsible only to yourself. And what *you* want is as important as what anyone else wants from you."

"But what if..." I wiped my tears, took a breath to settle my jumbled-up insides. "What if I don't know what I want?" *And what if I figure out what I want, but can't have it?*

She squeezed my arm, then handed me a tissue. "You will, Lucy. I promise, you will."

22

A small notepad rested on the table between us, and Matt was grinning.

"What's up?" I asked, somewhat nervous about the eagerness with which he had pulled me over to the table and asked me to sit. Barely giving me a chance to get my coat off after I came in from my session with Dr. Kay, the sting of Daniel forgetting about our coffee date lingering. It was nearly dinnertime and I could smell something delicious wafting out of the kitchen. The table was set with two plates, silverware and water glasses, but there was also a long row of spoons and forks down its center, along with a dozen wineglasses.

Matt continued grinning but didn't immediately answer my question. Or fill me in on why the table was set like this, or the reason his fingers tapped excitedly against the notepad's cover. "When did you get home?" I asked.

It was only 6:05 p.m., and by the look and smell of things Matt had to have been home for at least a couple of hours. Consultants at Jameson Porter—especially those on partner track—typically didn't leave the office by five o'clock, let alone earlier.

He shrugged. "I came home after lunch." I saw his laptop sitting open but asleep on the coffee table and felt guilty about how much work likely lived behind that dark screen. He had taken so much time off these past two months and I couldn't help but worry what that meant for his upcoming bid for partner.

Turning my attention back to Matt and his blatant excitement, I slowly unwrapped the scarf from my neck. "So, are you going to give me a clue here? What's the occasion?"

"This," he replied, holding up the notepad and then slapping it against the open palm of his other hand. I stared at the notepad, then at him, and my eyebrows rose with impatience.

"A notebook?"

"Not only a notebook," he replied. "I've been doing some research—on memory—and it gave me an idea for how to get some of the missing pieces back."

My heart sank as I took in his words. I had the distinct feeling I was about to be tested or something, and knew inevitably I would fail at whatever he had planned and we would both feel worse about everything for it.

But all I said was "Okay…"

"Okay." Matt pulled his chair in and opened the notebook. He held up a bookmark that had been tucked into the notebook's pages—it was made of a caramel-colored wood, with a leather toggle on its end and bicycles etched into its surface. "I know you won't remember this, but you hate that I dog-ear pages of books. And you especially hate how I fold the bottom corner instead of the top."

"I do?" I tried to recall this hate he spoke of but couldn't. I did, however, remember the first morning I was back home and noting how Matt marked the spot in the book he was reading. While I had found it odd, I couldn't remember any stronger emotion about it.

He nodded. "You do. So you got me this bookmark shortly after we moved in here." He held it out to me and I ran my finger over the etched-in bicycles, along the stiff leather toggle strings. It had barely been used.

"I've tried," Matt said, as though reading my thoughts. "But, well, old habits die hard." He grinned and showed me the edge of the notebook, where I could see a dozen little corner folds along the bottom of the pages.

"Back to my research," Matt began, setting his finger on a line of text on the first page of the now-open book. "I read up on memory loss and treatments, and it seems spontaneous recovery is a real thing. Lucy, you could get your memory back—all of it, even—one day, like, poof." He made a fist near his head and then pulled it away, opening his fingers quickly as he did. I nodded, because this was not news. The doctors had mentioned spontaneous recovery, which was how they often handled amnesia in movie plot lines, the character getting a second whack to the head and remembering everything.

"Right," I said, my tone guarded because I wanted to acknowledge the possibility but without too much enthusiasm. Clinging to something as unpredictable as spontaneous recovery wasn't a good idea for either of us. Maybe it would happen, but more likely not. I—we—had to learn to live with present circumstances, including my false memories.

"I know it's a long shot, don't worry. But then I came across this thing called 'reminiscence therapy,' where we would talk about past experiences and use tangible cues—like scent and taste—to help trigger your natural recall." Matt was animated, his words tumbling out. "We've already been doing that a bit, right? With the photos and your list. But this is more specific and not just visual, what I'm proposing we try."

I nodded, but even though he told me not to, I worried about his excitement. Was concerned about the possible (probable?) disappointment. The photos *had* unveiled one memory, of the ski trip, but unfortunately it triggered the confabulation rather than the real thing.

"It's not a quick fix and it may not work at all," Matt continued, watching for my reaction. "But I thought maybe it was worth a try."

I hesitated only briefly. "I'm game," I said. "So how do we do this?"

"Great. Amazing." Matt exhaled, ramping back up again. "I made a list, wrote down a few experiences to get us started."

"Lists are good," I said, smiling.

"Lists are good," Matt replied. "I've also got props, like more photos and food. Oh, and wine."

"Wine is also good."

Matt smiled, and it went practically ear to ear. *Please don't let me disappoint him again.*

"First thing is the infamous Halloween party. I know I already told you about it, but I think we're supposed to talk about the experiences multiple times. Plus, I found a picture." He shuffled through the photos on the table and put one on the top. My hair was whooshed to the side, as was Matt's tie, and we did look as though we had been hit by a huge gust of wind. We also had that decidedly drunken look—heavy-lidded eyes and disheveled smiles—and were tangled into one another, me tucked into Matt's arms, his chin resting on my head, our hands holding up a huge bottle of tequila.

Matt snapped his fingers and jumped up. "Hang on, almost forgot." He disappeared into the kitchen for a minute and came back with a bottle of tequila—same brand as from the photo. He cracked the lid and poured the clear alcohol into two shot glasses and handed me a slice of lime. "Tequila requires lime. But don't worry, I washed it."

I had a strange feeling in my belly when I looked at the lime in my hand, but it was gone before I could figure out why. "Thanks," I said, turning my attention back to Matt.

"So I already told you about that night when you saved my sorry ass from having no costume and we won Most Original and then got very drunk on that tequila right there." He pointed to the picture. "But what I didn't mention was that was one of the best nights of my life." His voice softened, and I felt a lump grow in my throat, along with a twinge of jealousy at how intact his memory was. Matt handed me one of the shots of tequila and then took the other one, clinking his tiny glass to mine. "Bottoms up."

We tossed back the tequila, which burned all the way down, and chased it with the slice of lime, the sourness puckering my lips.

Matt then proceeded to tell me the whole story again and I listened carefully, laughed and smiled and blushed in all the right places, and did two more tequila shots while staring at the photo. Still, nothing happened.

"It's okay," Matt said when I admitted it didn't seem to be working. "Remember, this isn't a quick fix, right? I'm grateful you're even willing to try. I know this can't be easy for you. Ready for the next thing?"

I nodded, warmed and bolstered by the tequila. "Ready. But I have a feeling I could end up very drunk tonight." I glanced at the row of wineglasses. "This could get messy."

"Don't worry," Matt said, smiling. "I'll take good care of you."

I did get drunk. Very drunk. There was no spontaneous recovery, but at least the process felt productive. Like we were *doing* something. And if nothing else, it reminded me I couldn't wallow in what had happened to me. Moving forward was the best option, and with the sort of clarity one gets from consuming too many shots of tequila and a lot of good wine, I decided that was exactly what I was going to do. *Put the past in the past, and embrace the future.* I repeated the mantra a few times out loud, and soon Matt joined me, becoming the thing we said prior to doing yet another shot.

Matt took me through a handful of experiences. There was the walking ghost tour in Niagara-on-the-Lake, but we'd visited too many wineries prior to the tour and were so tipsy by the time it started we couldn't stop giggling, distracting the tour guide and other guests. Then after I jumped from behind a door at one of the supposedly haunted houses and shouted, "Boo!"

nearly giving a retiree from Ohio a heart attack, the unimpressed guide took us aside and suggested we might do better with a different sort of tour.

Matt liberally poured wine from what he said had been our favorite winery on that trip, and produced a photo of me making a scary face behind some unsuspecting white-haired tourist, the flash causing my face to go whitewashed and my eyes red. I laughed hard, choked a little on the wine but still couldn't remember.

He also cooked a meal we'd enjoyed during a trip to Austin— a work trip for Matt but one I had apparently tagged along for to partake in a long weekend. The photo showed me standing in front of a food truck, my hands weighed down by two grocery bags each holding enough food for a small dinner party. Matt said we ordered one of everything, including four kinds of barbecue, blue cheese coleslaw and banana pudding for dessert. Tonight he'd made the coleslaw and pulled pork shoulder— now I knew what had smelled so delicious— even attempting to replicate the sauce, which he had tried to procure but was a well-kept secret and he hadn't been able to sway the food truck's owner to share it.

And with every memory Matt recounted, every experience we'd shared, every bite of food and sip of wine that had meant something to us, I hoped it would be the thing that did it. We ate until I thought I might burst and drank until things became blurry and beautifully uncomplicated, but still I remembered nothing.

23

It took me two days to recover from the hangover, and I still wasn't a hundred percent by Wednesday when I got a text from Matt midday telling me to be ready to go out for seven o'clock and to dress casually, but in warm layers. Also to pack an overnight bag (we were staying downtown somewhere) and to drink as much water as I could stomach to counteract the alcohol we'd be consuming. I groaned at that last part but promised to be ready, warm and hydrated. I also texted, So which T-shirt is my fave? and then with his response packed Matt's ancient, buttersoft Toronto Maple Leafs shirt into my bag to sleep in. I was going to do everything I could to make tonight a success, even if I had no idea what that entailed.

Dressed and waiting by six-thirty, I set a huge glass of ice water beside me and flipped through my memory confidence list (I added the T-shirt note), wanting to do some work on it before my Friday appointment with Dr. Kay. But I couldn't concentrate, my mind on what Matt had planned for us. I gathered it had to do with this reminiscence therapy, and expected tonight would be another test I couldn't prepare for. Like when you dream you show up to a class you aren't registered for—organic chemistry was always the one in my dreams—and surprise! There's an exam, but you didn't study for it because you're not actually taking organic chemistry and it's worth a hundred percent of your grade, and with rising panic you realize this can't end well.

I tried to reassure myself this wasn't actually a test; I couldn't pass or fail. But running alongside that mental track was one telling me Matt had probably planned a night full of things I should know—used to know. Of course, there was always the chance something would trigger a memory and I could only hope it would happen while I was with Matt—and be *about* Matt. The last thing either of us needed was for another memory of Daniel to expose itself, taking over valuable real estate in my mind.

I wiped my damp palms against my jeans and tried to decelerate my heart rate. I wanted—no, *needed*—for this to go well. By 6:50 p.m. I'd worked myself into a mild frenzy, anxious about the date but unable to stop thinking about Daniel. About how much simpler things would be if I were waiting for him to get home instead. The guilt was swift and overwhelming and I needed to alleviate it before Matt walked through our front door. And so I was downing a second glass of wine—the ice water untouched—when I heard his key in the lock.

"Luce?" Matt called out from the foyer. He stood by the front door, unclipping his bike helmet. "Hey there. Wow. You look *hot*," he said, smiling at my multiple layers of clothing—jeans, ski socks and a wool sweater over two long-sleeved shirts. "And I mean that both literally and figuratively." I laughed, more relaxed now thanks to the wine.

Fifteen minutes later Matt had changed, tossed our bags into the car, and we were on our way. "How was work?" I asked.

Matt gave me a quizzical look but kept the smile on his face. "Good. Nothing new to report since the last time you asked. Five minutes ago."

I put my hands over my face, the wool from my mittens tickling my nose. "I'm sorry," I said, my voice muffled with my hands. "I'm nervous!" I was obviously doing a terrible job pretending not to be, so I might as well be up front about it.

He reached over, keeping one hand on the wheel, and pulled

my hands away from my face, holding on to them and squeezing. "Don't be nervous, okay? Tonight is about nothing more than having fun. I promise. No expectations."

I smiled at him, leaned my head back and closed my eyes. "Was I this neurotic about stuff? Before, I mean?"

Matt laughed, and I turned to look at him. "Honestly? Yes. You're a bit of a worrier."

"Good to know." I laughed, too, still holding his hand. A couple of minutes later we pulled into a Green P lot and I recognized where we were. "But it's April," I said, glancing at him as we walked near the waterfront. "The ice is gone, isn't it?"

"It is," Matt said. "But we don't need it. Come on." He pulled me toward the outdoor rink, which had now reverted back to its postwinter concrete surface, and we sat on a bench on its edge. Matt had one of those reusable canvas grocery bags at his feet, from which he brought out a tall thermos and paper cups, doubled up to protect our fingers from the heat of the beverage. Handing me the cups, he opened the valve on the thermos and poured the dark brown liquid.

"Hot chocolate?" I asked, the smell wafting into my nose. I brought a cup closer and sniffed, the scent sharp. "Ah, grown-up hot chocolate. Nice."

"When I was a kid, I wanted to be a hockey player." Matt sipped at his steaming-hot cup, blowing a few times across its surface. "But I was a terrible skater. Like, worse than you can imagine. 'Two left feet,' my grandfather used to say."

I laughed, sipped the hot, boozy beverage. "What's in here?"

"Bourbon," Matt said. "My grandmother used to make a thermos of it for my grandfather when he took me skating at the outdoor rink by their house. He was determined to teach me to skate but apparently needed something to smooth out the frustration. We spent a lot of weekends on that rink, and still I never learned to skate well."

Looking out at what used to be the ice-skating rink, I wondered about why Matt had brought me here tonight. He seemed to know what I was thinking, pointed to the left side of the rink, and I followed his hand. "See that spot right there? Over by the bench? That's where I wiped out on our first date. I twisted my ankle and you had to help me off the ice." He grinned and I tried to picture it. Matt grimacing with pain, me supporting his lanky frame.

"You brought me ice skating on our first date? But why? If you can't skate?"

"Because you said you loved ice skating but didn't get to do it much anymore." He shrugged. "So I thought it would be romantic. Keep in mind, it was a couple months past the costume party, and I knew Jake had asked you out and I wanted to make a big impression." He laughed, big and genuine. "And that's exactly what I did. But not in the way I'd hoped."

It had been February 15 and apparently very cold, but it hadn't snowed in close to a week, so the rink was bare aside from the thousands of blade slices marking its surface. It was busy, Matt said, and so being agile was critical. Otherwise, you could take out an entire family with one wrong move. "We started with skating and spiked hot chocolate, then I'd made a reservation at Bymark so you could try that thirty-dollar burger." I nodded appreciatively, perking up at the restaurant's name and famously overpriced hamburger.

"Don't get too excited," Matt said, nudging my shoulder. "We didn't make it to Bymark because of my ankle, so that's not next on our agenda."

"Bummer. I'd like to know what a thirty-dollar hamburger tastes like."

"It's even more now, close to forty, I think. We'll put it on the to-do list, okay?"

"Okay. So, what happened next?" I asked, the hot chocolate warming both my belly and my hands.

"I'd been presumptuous and booked us a hotel so we didn't have to deal with our roommates." He paused, waiting to see my reaction to this as by now I'd figured out what those overnight bags meant—he was taking me back to the same place where we'd spent our first date night. "Because we'd missed our reservation but were starving, after you practically carried me off the ice, we grabbed a taxi to the hotel and ordered room service instead."

"Are you that bad of a skater?" I asked, still imagining us on the crowded skating rink, me trying not to laugh as Matt stumbled but tried to appear like he knew what he was doing.

"Terrible. Horribly unskilled. I'm pretty grateful the ice has melted so we don't have to re-create that particular part of the night."

I leaned over and quickly kissed him on the lips, then smiled as I pulled back. We were apart for only a moment before he put his cup down on the bench and placed his hands on either side of my face—his palms warm against the coolness of my cheeks—and kissed me deeply. Closing my eyes, I gave myself over to him and to this night, to the memory of us. When we finally broke apart, both of us a little breathless, Matt asked if I was ready for part two. I nodded and let him pull me up from the bench. He tossed our half-full cups of hot chocolate in the nearby trash can, then pretended to skate across the concrete, dancing me around in a spin. I threw my head back and laughed, the stars above twirling in a dizzying pattern as I did.

The room was beautiful, luxurious, and probably cost per night about the same as our monthly rent. "The Four Seasons?" I'd whispered as we walked through the sliding glass doors— holding tightly to each other's hands—into the opulent lobby. "You were trying to make an impression."

"I had to go all out," Matt said with a grin. "I knew the skating could go either way—though I didn't plan on an embarrassing ankle injury that would land me on crutches for a week." I cringed at this, and Matt leaned over to kiss the frown off my lips. Perhaps it was the alcohol, or the sweetness of how much effort he had put into re-creating this night, but I wanted to do nothing but kiss him. And then some, which I took as a good sign for the rest of the evening. *Maybe I will remember something. Maybe I can put Daniel back in the past where he belongs.*

At the thought of Daniel my good mood faltered slightly, but Matt didn't seem to notice—he, too, was enamored with how our evening was going so far. I forced Daniel from my mind. *Tonight is about Matt. Tonight is about us.* "I figured a good meal and a nice hotel room would make up for my lame rink skills."

After we ordered room service, Matt pulled out a bottle of wine and two tumblers from his overnight bag, and something in a brown paper sack. Opening the wine, Matt gave me a wink and said, "I hope you took my 'drink lots of water' seriously, because this is only the beginning." I was grateful for the wine—for the idea of getting right drunk tonight—because I had discovered how nicely alcohol softened the rough edges of my current situation.

We clinked glasses and I took a long, slow sip. It was delicious— smooth and oaky, a hint of vanilla—and with a jolt I realized I recognized the flavor. "I think I know this wine," I said with surprise, and Matt beamed. It didn't matter whether I remembered it because of this night (which I could tell was what Matt decided to believe) or because it had been a regular go-to for years; it mattered I'd remembered it at all. "I think I love this wine."

"You do," Matt said. Then he seemed to make a decision, putting down his glass and grabbing the paper bag. "I'll be right back. Sit tight, okay?"

I poured myself another glass while Matt was in the washroom. I could hear water running and wondered what he was doing—taking a shower? Waiting, I took my glass over to the large floor-to-ceiling glass window and drank it down as I gazed upon the lights of the city in front of me. A moment later the water stopped and Matt came out of the washroom. He seemed eager, but also nervous—he shifted from one foot to the other, his shirtsleeves rolled up past his elbows.

"Will you come in here with me?" Matt asked, his voice

gentle—almost pleading. He held out one hand, and I took it, following him. The air was warm and humid, and it smelled gorgeous. Like walking into a blooming flower shop. The bathtub was three-quarters full of water, and there were dozens of pink rose petals floating on its surface. I froze at the sight of the petals.

"Lucy?"

I couldn't stop staring at the tub. At the floating rose petals. At the faucet, which was positioned in the middle of the far side of the bathtub, and would have left a perfect circle of a bruise if you happened to bend your knee up hard against it. "Hey, you okay?" Matt gently put a finger on my chin and turned my face toward him. His forehead was creased with worry, and I could also see regret there. "I thought…what if we could go back to the beginning, you know? Start over." He took in a long breath, eyes never leaving mine. "I'm sorry. This was a bad idea. Let's go back out and drink that wine you love, okay?"

I started crying, which made him look even more desperate to cut this part of the evening short. "Please, Luce. Let's go. Do you want to leave? The hotel, I mean."

Shaking my head, I tried to explain. Tried to talk through my tears, which had now turned to gulping sobs. I sat down on the closed lid of the toilet and tried to pull myself together. Matt crouched in front of me, his hands on my thighs, every now and then reaching up to wipe a tear off my cheek. One stray rose petal was stuck to his forearm, and I gently peeled it off, holding it carefully between my fingers. Finally I managed to say, "I remember."

He looked at me, not understanding exactly what I meant. "You remember…what?"

I gestured to the bathtub. "I remember this bath. The rose petals." I didn't tell him that when I had previously remembered this moment it had been Daniel in the bath with me and not Matt, because that detail was only important for me to know. What mattered now was I was finally remembering this moment as I should have from the beginning—as it really was—a memory of an intimate and romantic experience shared *with Matt*. I had not taken a bath full of rose petals with Daniel, and definitely not the night I originally believed—before our engagement party—because as Daniel had confirmed, my arm had been in a cast. Also—and I couldn't believe I was only now realizing this—the faucet on the bathtub at Daniel's place had been at the end of the tub, not in the middle like this one.

So, it had been Matt I rested back against in the bathtub, the warm, rose-scented water lapping at our skin as he kissed my neck and then some. My memory had righted itself—it had always been Matt. He had booked a hotel room at the Four Seasons, asking them to fill a tub with rose petals one day after Valentine's Day, which was both a little cheesy and a lot romantic. Matt had done that for me, not Daniel. "I ended up with a bruised knee, right? From the faucet?" Now I remembered Matt gently running an ice cube over my knee and the blossoming purple mark, later, as we lay naked in bed.

"That's right. You did." He sounded breathless, understanding creeping into his expression. Then he buried his face in the tops of my thighs, where his hands still rested, and I wrapped my arms around him. *I remembered.*

We stayed like that for a moment before I wordlessly moved his arms, stood and pulled him up with me, undressing and keeping my eyes on his as I did. He followed suit and then we slipped into the warm water, the petals clinging to our naked skin, the water cresting over the side with our slow and purposeful movements.

24

"Have you seen your mother today?" Dad asked. It was shortly after noon on Friday, and I was getting ready to see Dr. Kay. We were down to once-a-week appointments—to better accommodate my upcoming back-to-work schedule. I was still floating high after my date night with Matt and I couldn't wait to tell her about my memory breakthrough.

I threw my notebook and a pen into my purse, tucking my phone between my shoulder and cheek to not drop it. "I haven't," I replied, and Dad sighed. I stood up straight, held the phone tighter to my ear. "Why? Was I supposed to?" For a brief moment I wondered if I'd forgotten I had plans with my mom.

"No. I don't think so," Dad said. "I'm sure she's out with a friend or at the market. I only got home an hour ago myself."

"Okay," I replied. "So why do you sound worried about where she is, then?"

"Oh, do I? Well, sorry about that, pumpkin. It's fine. We have an appointment with the Realtor in five minutes and she's not here and you know your mom. She's never late for anything."

That was true. And five minutes early was actually late to my mom—in fact, anything less than fifteen minutes early meant you were already behind schedule. It was one of my mother's idiosyncrasies I'd long ago given up trying to understand or rationalize.

"Did you try her cell?" I asked, glancing at the time. I had to be out the door in two minutes.

"Yes...yes. It went to voice mail." He sounded distracted, and I could hear him unloading the dishwasher.

I continued walking through the apartment and tossing things into my purse—a granola bar and bottle of water, a small pack of tissues in preparation for the inevitable tears that came with a Dr. Kay appointment, despite my best intentions to hold it together. "Speaking of the Realtor, where are things at with that?" I hoped they wouldn't sell the house. I had a lot of memories there— great ones—and for whatever reason it felt like if they sold our house they were selling those, too, right out from under me.

"Just a meeting. Oh, there's the doorbell. I'd better go. Let me know if you hear from your mom, okay? Though I'm sure she'll be home any minute. Any minute. Maybe that's her now."

"I will," I said, and was about to comment Mom probably wouldn't be ringing the doorbell to her own house when I realized Dad had already hung up. Staring at my phone for a moment, I wondered if he was okay. He sounded so scattered, which was unlike him. My dad was the most even-keeled of all of us. But I knew they'd had a lot on their plates since my accident—because of my accident. And with my mom pushing for a possible move to her dream town house with the "gor- geous north-facing morning sun, perfect for painting," he was likely feeling pressure to make that happen, too.

I slung my now-heavy purse over my shoulder and headed out the door, my conversation with my dad already pushed out of my mind as I focused on whether I still had time to take the streetcar to Dr. Kay's office or needed to grab a cab.

As soon as I got out of my appointment with Dr. Kay there were three messages on my phone. One from Dad, saying he found Mom and everything was fine, though his voice was strained and I wondered again what was going on. Maybe they had decided to sell the house, after all, and were worried about telling me. There was another message from Matt, asking if I'd talked with my dad and did I want to go out for dinner tonight, and one from Alex asking me to call her immediately.

"What's up?" I asked when Alex answered, fumbling to hold my phone and get a token for the streetcar out of my wallet without dropping everything.

"Move the ladder," Alex said.

"What? Are you talking to me?"

"No, sorry. Hang on a second," she said.

"Are you talking to me now?" I asked.

"Yes. But ignore me for a moment while I try to get these clueless people into their places." Her voice was low so only I could hear. But then I had to move the phone away from my ear as she yelled at someone again about the ladder.

"Okay, sorry about that," she said to me. "I'm doing a tableau on climbing the corporate ladder and they're insisting on using an actual wooden ladder in the shoot. Uninspired but well-paying assholes." She raised her voice back up above normal levels. "Fantastic. That's the right spot. Yes. Leave it. Right there. Okay, I'll be with you in a minute.

"Amateurs," she mumbled, and I laughed. "Okay, I'm back. What's up?"

"Alex, you called me and told me to call you. *Immediately.* Remember?"

"Right! You'd think I was the one with the fucked-up memory, huh?" She chuckled and I rolled my eyes. Alex wasn't known for her tact. "Mom was in the hospital."

I stopped walking, right in the middle of the sidewalk. "Watch out!" someone said from behind me, and my purse dropped from my shoulder when the fast-moving pedestrian collided with me. I mumbled an apology and stepped to the side, out of the flow of foot traffic, my purse dangling from my fingertips.

"What do you mean Mom's in the hospital?" My breath

caught in my throat, my fingers felt tingly and I thought I should find a place to sit down before I fell down. "What happened? Is she okay?"

"Relax, Lucy. She's fine. Her blood sugar was out of whack. She got dizzy at the market or wherever she was. You know, I assumed it was the market because she goes there so flipping much, but—"

"Alex!" I shouted. After some forty years Mom had her condition under such good control it was easy to forget she was diabetic, except for the insulin pump monitor she always had clipped to her pants. I couldn't remember her ever having to go to the hospital because of it. "Did something go wrong with her pump? What happened?"

"I don't know exactly because I could only chat quickly with Dad. They took her to emerg as a precaution. Whoever she was with apparently panicked and called 911 when she got light-headed."

"Who was she with?" I was trembling, caught up in one of those emotional tidal waves where my reactions were excessive for the situation. *Mom is fine.* Alex would never lie about that, so why did my body feel like it was going into shock? "Everyone knows she's diabetic. She wears a bracelet. She has a monitor clipped to her at all times."

Alex shouted something else about the ladder. "Listen, I've got to run before these yahoos screw up the entire shoot. Call Dad, he'll fill you in. Love you." And then I heard a few choice words she mumbled under her breath about the *goddamn ladder* before she disconnected the call.

I tried Dad, but he didn't pick up. I was struggling to figure out what to do next, as it seemed my brain had stalled during Alex's call and wouldn't reboot. I considered going back to Dr. Kay's office, slightly worried something more serious than a panic attack might be going on with me. With the splitting headache that had settled behind my eyeballs during the call and the strange tingling I had through my limbs, I couldn't be sure I wasn't having a stroke.

Call Daniel. He popped into my head, and it felt so obvious. *He's your husband, call him.* But just as quickly came this: *Daniel is not your husband, Lucy.*

He never was your husband. He's married to Margot.

Matt is your boyfriend. You should call Matt.

I sat heavily on the stone steps of the closest building and called Matt. Unable to stop it from happening, I started crying the second he picked up.

"I need you to come get me," I said as best I could.

"Lucy? Are you okay? What's the matter?" So many questions, so much worry in his voice. Then, more firmly, "Tell me where you are."

25

Matt was there within minutes, flying out of the taxi so fast he left the door open. I had calmed down somewhat, though my parents were still not picking up their phones, and was able to tell him what happened. He wanted to take me home to rest, but I insisted we go straight to my parents' place. I apologized multiple times on the way there, worried about dragging him away from work, but he held my hand tighter each time, saying, "That's not important right now."

Our taxi finally pulled up to my parents' house and I jumped out, practically running to the front door. I let myself in with my key and left the door open for Matt, who was a few steps behind me.

"Dad? Mom?" I called out, sliding my boots off on the sisal mat by the front door. It was quiet inside, and the sound of Matt shutting the door behind him echoed down the hallway of the foyer.

"Are you sure they're here?" Matt asked, slipping out of his shoes and unbuttoning his jacket. He put his hands on my shoulders from behind and rubbed gently, and we walked that way into the kitchen.

I saw both their cell phones sitting in the wicker basket on the counter and groaned with frustration—no wonder they hadn't picked up. The clock over the fridge ticked loudly, but there were no other sounds in the house. I called out again, then heard, "Down here!"

We headed downstairs to the basement rec room, found my parents sitting on the sectional. My dad was marking student essays; my mom had a sketchbook on her lap and colored pencils splayed out on the coffee table. She pushed her glasses on top of her head, nestling them into her silver hair. "Lucy, Matt, hello!" Mom said, smiling as though it was perfectly normal for us to visit in the middle of a workday. "What are you two doing here?" Then her expression darkened and she shifted to the edge of the couch. "Are you okay, honey? Did something happen?"

I stared at her. My concern turned to confusion. *"Did something happen?"* I asked. I felt Matt rest a hand on my lower back, and I looked between my parents. They both wore a neutral expression, though I could see something lingering behind Dad's gaze…a little worry he was still harboring. "Mom, I talked with Alex."

Mom gave a dismissive wave, leaned back into the cushions. "Your sister is always embellishing for dramatic effect. It's the artist in her." She said that last part with pride. Mom had always wanted to be a recognized artist, and it brought her great joy to see Alex making her way in the world, one photography award at a time.

"So what happened?" I looked at Dad this time, held eye contact until he looked down at the paper he was grading, clipping his pen to the page and setting it down beside him.

"Your mother had a bit of a spell, but she's fine," Dad said. "As you can see. Perfectly fine."

Mom put her glasses back on her face, smiled brightly. "I was at the St. Lawrence Market with a friend buying some fish for dinner and I got a bit faint. My friend overreacted and called an ambulance. It was incredibly embarrassing. But like Dad said, I'm fine, love. *Good as new.*"

"What friend?" I asked, frowning. Everyone knew Mom

was diabetic, and all her friends knew what to do in case of an emergency.

Mom did look fine, but she also seemed uncomfortable—she wouldn't look at me straight on. And neither would Dad, I realized. He was fiddling with the stack of essays, running his thumb along the edges and letting them fan out one way, then the other.

"No one you know." Her tone left little doubt she was no longer interested in this line of questioning. She got up from the couch, came over in front of me. "Darling, please settle down. It isn't good for you to be so worked up," she said as she tucked a stray piece of hair behind my ear. "How about a nice cup of tea? I got a gorgeous oolong at the market. Matt?"

"Sure," Matt said, taking off his suit coat, realizing we'd be staying for a little while. "That sounds great."

They all started to move, heading up toward the kitchen, but I was rooted in place.

"Lucy? Are you coming?" Mom said, pausing on the bottom step. Everyone turned to look at me.

"Would someone please tell me what's going on?" I said. "Is this about the house? Are you selling it?"

Dad, who was the closest to me, cupped my elbow and spoke gently. "Sweetheart, let's go have that tea."

I pulled away, took a step back. I wanted to settle down, to drink tea and be happy Mom was okay, but I was struggling against the anxiety threatening to overtake me. My fuse was shorter since my accident, my ability to stay calm in situations that felt stressful diminished. "I don't want tea, Dad. I want you all to stop treating me like I might break if you say the wrong thing! Yes, my brain is a bit of a mess, and if I'm being honest, I am, too. But if you think keeping things from me is going to help, it isn't."

Dad and Mom exchanged a glance. Matt looked down at his socked feet.

"So. What are you not telling me?" I asked again, hands clutched together to hide the shaking.

Mom pulled her shoulders back, stood as tall as her five-foot frame would allow and glanced briefly at Dad before looking back at me. "Okay, Lucy." She sighed. "Your father and I are separated."

All the frustration and anxiety left me like a wave going back out to sea. "Sorry...what?" I swiveled between them, feeling weak-limbed, similar to how I'd felt on the street when Alex had told me Mom was at the hospital. "But...how? When? You had your anniversary, like, six months ago. We had a party!"

"No, we didn't," Mom said. Matt now stared at the ceiling, his hands on his hips. Dad watched Mom.

"Yes. We did." I was sure of it. It was one of the memories I'd managed to retain from the past few years. "It was at that restaurant you and Dad love. What's the name of it again?" I snapped my fingers impatiently, trying to recall the name. "You know, the one with all those twinkle lights running across the ceiling." No one said anything. "The food was amazing. Re-member the mini Caesar salads in bacon cups?" Now I looked at Matt, held my hand in a cup as though I was holding one of the little salads. "You were there, right? Remember those salad cups? How good they were?"

The corners of Matt's mouth were downturned, and he watched me worriedly. "I *do* remember—"

"See! Matt remembers! How can we go from there—" I used my hand to cut through the air in a chopping motion "—to here, in only a few months?"

Matt cleared his throat. "I do remember, Lucy, but, uh..." He glanced at me, then at my parents. They all looked terrible, and a sick feeling settled into my stomach. "That anniversary party was for *my* parents. In California, last fall. Remember? I showed you the pictures."

"What? No. No." I shook my head repeatedly. "It was here, in Toronto, with *my* parents. It snowed, I remember. I wore that…" I paused, trying to remember back to what I had worn for the party. Came up blank.

Matt cleared his throat again, shifted his weight from one foot to the other. I could see he had a small hole in one of his socks, by his big toe. "You wore a yellow dress. And you're right, it did snow. But not at the party. At Heavenly Mountain Resort, where we went skiing for a few days later."

The picture with the yellow dress, the champagne toast with his parents and sister, the ski selfie. I stopped breathing when I realized the truth. My parents were splitting up and I didn't remember anything about it.

"Lucy Bear, your mom and I told you and Alex about this only a month or so before your…your accident. But when you didn't remember after you woke up, well…" Dad said, throwing his hands up. "We decided to wait. Hoped you might remember on your own."

"So that's it, then? You're separating?" I asked, stunned and upset by the news and the fact they'd all kept it from me, once again.

"Separated," Mom said quietly, correcting me.

"Is this why you've been meeting with the Realtor?" I asked, my voice breaking. "You're selling the house because you've split up?" I wiped a tear away hastily, frustrated to be so emotional. But while I understood we'd already done this once before— when they told me the first time—I couldn't help my reaction to the news my parents' relationship was over.

"We're looking at our options," Dad said, sitting down on the stair he was standing on, letting his bent elbows rest on his knees. He looked tired, and sad. "That part is true."

"Where are you both living now?" I asked them, thinking back to our interactions over the past month. Realizing how little time we'd all spent together, and understanding now the reason why.

"I'm staying here," Dad said. "Your mom is staying in the

west end with a friend." There was something in the way Dad said "a friend" that gave me pause.

"Is this the same friend you were with at the market today?" I closed my eyes and rubbed my hands over them. The headache was only getting stronger and I wished I could lie down. Pretend like this moment was actually a confabulation—and in reality my parents were as happy together as they'd ever been.

A pause, then, "Yes. His name is Carl. He's an artist I met at my watercolor class." Good grief, not only were my parents separated, my mother had a *boyfriend*.

"Did I know about this Carl? Before my accident?"

Mom nodded, and I had a very clear sense everyone was holding his or her breath as I tried to digest what I'd learned this afternoon.

"We understand this is a lot to accept all of a sudden, but imagine it from our side, pumpkin. We already *had* this difficult conversation," Dad said. "We've hashed this all out, have been living with it for months now."

"*You* have all been living with it for months."

"Lucy, I'm sorry you had to find out like this, honey. But you have to know we didn't mean to hurt you, or to keep it from you," Mom added.

"Of course you meant to keep it from me," I replied, my voice weary. "Otherwise, why wouldn't you have told me right away?" I'm sure it was hard enough the first time, certain they thought they were doing the right thing. But it didn't make this moment any easier.

Heaving a big sigh, I walked over to the couch and sat down, pulling out my notebook and pen from my purse. Then I leaned back into the cushions, crossed my legs and rested the pad on my knee, flipping to a blank page. I set the point of my pen on the paper and pressed down hard to create a bullet point. "Okay, then. Here's what we're going to do. No more secrets or surprises. Everyone sit down, right now, and tell me *every single thing* I've forgotten about in the past four years."

26

That evening Matt caught up on work and I read through emails and project notes Brooke had sent to prepare me for Monday's return to the office. We didn't speak again about my parents' separation, which I suspected made Matt uneasy by how often I caught him glancing my way.

I could tell he expected something from me around today's revelation. Either to lash out, or be upset, or maybe to drone on about what a shock it had been. But I had no interest in doing any of that, and so I chose to act as though none of it had happened. Pushed it to the back of my mind, where things were cobwebby and convoluted. We had dinner, watched mindless television and went to bed far earlier than normal, under the guise of exhaustion, but I think we were both tired of playing the game. Matt was soon asleep, but I knew it would be hours before I drifted off, my mind swirling and confused.

There are no distractions in the quiet dark of night, so your mind can get the better of you. Slipping out of our bedroom, I closed the door softly so as not to wake up Matt, then grabbed my memory journal from the coffee table. Boiling the kettle for tea, I read over the most recent pages of questions and added a couple of notes about what had transpired today so I wouldn't have to second-guess myself later. I flipped to the page where

I'd planned to capture any other big revelations my family and Matt had to share, but the paper was blank aside from one lonely bullet point.

After I'd sat on the couch and demanded they tell me everything, there had been silence. Then some stammering followed by blank looks, and finally assurances there was nothing else. I'd pushed, reminding them these sorts of "surprises" weren't helpful. Were in fact detrimental to my mental health and well-being and eroded my trust—at a time when I needed to be able to trust them the most. But the three of them claimed there was nothing else they could think of, and in the end I had no choice but to believe them and so the page remained empty.

I wasn't upset about my parents' separation; I was upset about everything. And, maybe irrationally, I was most upset with Matt. We had been doing so well—his reminiscence therapy efforts so sweet, the date night exceeding expectations, especially because it triggered an important memory of the two of us. But then we sat in my parents' basement and I learned they had split up and no one had bothered to tell me—including Matt. *Especially Matt*, who had a million opportunities to give me the truth and who had the most up-close view of how much I was struggling.

Maybe it was juvenile for a grown woman to be upset about her parents splitting; maybe it was unfair to expect Matt to be the one to tell me about it. He would probably say it hadn't been his news to share, and there was truth in that. Hell, any of them could have told me—and I should be equally pissed with my parents, and Alex (and I was). But even if my rational brain told me Matt was doing the best he could in a situation with no rulebook, I couldn't help the simmering anger, the relentless burn of disappointment that he'd let me down.

Still restless and frustrated two cups of tea later, I picked up one of the novels on the table—a book I had apparently been reading before the accident, the bookmark at page 132. I read that page, and the few before it, but there was no memory jog and soon I set it down with a frustrated sigh. Checking my phone, I scrolled through social media, then decided to search for Daniel so I could finally "friend" him. A few seconds later I had found his profile and sent a friend request, ignoring the lingering humiliation that he'd stood me up on Monday. Expecting I wouldn't hear anything until the morning (if at all, because it didn't appear he was active on the social media site), I was surprised when a notification popped up saying Daniel London had accepted my friend request. A moment later a message box appeared with a note from Daniel.

Hey, Lucy, how goes it tonight?

I typed back, Good! Can't sleep, though. You?

Messenger showed me he was typing, the three little dots dancing while I waited for his note to load onto my screen.

I'm studying. Going to be a late night. Any chance you want to meet for a drink? Give me a break from these books for an hour?

A drink? This was unexpected, and I had no idea what to do. I shouldn't go. It was well after ten. Matt was sleeping and would be worried if he woke up and I was gone. Plus, it was Daniel. What about Margot?

I shouldn't go.

But my fingers typed back my answer before I considered it too seriously.

A drink is exactly what I need to cure this insomnia. Where?

We made plans to meet at Goods & Provisions, a restaurant and bar only a few blocks from my place. I wrote a quick note to Matt, left it on the kitchen table and hoped he would find it if he woke up and wondered where I was.

Out for some fresh air. Back soon. —L

It was vague (I never went out for "fresh air" at 10:00 p.m., especially alone), but I had weighed the level of his worry for both scenarios—him waking up, finding me gone but having no clue where, or seeing the note and at least knowing where I was, even if it meant he'd probably come looking for me—and decided at least some information would be wise.

I went back to the note and added *Don't worry—I'm fine* to the bottom of the page and then set out to meet Daniel. It was chilly, April not yet providing the consistent springlike weather the city was pining for after a bitterly cold winter, and my breath came out in curled wisps of frosty air as I walked.

With every step I considered canceling, wanted to race back and rip up the note to Matt and get back into bed, where I knew I should be. When I arrived at Goods & Provisions, cold fingers gripping the door handle and standing under the brown-and-beige-striped awning, I gave myself one final chance to turn around and go home. But seconds later I pulled open the door and walked in, the dark wood paneled walls and dim lighting adding to the tiny bar's charm. Shaking my hair out after taking off my toque, I saw Daniel a few feet away at the narrow bar, his own hat and gloves stacked beside him.

"Hey," I said, coming up beside him and taking a seat. I tried to act casual, like meeting my married ex on a Friday night while my boyfriend slept in our bed at home was a perfectly acceptable thing to do. But my heart raced inside my chest. *Daniel.* I still had a visceral reaction to being near him, like all the cells in my body were straining to get closer. I felt awful thinking it, but the truth was I wanted to kiss him. Press my chilled lips against his and close my eyes. I knew I was blushing, but I hoped with the dim lighting it wasn't obvious. "I'm surprised you beat me here."

"I really needed the break," he said, smiling, lifting his drink. *Damn, that smile.* Another rush of longing shot through me and I busied myself with the menu.

"What are you drinking?" I asked, eyeing his glass, now only half-full. A semicircle of lime lay discarded on a napkin on the bar in front of him, a swizzle stick holding a piece of sugared ginger beside it.

He lifted it up and smiled again. "Dark and Stormy."

A memory flooded my mind, and I inhaled sharply as it did. The night I met Daniel, that was what I had been drinking. I considered whether the memory was real, but I felt fairly sure it was. Things were mostly intact from that time of my life. It was only the past four years or so that were muddled. "Since when do you drink those?" Daniel was a beer drinker. Maybe some Scotch, here and there.

He glanced at me oddly, took a sip and set the glass back down. "Since the night we met."

The bartender appeared in front of me. "What can I get you?"

"I'll have what he's having," I said, gesturing to Daniel's glass.

"You got it," she said, adding, "Another? No lime this time?" to Daniel. He nodded, murmuring thanks.

"So how's school going?" I asked, settling onto my stool and trying to clear my mind so I could focus on our conversation. I clasped my hands together, wishing I already had a drink to hold.

"Pretty good," Daniel said, shaking his now-empty glass a little, making the ice rattle against its edges. "It's not entirely different from law actually, which has made the transition easier."

"What exactly are you studying? You said it was grad school and something to do with education?"

"Social justice education," he replied. "I'm hoping to get my doctorate. Teach, eventually."

"Oh, yeah?" I said. "That's great. Sounds perfect for you." I had no idea why I said that last part. I had never known Daniel to be interested in teaching in any way, and a doctorate in social justice education didn't line up with the Daniel I knew—who had been following in his dad's footsteps as a personal injury attorney.

Which also forced me to admit the truth: I didn't know this version of Daniel. I also had to wonder how much influence

Margot had had on his decision to leave law and become an educator, which lined up nicely with her own professional ambitions. I thought about asking what Margot was doing—not tonight, but in general—but also didn't want to bring her name up. I wanted to drink and pretend for a while.

Our drinks arrived, and Daniel cocked an eyebrow and pointed at the lime wedge on the rim of my glass.

"What?" I asked, glancing between him and my drink.

He chuckled, then shook his head. "I thought I had more power than that."

Confused, I frowned. Felt the uncomfortable prickle of understanding that my memory had failed me again. Daniel could see I was getting upset, and quickly changed tact.

"Hey, sorry. I'm kidding around, Lucy. But..." he began, gesturing to my drink. "I was surprised to see you back on the lime."

"'Back on the lime'?" *What in the hell was he talking about?*

"You don't remember." He smiled, the corners of his eyes crinkling as he did, and I felt instantly lit up inside. No longer upset, now I was curious.

"I don't remember." Then I laughed. "I can't tell you how many times a day I have to say that."

He turned to me quickly, exaggerated shock on his face. "I'm hurt."

"Okay, so what's the story with the limes?" I grinned and took a sip of the drink, the dark rum strong, the ginger beer sweet and spicy. "I hope it's worth it."

"Lucy Sparks, *the lime* is where it all began."

27

It was hot, too many bodies crammed in the room, and the night was only getting started. Lucy pulled her black silk top away from her skin where it clung with sweat, and billowed it out from her body a couple times. Scanning the crowd from where she stood by the outdoor bar, she couldn't find Jenny, who had said she'd be right back, almost fifteen minutes ago. The music reverberated in Lucy's chest as she swirled the slim red straw in her Dark and Stormy, the ice nearly melted with the heat of the room and her hand holding the glass. Stabbing the lime floating lazily in her drink, she brought it to her mouth and sucked out the juice and some of the pulp.

The Madison Avenue Pub was a local watering hole near the university—three old mansions that had been combined and converted into a bar and English-style pub where students drank too much and made memories they'd reminisce about for years to come. It was a maze of rooms connected by grungy, maroon-carpet-covered staircases, with a huge wooden deck off the back that was usually teeming with students on weekends.

Tonight Jenny and Lucy were meeting up with some other friends, and Lucy had heard Evan McAllister—a guy she was interested in but didn't know well yet—was also coming. Evan and Lucy had flirted at another bar night similar to this one and had run into each other a few times on campus. They were also in the same psychology class, though there were four hundred people in the class, but Evan always waved and smiled when he saw her. There was chemistry between them for sure—at least enough for a few nights of fun, and at twenty-one, Lucy was all about fun.

"That's a mistake," someone said, and Lucy looked up from her glass to the guy standing in front of her. Clearly intoxicated—bleary-eyed, body swaying slightly, damp hair stuck to his forehead—but with a nice smile, dimples on either side piercing his cheeks. Lucy wasn't short at five foot six, but this guy had only a couple inches on her. He also seemed a few years older, maybe a graduate student.

"Sorry?" Lucy replied, unsure if he was actually talking to her or not.

"Eating the lime. They never wash the fruit before it goes in the drinks," he said, shouting to be heard over the cacophony of voices and music. He pointed over her shoulder at one of the bartenders preparing a row of cocktails. "See?" he said. "He's grabbing those slices with his bare hands. And who knows where those hands have been." He raised his eyebrows, swayed a little more and held up his own hands while somehow managing to keep a grip on his beer bottle.

"Thanks for the tip." Lucy set the lime peel on the bar's countertop and grimaced as she watched the bartender wipe his sweating brow with the back of his hand before slinging fruit slices into drinks.

The guy gave a sloppy wave, as if to say, *Happy to help.*

Then he squinted at her, leaned in enough she instinctually leaned back, if for no other reason because of the waft of alcohol following his breath. "Have we met before?"

Lucy had to laugh. "Has that line ever worked for you?" She sipped from her watered-down drink, missing the lime.

"Not really," he said, looking sheepish. "But seriously, you do look familiar."

"I hear that a lot," she said, which was true. With her shoulder-length bob and all-black outfit, she in fact looked like at least seventy percent of the women in this very bar. The guy shifted then, and one of the spotlights illuminated his shirt. It was navy, with a white arrow pointing up toward his chin and Keep Calm and Kiss the Groom emblazoned on the front.

"Nice shirt," Lucy said, gesturing to his chest. "How's that working for you tonight?"

He tugged out the shirt as if he was noticing it for the first time, then read it upside down. "Not much better than the line, if I'm being honest," he said, and they both laughed. Then he jumped in a semicircle so she could see the back of it, which he tried to read over his shoulder. "What does it say? They wouldn't let me look."

Hi, my name is Daniel.
If I'm too drunk and seem lost, please call me a cab.
(There's twenty dollars and my address pinned inside this shirt.)

She laughed, and he asked again what it said, but she told him it was the same as the front. "What's your name?" he asked.

"Lucy." She held out a hand and he shook it. "And I'm guessing you're Daniel."

"I am," he said. "Wait, how did you know?"

She shrugged, smiling. "Lucky guess."

He nodded as though that was a perfectly acceptable answer and pointed to her nearly empty drink. "Well, Lucy, can I buy you another?"

"Sure. Thanks," she said. "Dark and Stormy. This time without the lime, I guess."

"Coming right up." A few minutes later he was back with her drink, and one for him, as well. "I've never had one of these. What's in it?"

"Dark rum, ginger beer and lime juice."

"Hmm, sounds good," he said before trying a sip. Then another. He gave a long blink, swayed a little again. "You have good taste in cocktails, Lucy."

"Thanks?" Lucy laughed again and wondered about Daniel's story. He was engaged, if his T-shirt was to be believed, but he seemed to have forgotten that detail as he flirted with Lucy and sucked back his drink.

A group of ten or so guys, all wearing navy blue shirts that read Team Groom, engulfed Daniel and dragged him laughing back out into the dark sea of people. He waved as he went, and Lucy gave him a wave back right as Jenny returned, bumping their shoulders together. She handed her another drink and Lucy immediately took the skewered lime out of the glass and lined it up beside the other one on the bar.

"Who are you waving at?" Jenny asked.

"Some guy named Daniel. He seemed to know a lot about bar limes and is apparently getting married soon."

"You know, you might have better luck if you stick with the *single* ones," Jenny said.

Lucy rolled her eyes. "So where have you been?"

Jenny sipped her own drink. "I ran into Jackson."

"Jackson?" Lucy asked, trying to remember which one he was. "English lit Jackson?"

"No, that's Jack. This is CrossFit Jackson," Jenny replied, a contented smile spreading over her lips.

Right. Jenny's latest fitness craze was CrossFit, and Jackson was one of the guys who ran a few classes a week out of the university's gym. He was muscled in a way that made Lucy both curious and concerned, and Jenny had been going to a lot of classes lately.

"He's here with a few other guys. Thought we might want to join them?" She gave Lucy a hopeful look, and Lucy glanced at her watch. With every passing minute she was getting drunker and less certain Evan was going to show. Jenny covered the watch face with her hand and shook her head. "Nope. No. You do not get to pull the 'It's getting late, I'm going to cab it home' thing." She puffed out her cheeks, gave Lucy her best annoyed pout. "It's barely midnight. You promised fun-Lucy tonight."

"You're right, I'm sorry," Lucy said. "I'm all yours tonight. Fun-Lucy is ready for anything." She gulped the drink Daniel had bought her, the burn of the alcohol and sharp ginger mingling uncomfortably in her mouth with the cold of the ice cubes. Crunching the ice with her teeth, she set her now-empty glass on the bar beside the fallen lime soldiers, picked up the drink Jenny had brought her and pointed into the crowd. "Let's go find Jackson and his shockingly fit friends."

Jenny smiled and kissed her on the cheek, then grabbed her hand, and Lucy let herself be pulled deep into the pulsing sea of bodies. Later, she would run into Daniel again. They would literally bump up against each other on the too-small dance floor and Lucy would fall right on her ass. He would crouch in front of her, not so drunk he wasn't horrified to have knocked her over, and Lucy would laugh at his clumsy attempts to help her up, then let him buy her drinks with the twenty dollars from inside his shirt. She would learn he was a few years older, a soon-to-be lawyer currently articling, and was getting married in a couple of weeks.

Lucy would give him her number because she had had too much to drink and was young and single and didn't care whether or not that was appropriate. And a month later Daniel would call her, out of the blue while she was studying for midterms—now dating Evan, even though she liked the idea of him a lot more than the reality, as it would turn out—and he would ask her out for a drink. He and his fiancée had broken up before the wedding. Lucy never asked why, only if it was for good (it was, he said), and if he was okay with it (which he assured her he was).

Three weeks later Lucy was Daniel London's girlfriend.

28

"I can't believe I forgot about the lime," I said. But I hadn't forgotten-forgotten, like the way I'd forgotten I liked eating meat and my parents were separated and Matt was my boyfriend. This particular detail—so small and insignificant in the grand scheme—had been pushed aside. Easily retrievable with a little reminiscence therapy, which was what Daniel and I were up to tonight.

There was a brief flit of guilt in my belly as I thought about Matt and his reaction when I asked for extra lime in my drink at Jake's party, and the tequila shots from the other night (*this must have been what I was remembering about the lime*), but I pushed it aside.

"I shouldn't be surprised, though. My brain is a bit of a mess." I tried to laugh, but it got caught in my throat.

"You okay, Lucy?" Daniel asked gently. "Maybe I shouldn't have brought up the lime thing? Let you live in blissful denial?" He was trying to make me smile, and it worked.

"It's not the lime thing," I said, my smile fading. "I got blindsided by something today, and, well…" I held up my drink. "Let's say I needed this Dark and Stormy tonight."

"So what happened?" Daniel asked, holding up two fingers for the bartender before turning his gaze back on me. I saw his ring then, and my head was spinning and I felt unpleasantly warm. I looked away from his hand, from the ring and what it meant.

"I found out my parents are separating. Or are already separated, months ago."

"Ah, I'm sorry. You didn't have any idea?"

"I guess I *did*," I said. "But I don't remember, and they've been keeping up this whole 'we're still happy and together' charade since I got out of the hospital. My mom is even *dating* apparently." I shuddered, and Daniel laughed.

"This is not funny," I said, though the smile crept back onto my face.

"The nerve of our parents, doing things we don't like," he quipped, and I laughed. "My parents should have split years ago. Neither of them is happy, but after Nan left Gramps it created such a mess within the family my mom once made the comment being unhappy was part of being married. A 'suck it up, buttercup' arrangement." He raised one eyebrow, smirked. "Nice, right?"

"That's sad," I said.

"It is sad. But my grandparents got back together and now they act like newlyweds, so who the hell knows."

"They got back together? Huh. Maybe there's hope for my parents yet."

"Nan and Gramps married when they were seventeen," Daniel said. "Nan said she needed to 'know' another man, aside from my grandfather. It was apparently on her bucket list." He cringed and I chuckled. "Look, I'm sorry you're going through this with your parents, Luce. They always seemed so solid."

"I know. And it sucks. But the worst was finding out they've been lying about it. Plus, everyone else knew and kept it from me, too." I picked up my third Dark and Stormy, which had magically appeared in front of me. "There's nothing worse than being the last to find out."

"I bet," he said, draining his glass. I wasn't sure if he was ahead of me or not at this point, but he definitely seemed less intoxicated than I was.

"You want to know the shitty truth?" I asked.

"Always," Daniel said. "Hit me."

"I have no idea what other secrets are locked inside my brain. They could be big. Important, life-changing secrets. And what if I never remember?" I said. "What if I can never trust my memory again?"

He sighed, shook his head. "I don't know, Lucy."

I held up my glass a bit sloppily, and some of the drink spilled over its edge. "And the award for the most honest reply yet goes to Daniel London!"

Daniel chuckled as he watched me try to mop up the spill with a tiny napkin. "I think you need another drink," he said.

"Ha! That's probably the last thing I need. But why the hell not?" I said, slurring a little now. "One more couldn't hurt."

"That's the spirit," Daniel said, and soon we had another round going and I was sucking it back like it was water.

The rum had loosened my tongue and so my curiosity finally won out. "Where's Margot tonight?" I asked when there was a lull in our conversation. I hoped my tone sounded light and nonloaded, even though I was quivering slightly on my stool.

"She's out," he said. "Girls' night." He was saying something else, about someone's birthday or something, but I was fixated on his lips. I had the sense everything would be all right if I moved closer…closer again…

"Easy, Lucy." Daniel laughed as he helped me right myself after I nearly slid off my stool. "As much as I'm enjoying this, maybe it's time to call it a night?"

"Prob'ly good idea," I said, my words blending together. Daniel paid our tab and tucked his arm through mine as we left the bar. I let him take some of my weight because it turned out that last drink had in fact been a terrible idea, and I swayed more than walked back to my place.

"So what is the lovely Margot doing these days?" I asked, like it was perfectly ordinary to discuss her. Like it didn't hurt me to say her name, to know she filled the space in Daniel's life I believed was mine even though it wasn't. "She wanted to be a professor, didn't she? Is she teaching or something?" I was trying hard to be coherent, but it was a battle I wasn't winning.

Daniel shook his head, used his free hand to pull his collar up higher against the chill. "You'll never believe it, but she's an interior designer now. Does some TV work, too."

"Shut up!" I slapped his arm but missed and lost my balance. Daniel put a firm hand on mine, which was clutching his arm for support. "You're kidding. Television, eh?"

He laughed, took a step back so we were side by side again, and I had mostly regained my balance. "I told you it was unbelievable."

"But...but...she used a sleeping bag instead of sheets when we were at school! Hated having her picture taken. She always used to hold her hands in front of her face during photos, said smiling on demand was demeaning."

"I know." Daniel let out an even bigger laugh this time. "That was a long time ago." He smiled at me, and a flutter filled my belly. I couldn't stop staring at him, the feelings inside me swirling and growing, at least in part thanks to all those drinks.

"You should see how many accent pillows are on our bed now. It takes me five minutes to move them every night." He didn't sound like he minded, though, and again I was hit with the truth that Daniel had married Margot. He chose her, even though I was the one who used to wear an engagement ring he put there.

The sadness was swift and crushing, and I started walking faster for fear if I didn't I would sit on the cold sidewalk and cry. "You sound happy," I said, because it was true, and though it hurt me to know the reality of Daniel's life now, I was glad for him. Wanted him to be content with his life.

"I am. Life is pretty sweet," he replied. "Though I could do without the pillows, if I'm being totally honest." I smiled and tucked my chin into my coat, which allowed me to let my smile drop without him noticing.

Things were quiet between us as we walked the last block to my place, and I slowed as we approached the front steps of the building. "This is me," I said, pulling my arm out from his.

Daniel looked at the building. "Nice place. I remember when they were building these." I followed his gaze, appreciated again how much I loved where I lived. It was an old bank that had been converted into four loft town houses, with exposed brick and beams inside and plenty of character on the facade. "Bet it's great inside."

I bit my lip, held in the desire to say, *You know it is*, because even if my mind tried to remind me this was *our* place, Daniel had never stepped into my building. "It is" was all I said instead.

"Thanks for the drinks, and the walk home," I added, thinking in any other scenario this would be when I invited him up for another glass of something neither of us needed.

"It was nice to hang out," Daniel replied, sensing none of my conflict, blowing into his gloved hands and jumping a couple of times to stay warm. "We should do it again."

"We should," I replied, though I didn't think that would be the best thing. For me, anyway, because there was too much between us and I could still feel the current connecting me to Daniel. I wondered if he could feel the threads, too. "Well, okay. Good luck with the studying. I hope you aren't up all night now."

"Don't worry about me," he said. "I've got all weekend." And still, he didn't leave, as if there was no other place in the world he'd rather be.

I did it without thinking, and it shocked both of us.

He took a quick step back and placed his fingers to his lips (which I had just kissed) and I stammered an apology, suddenly sobered, followed by a quick goodbye before nearly running up the stairs to the front door. But Daniel was right behind me, gently holding my arm, and he turned me to face him before I made it through the door. I was mortified by my lack of judgment, my lack of respect for Matt, Daniel, even Margot.

"Lucy, wait," Daniel said, his voice gruff. "It's okay."

I shook my head, tears close. "It's not okay." Even though I couldn't seem to separate the truth from memory, I was still in charge of my decisions. And I couldn't blame anyone else for what had led me to kiss my ex-fiancé in front of the condo I shared with my current boyfriend.

"I'm sorry," I said again, pulling away from Daniel. "I shouldn't have come out tonight. And I should never have…" I left it at that, because we both knew what I was apologizing for. I looked into his face, saw compassion there and something else. *Pity*, I thought, which made my insides feel as chilled as my outsides.

"You're married. I have Matt. Who is sleeping upstairs and has no idea I'm out with you tonight and has been perfect through everything and doesn't deserve any of this."

"Please, don't cry, Lucy," he said. "What's really going on with you?"

I let out a sharp laugh, and Daniel looked confused. And then I did the second thing I knew I'd probably regret later—I told him the truth about my memory.

There were a few moments of stunned silence as I stood there, shaking with the cold and adrenaline, as Daniel searched for the right thing to say. "That explains a few things," he finally offered, and then he smiled that smile of his and I felt like everything might be okay. Soon we were laughing, so hard tears streamed down my face from the release, and I held my stomach as I tried to catch my breath.

"God, I needed that," I said, taking in a deep breath. The cold air tickled my throat as I gulped in a few desperate breaths, but it felt good.

"So, when you say you remember us being married, you mean you have a memory of the actual wedding? The one that didn't happen?"

"Yes, I have this very vivid memory of our wedding."

"No kidding," Daniel said, eyes widening. "And it feels real? Like, really real?"

"Honestly it feels as real as all my other memories," I said. "It's been somewhat confusing, to say the least." This last part I added quietly, because I was feeling exposed in a way I wasn't prepared for.

He exhaled loudly, as if he had been holding his breath. "And the award for the biggest understatement of the night goes to… Lucy Sparks!" He was trying to inject some levity into the moment, but his voice fell flat by the end.

"I didn't plan on telling you about, you know, all this." I gestured in circles beside my head. "I know it's weird, and I'm sorry to lay it all on you tonight."

"I'm not sure exactly what to say, Lucy."

I grabbed his arms with vise-grip–like fingers. "*Nothing.* You don't need to say a thing. Daniel, you know I don't expect anything, right?" I shook my head, released his arms when I realized how tightly I was hanging on. "Okay, that didn't come out the way… Sorry, I meant I don't want you to do anything." I groaned and he laughed, which made me feel immensely better. "Like I said, things are a bit of a mess. Can we pretend none of this ever happened?"

"Lucy, stop. It's okay. It's not what I was expecting you to say obviously, and I can't say I totally get what's happened here, but it's *fine.* I've forgotten all about it already. Promise."

"Phew, good," I said, nodding, trying to act like what had transpired between us was meaningless and insignificant. Which to Daniel it likely was, at least in the long run, but for me…well, it confused me even more and I felt like a million fire ants were crawling under my skin. I shivered violently.

"Are you going to be okay to get upstairs?" he asked. "You're pretty drunk."

"Oh, I'm long past drunk," I said, snort-laughing as I did. I clapped a hand to my mouth, embarrassed by the outburst, but

Daniel smiled. "But I'm okay. Hey, thanks again for being so great tonight."

"Anytime," he said. "Honestly, anytime." My chest constricted and I forced myself to key in the door code without looking back at him, to step through the door and have it close behind me, only then turning to wave a final goodbye to Daniel, assuming it would be the last time we saw each other.

29

I took the stairs slowly, pausing on the landings between flights to catch my breath and compose myself before walking through our front door. In part I was relieved. I'd told Daniel the truth and nothing terrible had happened. We said goodbye and all was fine, or at least mostly fine. I was embarrassed and wished I could take it all back—hit the rewind button to when his message arrived and stayed at home instead—but it was done. I survived, like Dr. Kay said I would.

But I was also deeply disappointed. I'm not sure what I hoped might happen, but I would be lying if I didn't admit to having fantasized about the moment all was revealed. How by some strange mechanism Daniel believed my memory of us being married, or it shook things loose in my brain so everything could return to how it was supposed to be. The memories of Daniel would disappear, and the ones with Matt would take their place and life would make sense again.

I climbed the last flight of stairs, stumbling on the second to last riser and taking an epic fall, banging my chin on the smooth concrete floor when my hands missed their mark and my face took the brunt. My teeth slammed together when my chin hit, and pain reverberated through my skull. *Shit.* The last thing I needed was to give myself another concussion. I should have much, much less to drink going forward. I pressed a gloved hand to my chin and was glad to see there was no blood.

Getting up with some difficulty, all the layers bundling me from the cold also making it difficult to recover gracefully, I finally found my house keys deep inside my coat pocket. Holding my breath as I slid in the key, I turned it slowly to avoid the noise of the lock disengaging. Opening the door gently, I stepped inside and tiptoed into the living room.

I shouldn't have bothered being so quiet, and I'm not sure how I didn't notice the lights on, but there sat Matt, on the couch, arms crossed over his chest. He did not look happy. He also held my phone in his hand. *Oh, no.* I had forgotten to take my phone with me.

"Why are you up?" was the first thing I thought to say. And based on his expression, the deepening of his frown, it was not the right thing.

"Where were you?" he asked, anger seeping into his words. I knew he had probably been more worried than angry, but now that I was home and he could see I was fine, anger trumped concern.

"I left you a note," I replied, hearing how lame it sounded as it came out. I pointed to the table and saw the note was still there. "I couldn't sleep."

He stood and came toward me, taking stock of my face. "What happened to your chin?"

My hand fluttered to my face, and my fingers—now gloveless— felt a growing lump on my chin. "I slipped on the stairs."

"Have you been out *drinking?*"

I took a step back, busied myself with wrestling off my coat and hanging it on the hook by the door. But all the rum had messed with my balance, and I missed the hook, stumbled and slammed into the brick wall to prevent myself from falling over completely. Matt tried to grab my arm to keep me from falling, but he wasn't quite fast enough and so the wall caught me instead. "I had a drink." It was true, I *had* had a drink. And then a few more.

"Where? By yourself?"

I finally managed to get my coat on the hook and pushed past Matt into the living room, then to the kitchen, where I ran the tap until the water was cold before filling a glass. He followed me. "Why the third degree?" I said, knowing I was only inflaming the situation by not answering his questions directly. I gulped down the cold water, then filled the glass again. "I couldn't sleep, so I went out for a walk and stopped for a drink."

Matt didn't say anything but followed me again as I took my water back to the living room, finally settling on the couch. I was drunk, but I was hoping I could hide exactly how drunk. But that was naive because while I didn't remember my life with Matt, he knew me inside and out. Hiding things from him wouldn't work.

"Why are you lying to me?" His eyes narrowed and his tone was harsh. It shook me, how he was looking at me, like he was disgusted by what he saw. So far Matt had mostly been treating me with kid gloves—everyone had—but tonight was going to be different, I could tell. I had pushed the bounds of his patience and understanding too far.

"I'm not lying!" I said. "I went out for a drink."

"Alone?" Matt asked.

A moment of silence, then, "No."

"Who did you have a drink with, Lucy?" And in that moment I understood he knew I had been with Daniel. Because even rum-soaked, I had enough mental acuity to realize if I had been with Jenny, or Alex, or even with my parents, I would have already admitted it. The only reason I would be hedging was if the person I had a drink with was someone Matt wouldn't be happy to hear about.

"Daniel."

The effect of speaking his name was significant in our living room, where it hung like a heavy curtain blocking out all light and sound. We stared at one another, and I tried to keep my face as neutral as possible, but all I could think about was how I had kissed Daniel. Sickening guilt hit me and I thought I might throw up all those unfortunate Dark and Stormy drinks onto our living room rug.

"I see," Matt said. I braced myself for the onslaught of questions. The inevitable "What? How? Why?" I expected to follow. But he asked nothing. Only said, "I'm going back to bed," and then promptly dropped my phone onto the couch beside me, where it landed with a soft plop, before walking into our bedroom and shutting the door.

My heart hammered, and I finally took in a breath. Then I looked down at my phone, which had landed faceup, and on a hunch pressed the button to wake up the dark screen. There was a text message, from Daniel.

Hope you got upstairs okay. It was nice to see you. And like I said, already forgotten.

He'd closed the message with a winky-faced emoticon, and I felt another rush of nausea when I glanced at the time stamp. It had come in only moments after we'd said goodbye; he had probably sent it while he walked down the street to catch a cab, and without question Matt had my phone in his hand when the message lit up my screen. Which meant he saw it, probably as I sat on the landing after my stair tumble, trying to reconcile what I had done.

I glanced at the closed bedroom door. Should I go in there and apologize? Tell Matt the whole story about how we'd run into each other at Jake's party and had a (very innocent) coffee? How tonight sort of happened and nothing about it was premeditated? But I decided if Matt wanted to know why my ex was texting me, why I'd gone out with Daniel without telling him, he would have asked. He wouldn't have shut the conversation down by walking away.

Regardless, I should have gone in there and pulled back the covers and lain down beside him and unloaded everything in gentle whispers in the dark. With kindness and honesty, admitting my imperfections and letting him know I wanted to do better for both of us. To tell him the truth about how conflicted I felt and how I was trying my best. That I was sorry I kept hurting him, because he didn't deserve it.

But instead I retreated to the guest room and flopped down on top of the bedding, pulling the quilt over me like a burrito wrapper before sinking into a dreamless, alcohol-heavy slumber.

30

The next morning when I woke up, cold and uncomfortable because the quilt was on the floor, I lay still for a few moments so the events of the prior evening could load into my brain.

I met Daniel for a late-night drink, which turned into a few too many. *I need to stop drinking so much.*

I kissed Daniel and told him I remembered us being married.

Matt knew I went out with Daniel, and that I'd lied to him.

With a sigh I ran a hand over my face, tried to clear the sleep from my eyes. Everything hurt—my head from the booze, my chin from where I tripped and fell on the stairs, my body from an uncomfortable and restless sleep. But I could hear footsteps outside the guest room, the sounds of Matt moving around in the kitchen, and then my nose picked up the smell of brewed coffee and something frying.

I swung my legs to the edge of the bed and stood carefully, hanging on to the wall for support as things spun a little before settling into place. The sickly sweet flavor of ginger beer coated my tongue and mouth and I desperately wanted to brush my teeth. Pushing the door open as quietly as I could, I padded to the washroom—saw Matt in the kitchen standing over the stove, his back to me—and brushed my teeth while I peed. Then I looked at myself in the mirror, frowning as I did. There was a purplish-looking lump on my chin, my mascara had spread beyond my eyelashes and I was pale. With a quick scrub of face wash and some tinted moisturizer and blush I looked better, but still not great. But I couldn't do anything about my insides, which felt a thousand times worse than how I looked on the outside.

Despite my lingering nausea, the smell of pancakes and bacon frying on the stove piqued my appetite. A full pot of coffee sat waiting to be poured, and Matt was in his sweats and a T-shirt, his hair still shower-damp, a dish towel thrown over his shoulder.

I paused a moment longer, taking in the scene and wishing, again, that things could be different. Only months earlier I had been in love with this man. I had no relationship with Daniel and, from everything I had been told, had completely walked away from him when we broke up—never looking back. It must have been so nice, to be confident about and content with my life, and to have no doubts. The pain of what I'd lost hit me hard as I watched Matt, and I held back the sob trying to burst from my lungs.

Clearing my throat so he would know I was there, I walked into the kitchen. "Morning," I said, heading to the fridge to pour a cold glass of juice.

Matt looked up from the pan, a spatula in his hand. "Morning." He smiled, the same smile he had been giving me every morning since I got home—warm and reassuring—and for a brief moment I wondered if I'd imagined everything. Maybe my mind was playing tricks on me again. But then I touched my chin and the shot of pain from the bruise reminded me last night had been real.

Matt took the coffeepot and held it over a mug. "Coffee?"

"Uh, yes, please," I said, my voice croaking. I took the mug and held it tightly in my hands. "Thanks."

"Hope you're up for some breakfast." Matt still hadn't looked at me except to give me that brief smile, and I wasn't sure what I was supposed to be doing. So I stood where I was, in the middle of the kitchen with my mug in my hands. "Did you sleep okay?"

Did I sleep okay? Again, I considered maybe my memory of last night was a bizarre confabulation, but then Matt said, "Your phone is charging, in case you were looking for it." He plated our pancakes and bacon, licked a bit of grease from his thumb. "Let's eat while it's hot."

At the mention of my phone my stomach flipped over, making it entirely possible I would vomit up all of last night's rum into my plate of pancakes. But I sat beside him at our kitchen table, pulled up my chair and tucked into my breakfast. My stomach didn't revolt after the first bite, or the second, which was a relief. "This is great."

He smiled, continued chewing his breakfast. Still said nothing about last night.

I wondered if this would be how things would go for the next while. Matt and me being excessively formal, tediously polite, as we tried to coexist in this new state where I had lied and he had found out and nothing was how either of us hoped or expected it to be.

Matt polished off his pancakes first, then worked on his bacon, dipping the strips into the pool of maple syrup on his plate. "I need to go into the office. But I'll be back for dinner."

I glanced at the clock; it was already ten in the morning. "You aren't going for a ride today?"

He dipped another piece of bacon into the syrup. "Already did," he said. "I went early."

Nodding, I swallowed the bite of pancake in my mouth and felt it stick in my throat. I needed to explain things now. I hated how the air around us felt—tense and strange, despite Matt's seemingly fine mood. But that was exactly the problem. He wasn't fine, couldn't possibly be, and the fact he was working so hard at pretending broke my heart.

"Listen, Matt," I began. He looked at me, holding the other half of the bacon strip in his hand, waiting. I looked down at my plate, hated myself for not being able to hold his gaze. "So that night at Jake's party? I...I ran into Daniel outside the bar as I was leaving." I was nervous, unable to cover the tremor in my voice. I still couldn't look at Matt, was afraid of seeing his expression. "We talked for a couple of minutes and then I went home."

Matt put the bacon down on his plate and sighed. "Yeah, I know."

I frowned. "You know? How?" I tried to remember if I'd told Jenny, or Alex, and wondered if they'd passed this information along to Matt. Maybe under the guise they were worried about my state of mind. But no, I had told only Dr. Kay. So how did Matt know?

"I saw you." He said it nonchalantly, like it was no big deal. Then he gathered his silverware and set them on his plate, then took it all over to the sink to rinse them.

"You *saw* me? Where? How?"

He dropped his plate into the sink, the silverware clanging so hard against it I thought the plate might have cracked. Then he whipped around and the look on his face slayed me. His eyes were wide, his cheeks puffed out, his hands clenched in fists even as they held on to the counter edge behind him. "I saw you, Lucy! I followed you outside because I wanted to make sure you were okay, and then..." He shook his head and then let it drop forward, his chin to his chest.

"I saw you talking to him," he said, looking back up at me with red-rimmed eyes. "I saw you laughing. With *him*." His voice was hollow, like he'd given up.

I stood quickly, walked around the table to stand in front of him. "I didn't plan it, Matt. It was a total fluke." I didn't dare touch him, though my instincts told me to. I wondered what that meant. Was it a desire to comfort Matt because he was upset and I cared about him? Or did my body, my reflexes, remember I loved him even if my mind didn't? "Honestly, we talked for a few minutes and then I came home."

"Did you see him again? Before last night, I mean?" he asked.

I wished I could lie, but instead I paused, and that was enough.

"I don't think I can do this anymore," Matt said, now openly crying. I was both anxious at his tears and sad in a way I couldn't quite reconcile. It was different from the grief I felt about Daniel—the realization that despite believing he was my husband, he didn't feel that way about me anymore—but it was still intense.

"Please, Matt, can we talk about this?" I grabbed for his arms, but he shoved off the counter and away from me. Opened the dishwasher, loaded in his plate, fork and knife.

"There's nothing to talk about." He no longer sounded angry, or hurt. He sounded indifferent and that scared the hell out of me.

"So, what now? This is it?" My breath came out in strange little gasps I was unable to control.

"This is it." Matt left the kitchen, me right behind him.

"Matt, stop." He didn't, headed into the bedroom. With a frustrated sigh I followed him again, then stood with my hands on my hips, trying to quell my too-fast heartbeat. Since I'd come home from the hospital Matt had been perfect and present—kind and patient, accommodating at every turn. And so for him to give up like this terrified me, because despite how screwed up everything was with our relationship, I needed Matt. He was the anchor I would be lost without. *How could I have been so stupid to not see that? To jeopardize things like this?* I knew it wasn't fair, to need him so selfishly, but it was the truth.

"Please, Matt. Stop," I repeated.

He did, paused with his jeans and sweater in his hands, his face holding none of the warmth I was used to. "What, Lucy? What do you want from me?"

I opened my mouth, but nothing came out. I let out another frustrated sigh. He shook his head and started to put his jeans on. "I'm going to work," he said. "Then I'll pack up some stuff when I'm back." He pulled his sweater over his head, grabbed his phone from the nightstand.

"Pack up some stuff? You're leaving?" My voice was thin and high-pitched. I was untethered and coming apart fast. "Shouldn't I be the one to leave?"

He ignored my question, and my reaction. "We'll talk later." Then he left me standing in the bedroom, staring at the empty spot where he had stood a few moments earlier.

A minute later the front door closed with a resounding click, and I sat down hard on the floor and tried to figure out what I was supposed to do now.

I had my legs tucked up under me on Jenny's couch—a futon that would also be my bed for the next while as I sorted out the mess I'd made—and was nursing a cup of tea she'd placed in my hands when I'd arrived with tearstained cheeks and an overnight bag. I had considered going to my parents' place but, still angry they'd lied to me, decided I couldn't deal with them right now.

When I'd texted Matt to say I was going to crash with Jenny for now so he could stay at the condo, I got a one-word reply (Okay). I'm not sure what I'd hoped for, because I certainly didn't deserve anything more. Matt had, over these past couple of months, been solid and selfless, and what had I done to show him my gratitude for his commitment? I kissed my ex.

"More tea?" Jenny asked, standing to fill her own mug.

I shook my head, stared into my still-full cup.

"So, what do you want to do?" she asked, adding water to her mug from the steaming kettle. She dipped the tea bag a few times, then settled back into the chair across from me.

"I don't know." I sighed and put my mug down, my hands shaking. "I screwed up, Jenny."

She took a tentative sip of her hot tea. "You sure did."

I laughed then. "Thanks a lot."

"Well, you did!" We laughed together, but it petered out quickly.

"Maybe you guys should try couples therapy," Jenny said.

"And talk about what?" I asked. "I'm not sure what a therapist would do with 'My girlfriend thinks she's someone else's wife... Any strategies for such a conundrum?'" I rolled my eyes and Jenny chuckled.

"You're right. Bad idea," she said. "Look, Lucy, I didn't have the chance to say this yet, but I'm sorry I didn't tell you about your mom and dad. And full confession, I agreed with them it was the right thing to do. Not telling you right away, I mean." She frowned. "You were dealing with so much and I think we all expected things would get back to normal. With your memory."

"Yeah, I think I expected that, too." And as I said it I realized I had, despite the warnings from my doctors and Dr. Kay about the possibility of my memory challenges being long-term. "It's okay. I get it, and I probably would have done the same thing."

She smiled gratefully at me, and we relaxed into a moment of silence.

"I've hurt Matt. Badly."

"You have," she said, then quickly added, "But it wasn't intentional, Lucy." True, I hadn't intended to hurt Matt. But even though my memory was in chaos, there was nothing wrong with my free will. Yes, I'd had too much to drink and my judgment was impaired, but I'd still made the choice to kiss Daniel. That was on me. "This is hardest for you."

"Is it? Is it hardest *for me*? I don't think I'm suffering any more than he is," I said. "But it feels impossible to transition from the Lucy who loved Daniel to the one who's happy with Matt." To box up what I connected with Daniel—that he took cream and sugar in his coffee, liked ginger beer and basketball but not hockey, how he shivered when I kissed a spot right below his ear—and shift to Matt, who liked his coffee black and was obsessed with the Toronto Maple Leafs and cycling and owned more shoes than I did and who knew how to make me laugh when I was upset better than anyone.

"It wrings me dry, the back-and-forth shifts, Jen. Sometimes

I forget who likes what and who I'm supposed to be when I'm with them, and mostly, what I want."

I pressed a hand to my forehead, closed my eyes. "Jenny, the way Matt looks at me. It's how..." I paused. "It's how I think I look at Daniel. But it's not real with Daniel, and I don't know how to stop—" My throat closed and I gulped noisily. "I don't know how to stop *all these feelings.*"

Jenny watched me for a moment, then sighed. "I don't know if you can."

"So what does that mean for me and Matt?"

She shrugged, which was answer enough.

"What were we like?" I asked. "Before, when I remembered everything and life was good and normal."

"You were happy," she replied. "Like, really happy." She sipped her tea, gave a small smile. "You two brought out the best in one another. And I know that sounds supercheesy and like a Hallmark card, but honestly, it's the truth." Jenny looked as though she was considering whether to say more, then made her decision. "You once told me Matt proved you'd never been in love before."

I nodded, then burst into tears.

31

Alex was licking peanut butter from a spoon and dipping it back into the jar. I scowled at her because it was Jenny's peanut butter and I was sure she wouldn't be happy about what Alex was doing. But I didn't say anything because I didn't want to argue about something else. We'd already had words about the separation, and her failure to fill me in—she joked Mom had bribed her with a new lens before admitting she agreed with my parents—so adding one more log onto a raging fire probably wasn't wise. "You know, I miss the days when you used to create a better version of the truth," Alex said, her mouth thick with the peanut butter. "Whatever happened to *that* Lucy?"

"What is that supposed to mean?" I asked, scowling more deeply now. "And stop double-dipping. It's disgusting." I was irritable and my back hurt from sleeping on Jenny's futon. Mom had also been calling incessantly, and when I wouldn't answer (or respond to the emoji-filled texts she sent immediately after each call), she sent Alex to talk with me. And so here we were, in Jenny's apartment while she was at work, eating peanut butter on Ritz crackers. But I didn't want to talk about what had happened. Or what I'd done to ensure no matter how fiercely Matt loved me (or how much I'd loved him) there may no longer be a relationship to cling to. No *us* to fight for.

"You used to be all about the silver lining. Like, remember when we got to pet those baby sharks at that aquarium in Sarasota, and I refused because I thought it was so sad they were locked up in there and you told me they were probably happier because they didn't have to fight for their food like they would in the wild?"

I frowned, remembering the smooth, rubbery feel of the shark's skin but not my comment about their happiness.

"Or when your bike got stolen and you told Dad it was probably some kid who couldn't afford a bike, so it was okay because they needed it more than you did?" I nodded, remembering that one. I'd known if I used that reasoning on dad he would buy me a new bike without too much fuss (he was a bit of a bleeding heart, my dad) and I would never have to admit I had left it unlocked, ripe for stealing.

"That's not creating a better version of the truth," I argued. "Silver linings go with the territory when you're a kid. Besides, I'm sure someone else *did* get a lot of joy out of my bike." It had been a great bike.

Alex nodded and licked her peanut-butter-coated lips. But she wasn't done with me yet, had a point (Alex always had a point) to drill into me whether I wanted to hear it or not. "Then there was that time your bestie, Nancy McPherson, stole your date in eighth grade. Remember what you said then?"

I paused, thought back, rejoiced quietly for a moment about how clear and secure my memories were from my childhood. "That it had been my idea," I said softly.

"Exactly," Alex said, dipping her spoon in one more time. "Silver-lining-Lucy."

But it hadn't been my idea at all. I had said that because I was embarrassed and hurt by what had happened, especially considering Alex had warned me and I chose to ignore her.

Nancy McPherson and I met in second grade, on a playground close to my house, and after finding out we lived two blocks from one another, we begged our mothers for a playdate.

We both loved the color green and wanted our own pet rabbit one day and thought Tiger Tail was the only ice cream flavor worth eating. In fifth grade we took a best friend blood oath (using one of my mom's finger prickers for her blood sugar testing) and Nancy barely even flinched, impressing me to no end. We were inseparable, and I believed Nancy would be my best friend forever. Then came the eighth grade, and a boy named Jordan Riggle.

I liked Jordan, and based on what I was hearing from mutual friends, he liked me, too. Nancy and I had brainstormed what to do. Sure, I could ask him to the dance, but the middle school rumor mill said he was planning to ask me, and so why not wait? *It will be epic*, Nancy had said, her voice swoony. *Being asked to the dance by Jordan Riggle!* I had agreed (I always agreed with Nancy) and decided to wait for Jordan to ask me. Though when I had broached it with Alex, looking for the older sister perspective, she told me to "Buck up, princess, and ask him first."

I had expected Alex to see things from Nancy's point of view, because I idolized both of them and thought they were the smartest people I knew. So I had argued with Alex—it *was* traditional for the boy to ask the girl, like Nancy said—and Alex had snorted her disdain and told me that was ridiculous. "You're going to regret giving Nancy McPherson so much power over you," she had said.

In the end Alex was right, having always been better at reading people than I was. I came down with the flu and missed three days of school. But Nancy came by every day to drop off homework and fill me in on "Operation Dance"—she said she was sure Jordan would ask me when I was back. By Friday I was well enough to go to school, and it was then I heard rumblings Jordan and Nancy were going to the dance together. I wondered if my delirious flu fever had returned.

But I wasn't sick, just a fool. Turned out Jordan asked Nancy if she thought I might go to the dance with him, and Nancy, my best friend for the past seven years, said I thought dances were stupid. So Jordan asked Nancy instead, and she said yes.

That was the day Nancy McPherson stopped being my best friend, and the moment I realized how horribly people could let you down and break your heart.

"You know, that dance fiasco might have been the last time you doctored the truth with your special brand of positivity," Alex said, pointing her spoon at me. "Until Daniel."

I sat up straighter at the mention of Daniel. "What do you mean?"

Alex shrugged. "Well, I could tell you weren't a hundred percent in, even though you were going ahead with the wedding."

Now I felt confused. "Why would you say that?"

"Because it's the truth. It was little things, these small clues. Like, you wanted to keep Sparks as your last name."

"But you didn't want me to change my last name. You told me that!" I sputtered, then added, "Hang on. I *did* change my name, so it's a moot point."

Alex's tone was direct, but not unkind. "No, you didn't, sweets. You didn't end up getting married, remember?"

"Of course I remember," I grumbled, then almost laughed at how ridiculous a statement that was. I had gaps in my memory from this time of my life, and some of what I did remember was a fabricated version of reality. "You know what I meant. So what else? Why would you think I didn't want to marry Daniel? Did I tell you that?"

She shrugged. "Not in so many words. In the beginning you seemed happy. But the closer you got to the wedding, the less you talked about it. About him." She licked a drip of peanut butter off her thumb. "And you're not exactly the type to go mute on something when you're excited. You used to drive me crazy as a kid because you never shut up when things were going your way." She smiled, but I found I couldn't return it.

I didn't talk about the wedding? Everything slowed down then. I wound back her previous words: *In the beginning you seemed happy. But the closer you got to the wedding, the less you talked about it. About him.* I took a deep breath and asked, "Alex, do you know what happened between me and Daniel?"

She stared at me for a moment. "I have an idea."

I was prepared to respond with "Oh, it's okay. No one else seems to know, either, especially me!" but then her words hit me.

"What do you know? Why haven't you said anything? Have you known this whole time what happened? Tell me. *What do you know?*"

She spread peanut butter on a cracker with the back of her spoon and held it out to me. I shook my head and she shrugged, bit it in half and chewed before saying, "I know Daniel London was an asshole."

Now I stared at her and waited for her to explain. She didn't. "Oh, give me a break, Alex." I tried to imagine it—thought back to everything I remembered about Daniel, how it had felt to see him recently. That kiss… I shook my head. "He isn't. He wasn't."

"I assure you, Lucy, he was. And probably still is." She dropped the spoon into the peanut butter jar, smacked her lips. "Hell, he was engaged, nearly married, when you met him, right? So I would say Daniel London is someone who always has one foot out the door, know what I mean?"

"No, I do not know what you mean."

Alex sighed and brushed a few cracker crumbs from her sweater. "The night of your engagement party I got there early. To 'oversee' things," she said, using air quotes, sounding like our mother, "because Mom was helping you get ready—you had a cast on your arm, but you probably don't remember that—and she was worried about the catering." I tried to control the small shake overtaking my body, afraid of what Alex was going to tell me but also afraid whatever it was wouldn't answer all my questions. "Daniel was already there, and he was at the bar, drinking and talking up a very attractive bartender."

"And so what?" Daniel had been flirting with the bartender. Big deal. It didn't explain anything.

"And so I confronted him—they were supercozy, Lucy, like inappropriately so. He had his hand on her arm. Left it there too long." Alex gave me a pointed look. "I cornered him and asked what he thought he was doing, being all flirty-flirty with the help, and he laughed. Said, 'Alex, calm down. I'm not married yet.' And then he winked at me and walked away."

I felt like I'd been turned inside out, but I also struggled to imagine the scenario she was describing. It sounded like an entirely different Daniel from the one I knew. And suddenly I was furious with Alex for only telling me this now. For tarnishing a memory I thought I could count on. "What the hell, Alex? Why now? Why didn't you tell me that night?" My cheeks flushed with frustration, and I let my anger toward everything—everyone—seep out at my sister. She took it without complaint, her voice calm.

"I did, Lucy. You just don't remember."

"Oh." The fight inside of me extinguished. "What did I say?"

"You were drunk—we all were—and we were up on the roof, polishing off a very expensive bottle of booze courtesy of Mr. and Mrs. London. I pulled you aside before we went back down to the party, told you I was worried about Daniel. That he'd been a bit too 'friendly' with the pretty brunette bartender earlier. A bit too handsy for someone about to get married to someone else. But you said Daniel would never do anything like that. Accused me of being jealous and suggested I should worry about my own 'nonexistent' love life. I think you even called me pathetic." Alex laughed, and I cringed. Strange how I remembered the night of our engagement party, and being up on the roof, but had conveniently blanked out on this particular detail.

"Sorry. I'm sure I didn't mean it. I *was* drunk, right?"

"Oh, you meant it, little sister. But it was fine, didn't bother me." I envied Alex's confidence, her ability to trust herself so completely. She had always been self-assured and cool, and I wished I could be more like her, especially these days.

"But why wait until now to tell me?"

"You weren't ready to hear it before."

I let out an exasperated groan. Her revelation didn't fully explain things but certainly planted some doubt in between my memories and feelings about Daniel. I wasn't in the mood to play games.

She held my gaze, repeated it again, slower this time. "You weren't ready to hear it."

"And what makes me ready now?" I threw my hands up in the air.

"You asked." I wanted to throttle her.

"I asked you before, Alex."

"No, you didn't. You asked if I knew *why* you broke up, specifically. And I don't. As far as I know you didn't talk about it, with anyone. Besides, it was a couple of months after the engagement party, so it probably had nothing to do with the bartender."

It seemed I *was* the only person who knew exactly what happened (aside from Daniel, of course), and there was a good chance I would never remember it.

"Hey, don't go dark on me now," Alex said, taking in my expression. "Silver linings, okay? If things hadn't gone south with Daniel, you never would have met Matt. And Matt is a good one, Lucy."

But I wasn't interested—yet—in seeing the positives here. Plus, it cut deep, thinking about Matt. What did any of it matter if I couldn't remember our relationship? "Well, silver linings are overrated," I grumbled. "Nancy McPherson taught me that valuable lesson."

"I think she taught you to never take bad advice," Alex said, a smirk on her face. "She was a piece of work. I never liked her."

"It's always a risk to fully trust another person." I spoke quietly, mostly to myself.

"That's depressing," Alex said in response. Then she screwed the lid back on the peanut butter. "Also, not true."

"Yes, it is! Think about it. Nancy. Daniel. Mom and Dad. Even Jenny and Matt." I enumerated them on my fingers. I tried not to get defensive and wondered when silver-lining-Lucy had disappeared. Maybe it was when Nancy McPherson stabbed me in the back and went to the dance with the boy I liked. Maybe I could blame Daniel, and whatever happened to end our engagement. I wished I knew, because maybe then I could figure out how to get that Lucy we all used to know back. "Seems everyone has let me down, especially recently."

"Oh, really?" Her sarcastic tone was hard to miss. "How so, Princess Lucy?" I hated it when she called me that—it had been a common nickname when we were kids, Alex often suggesting my parents treated me like the "baby" I was. In fairness to her, it had been true my parents focused more on my good behavior and more on Alex's rebellions, so I supposed things had been somewhat unbalanced. But even if I was seven years younger than her, we were adults now, and her pulling out this particular childhood jab incensed me.

"By keeping me in the dark about everything I can't remember!" I knew it was safe for me to lash out at Alex, and so I was going to let it come. "Can I trust Mom and Dad to tell me the truth? Do I believe Jenny when she says she has no idea why I broke up with Daniel? I mean, she's my best friend. I didn't tell her *anything*? And what about Matt? He's been holding stuff back right along with everyone else. Do you all have my best interests in mind? Because being lied to sucks, Alex. All I can count on is the truth, and you guys seem determined to keep even the smallest scraps from me."

"Hang on a second, killer," Alex said. "Now you're creating a *worse* version of reality." I glowered but didn't respond. She got up and put the peanut butter back in the cupboard, grabbing an apple from the fridge. "Want one?" I shook my head, and she came back to sit with me, polishing the apple against her thigh.

"Look, sweets. This blows, okay? No one would argue you got a crap deal here. But you know what I've been seeing? People going out of their way to accommodate you, and trying to make this better somehow *for you.* Mom and Dad keeping up this ridiculous 'we're still together and in love' ruse so you don't have to deal with the shittiness of going through their breakup. *Again.* Jenny has literally been sick with guilt about not giving you the exact lay of the land. And Matt, well, Lucy, Matt has been a mess."

"A mess?" I asked, feeling an uncomfortable heaviness spreading across my chest.

"Did you know he's been going to therapy, too? Or that he's lost, like, fifteen pounds because he's been so stressed about what's happened? Or that he's probably been pushed off partner track for the next year or two because of all the time off? Or that he's spent hours over at Mom and Dad's trying to figure out ways to jog your memory? All those photo albums? Matt put those together. In his 'spare' time, which with work and worrying about you has meant he's barely slept and, if you ask me, is holding his own life together by a thread."

She set the apple down beside her and took my hands in hers. "I'm not telling you this to make you feel guilty, so stop it. Stop feeling sorry for yourself." I was close to tears but nodded. "What I'm saying, Lucy, is this has never been *just* about you. Yeah, you're the one who slipped and hit her head and ended up with a memory like those moth-chewed dress-up clothes from Grammy's attic, but you aren't the only one suffering because of it. You're wrong if you think you can't trust us. Dead wrong."

I was quiet for a moment and Alex, satisfied to have said her piece, let go of my hands and bit into the apple. She chewed, watching me thoughtfully as she did. What Alex had said hit me hard. I had taken for granted how much they all loved me, how much my accident had changed them, too. *You are only as strong as your weakest link.* And I was the weak link, but not because of what I could or couldn't remember—because I had been pushing everyone away, unwilling to accept the help I desperately needed and insisting the problem was mine (and mine alone) to solve.

"I *wish* I didn't have to question everything," I finally said, my voice thick and shaky. I sniffled, wiped my nose with my sleeve. "I also wish I'd been wearing my winter boots and had ordered Matt's tie online. And that I hadn't hit my head in the first place."

"Me, too, Luce," Alex replied, then she laughed.

"What's so funny?"

"All your wishing reminded me of when you were little, and every time you made a wish—whether it was on the first star you saw at night or from blowing away dandelion fluff or a birthday candle—you used to screw your eyes shut and say, 'I wish for chocolate cake!'"

"I miss silver-lining-Lucy," I said, resting my head on her shoulder.

"So do I," Alex said, leaning her head against mine. "She's a hell of a lot more fun."

"Hey," I said, smacking her arm in protest.

Alex put her arm around me and squeezed. "Don't worry. She's still in there."

32

My mother was nothing if not persistent, and it wasn't long before I found myself sitting across from my parents at their kitchen table, a cup of lukewarm tea in front of me along with a plate of raw veggies and hard-boiled eggs. My mom, being diabetic, claimed to never having a sweet tooth, and so while another mother might serve fresh-from-the-oven chocolate chip cookies or banana bread with tea, mine believed savory snacks completely reasonable accompaniments.

They had told me the whole story, again, because I didn't remember hearing it the first time. They had decided to split up just after Christmas, though they were still living in the house together (in separate rooms) and planned to until they sold it and found other places to live. Dad had gone to Mexico with some of his golf buddies, without Mom, which explained his tanned arms in the middle of winter. Mom was dating, Dad was not, but he didn't seem to begrudge her for moving on and even managed to say what a nice man Carl was. Though if you asked me, he seemed a bit sad to be saying it.

"But the two of you," I began, trying not to get emotional. "You love each other. A lot. Am I remembering things wrong?" Did I confabulate a sweeter relationship than the one they had? The grateful smile Mom would give Dad when he asked if she needed a snack, always fussing over her and taking care of her. The way he would pat her bottom and give her a wink when he thought Alex and I weren't watching. The Sunday nights when they would go to bed early—saying we were not to bother them unless someone was bleeding or not breathing—and Alex and I naively thought they were tired. How Mom always went out of her way to make Dad—who had a serious sweet tooth—his favorite desserts, even when she couldn't eat them. How she would puff up with pride when she talked about what an amazing professor he was and how lucky the university was to have him, every chance she got. It made no sense.

"No, honey, you've got it right," Dad said, and he and Mom exchanged a smile. But now that I knew the truth I could see the difference between them. They cared about one another, but that spark—the love—it was no longer there. "Your mother and I will always love and respect one another. But sometimes what used to make sense doesn't make sense anymore." The frankness of his words hit me hard. Wasn't that exactly what was happening with my own life? "People can grow apart, even after thirty-some years."

I nodded and pressed my lips together.

"Do you want more tea?" Mom asked, but I hadn't even taken a sip. I shook my head. She pushed the plate of snacks closer to me and I ignored the vegetables, taking half a hard-boiled egg instead.

"So how did I take this news the first time?" I asked. I sprinkled a little salt on the egg, then bit into it.

They glanced at each other again. "Pretty much like this," Mom said. "Perhaps a little more angry, a bit less emotional."

"I wish you had told me right away," I said. "It wasn't fair, keeping it from me." I popped the rest of the egg into my mouth and Mom looked pleased for a moment—about what, I wasn't sure—before her face slid into a frown.

"We know that now, and wish we had, too, sweetheart," she

replied, heaving a big sigh. "Once we realized you didn't re-member things quite right—" *understatement of the year* "—your dad and I thought it would be easier to tell you later. After you'd gotten your feet back under you again."

"But we made a mistake," Dad added. "And we're so sorry, Lucy. We didn't want things to be harder for you, but, well... seems to be exactly what we've done."

I realized why they had done it, because it was exactly what I was doing with Matt. My parents had tried to protect me, to cushion me against the truth when my life had blown up into a million little pieces I might never be able to put back together. Their instincts were bang on even if their execution was flawed, and so I couldn't stay angry with them.

"It's okay," I said, and I meant it. "I understand why you didn't tell me right away. I probably wouldn't have told me, either." I smiled, and Mom grabbed my hand and kissed it, holding it against her cheek. "But no more secrets, okay?"

"No more secrets," Mom said, finally releasing my hand, and Dad nodded. I put another half egg on my plate, then noticed Mom looked sheepish as she watched me. "What? Why are you looking at me like that?"

"Well, you said no more secrets..."

"And?"

"And you don't like eggs, Lucy!"

I frowned. "Of course I like eggs." I thought back to my childhood, and Sunday morning breakfasts. Pancakes with real maple syrup and one sunny-side-up egg sprinkled with paprika. My mom always shoving hard-boiled eggs wrapped in waxed paper at us on road trips, to *keep your strength up*, which meant so we didn't have to stop to eat fast food. "I've always liked eggs."

"You used to, but then you got food poisoning from some egg salad at the deli in your office building a couple of years ago. You were so sick you had to get an IV at the hospital. Said you would never touch another egg again."

"What? Really?" I had no memory of that. Tried to see if I

could recollect anything, but I couldn't. I glanced at the egg on my plate and it looked delicious to me. "So, then why did you put eggs out? Doesn't that seem, I don't know, sort of mean?"

She shrugged. "I'm as surprised as you are. The eggs were for me. I thought you would just eat the veggies. You do need to eat more vegetables. But look, now you like eggs again!" She beamed at me. "See? It's not all doom and gloom, Lucy. Good things can still happen."

I wasn't sure we could make the leap from going back to liking eggs to other good things happening, but I smiled at her regardless. "Good things can still happen," I murmured, picking up the egg and biting into it, not hating it at all.

33

My office looked exactly as I'd left it. It was a relief to know where everything was, how to log in to the computer system, that it was easy to recall the client and project names I'd been working on before my accident. A giant balloon bouquet floated in one corner of my office, nearly identical to the one from my hospital room. Except these balloons said Congratulations rather than Get Well Soon. I wasn't sure what I was being congratulated on exactly, but it was likely hard to find the right sentiment for someone returning to work with a brain full of false memories.

Mary Steener, one of Jameson Porter's shared personal assistants who also handled reception duties for the communications team, was the first person I saw. "Lucy!" she exclaimed, holding a large flower arrangement of yellow, pink and orange tulips. She had to crane her neck severely to the right to see around it and into my office. "You look fantastic, sweetheart. Fantastic."

Mary was in her late fifties, a single mother who was never late for work and had been with Jameson Porter for nearly fifteen years. She was always dressed meticulously, nary a hair out of place or painted fingernail chipped, and she was also a well-known office gossip who often said the wrong thing for the situation. But she was bighearted and meticulous and hardworking, and so her wagging tongue and occasional lack of tact was overlooked.

She set the flowers down on my desk, the wide rainbow of tulips completely obscuring my view, and I shifted my chair over so I could see past them. "These beauties are for you. From upstairs." I knew that meant the flowers were from the consultants and strategy group (Matt's team), who occupied the floor directly above ours. "So how are you doing, honey? We're so glad to have you back."

"Thanks, Mary, it's nice to be back. And I'm doing well."

"You sure look it. Especially for someone who can't remember anything." She laughed. "I'm kidding, hon. Honestly, how could you forget us?" I smiled as hard as I could.

My second in command, Brooke Ingram, came up behind Mary and caught my eye. Brooke is two years older than me, and I was hired after her. I'd heard she was none too pleased when I was brought on—she had wanted the director job, but the partners felt she wasn't quite the right fit—but if that had been true, she got over it fast. She was great at what she did and I trusted her implicitly.

"Hey, Brooke," I said, and Mary turned to look behind her.

"Oh, hey there, sweetie," Mary said to Brooke. "I didn't see you there." Then Mary strode over to my desk and pulled me out of my chair for a hug, which lasted about five seconds too long. I finally disentangled myself, Mary's perfume lingering between us like a scented cloud, and straightened my suit jacket. Brooke tapped on her watch a couple of times and I nodded. "Thanks for bringing the flowers, Mary. But I need to go into a meeting with Brooke, so I'll talk to you later?"

"You bet. Have a great day, you two," Mary said, smiling as she exited my office. Then she leaned her head back in and lowered her voice. "I'll try to hold back your calls."

"Oh, that's okay. I'd like to take my calls." I smiled and Mary winked before turning to leave. I would probably have to go out later and explicitly tell her *not* to hold my calls. Mary was the type who believed she knew what people needed better than they did. She blamed it on having too much "mother energy."

"I should have had four kids," she would say. "But because I didn't, you'll all benefit!"

"Thanks for the rescue," I said to Brooke, who had taken a seat in one of the chairs in my office. I pushed the vase of tulips to the very far side of my desk. "I'd forgotten about Mary and her overabundance of helpfulness." I laughed but then stopped when I saw Brooke's face.

"Seriously?" Concern was etched on her brow.

"I'm joking!" I said. "But I probably shouldn't do that, right?"

"Probably not." Brooke laughed.

"So, what have people been saying? About me." I cringed, waited for her answer.

She shrugged but looked uneasy. "That your memory isn't what it used to be." She paused. "Is that true?"

I sighed. "It's true." I had decided there was no point in trying to fake anything or hide the issue. It would only fuel the rumors and I didn't need to be putting out those sorts of fires along with everything else. "For some stuff. But my work memory seems okay. So far I remember everything about this place." Brooke smiled, looking reassured.

"Or almost everything," I added. "I don't remember Matt. At least not my boyfriend Matt."

Now her eyes widened, but I could tell she already knew. "You can drop the act. I know you know. Everyone knows by now, I'm sure."

"Yeah, there has been some chatter," she said. "But it will all die down, now that you're back. Don't worry. There's plenty of gossip fodder around here. You'll be old news soon."

"Hope so," I said, a frown settling on my face.

"I, for one, couldn't care less about your relationship status. I'm just happy to have you back."

"Thanks." I smiled at her. "Especially for keeping things running smoothly while I was gone," I said, and Brooke seemed pleased. I glanced at my computer screen. "And judging by my nearly empty inbox, plus all the calls you handled the past couple of months, I owe you a lot more than a thank-you."

"You would have done the same for me," she said with a shrug. "But there's a Kate Spade bag I've been eyeing." We laughed, and then she gave me a serious look. "But don't do anything like that again, okay? We need you here. I need you here."

"Don't worry, I will always choose practicality over fashion from this point forward." I stuck one of my legs out from behind my desk. "See? Flats."

"Whoa. I don't think I've ever seen you in anything less than three inches," she said, then narrowed her eyes comically. "Are you *really* Lucy Sparks?" She laughed but then slapped a hand to her mouth. "Oh, not cool. I'm sorry. God, I'm as bad as Mary."

"Stop," I said. "You are far worse than Mary." Then I winked at her and she laughed, hard.

"Brooke, I'm used to it. I promise you. This is one of those situations where it's hard to know what to say, so don't stress." I raised an eyebrow and glanced at the balloons, and we both laughed at the message.

"There was a flurry of emails about those balloons," she said, still chuckling. "It was a tough race between Congratulations and Yay!"

"Well, Welcome Back would also have worked." I gave her a wry smile.

"Damn it, you're right," she said. "See? That's why you can't go anywhere. We're useless without you."

I avoided running into Matt for almost two days and then I had to go to a client intake meeting on his floor, which meant passing right by his cubicle. I considered skipping the meeting (Brooke would be there regardless), but that wouldn't be good for the rumor mill. I needed people to believe I was up to the task, which I was, for the most part. Sure, my emotional state was a land mine and my personal life a mess, but my coworkers didn't need to know that.

Jameson Porter knew about Matt and me. Dating a coworker wasn't against company policy, but you were required to disclose a personal relationship with another employee to human resources—which we had apparently done, according to Matt. So everyone at work knew Matt was my boyfriend, which was a strange thing because I still didn't remember our relationship, aside from the memory of the rose petal bath from our first date. However, I doubted Matt had said anything about our current status, which could be best described as "it's complicated." We weren't exactly broken up, more on a pause, but all of this meant I was dreading seeing him at work. It would be hard to pretend things were fine between us, and I was paranoid people would see right through the act.

But it was a Wednesday and so there was a decent chance Matt would be at the client's today rather than in the office. He had stopped traveling after my accident and was assigned to a project with one of the downtown Toronto banks. I'd felt bad about this, knowing how hard it would be for him to pass the client he'd been working with for close to a year to another consultant, but he acted like it was no big deal. Said he had almost wrapped up the project, anyway, and was looking forward to sleeping in his own bed rather than hotels.

Having convinced myself Matt would surely be at the bank today, I walked by his cubicle with barely a glance as Brooke and I chatted about the client…and then ran directly into him as we rounded the corner near the meeting room. He had a full coffee in hand and it splashed onto the floor between us.

"Oh!" I said, taking a step back to try to right myself. Brooke, beside me, somehow managed to escape the coffee splash.

We all stood there for a moment, everyone a little stunned, and finally Brooke broke the spell. "I'll grab some napkins," she said, ducking into the nearby meeting room.

"Did any get on you?" Matt asked. Aside from a small splash on my shoes, most of the spilled coffee had ended up on the ground and already disappeared into the dark gray patterned carpet.

"I don't think so." I shifted my folder to the other arm, wiped a few drops of the coffee from my shoes thanks to the napkin Brooke handed me when she returned.

"Do you need one?" Brooke asked Matt, extending a couple of napkins his way.

"Thanks," he said, taking them and first wiping his hands, then a splotch of coffee from his tie. It was then I realized it was the anniversary tie, the one I'd given him before every-thing went off the rails between us. My chest hurt to look at it, and the moment of uncomfortable silence stretched before Matt dropped his gaze. I also noticed he looked thinner—too thin—and thought back to my conversation with Alex, about what a "mess" Matt was thanks to my accident, my memory.

Brooke looked between us, then said to me, "Okay, well, I'll see you in there?" I nodded and she walked into the meeting room, leaving Matt and me alone.

"Why aren't you at the bank?" It came out somewhat accu-satory, but he didn't seem to notice.

"Oh, I was. But I have a meeting with Peter. I'm going back after." Matt scowled briefly, though he quickly corrected his ex-pression into one more neutral, and I wondered what was going on. Peter Cerelli, one of the senior partners, was well-known for working his associates harder than any other partner. Again, I thought back to what Alex had said, about Matt being pushed off the accelerated partner track because of me. For a moment I felt defensive—I never asked him to hand off his latest (and most challenging, he'd mentioned) oil and gas client—but then just as quickly I went from defensive to contrite. Consultants with oil and gas clients traveled nonstop—and like everyone had been reminding me, Matt was one of the "good" ones. He would never have spent so much time away while I was in such a fragile state and recuperating.

I wanted to thank him for giving this up for me, articulate

how sorry I was to have screwed up his career (his life), too, but all I said was "Is everything okay?"

"Yeah, sure." But he seemed distracted, and I knew there was plenty he wasn't saying. "How are you? I mean, how are things being back at work?"

"Things are good," I said, shifting the folder again more for something to do with my restless hands. I smiled. "Like riding a bike, right?"

Matt nodded, but he didn't smile. "How about with your... you know, with everything?"

"With my memory?" I asked. "Quite nearly perfect. I haven't forgotten a name or face or password yet." I smiled again. And again, he didn't return it. How cruel it was I remembered the less important things like my log-in password and that Mary was a gossip who drank peppermint tea with milk, but didn't remember I had loved Matt. My smile dropped.

"I'm glad to hear it. I've been worried." He cleared his throat, looked down at his mug, which was now wrapped in coffee-stained napkins. "I wasn't sure if being back would make things worse." I knew he wasn't only referencing the work. He also meant the stress of what was going on between us. Shame coursed through me as I thought about that night, about kissing Daniel.

"So far, so good," I said, looking for an exit because the guilt was making it hard for me to concentrate on anything else. "I guess I should probably get in there." I gestured to the meeting room, and Matt nodded.

"Sure thing. Okay, well, talk to you later." I said goodbye, and then he stepped around me right as I tried to step around him, and with both of us moving in the same direction we bumped into one another again.

"Sorry. Again," he said. "At least no coffee spill this time." He smiled, but I could tell how hard it was for him to do it. *Fix this*, I thought. *Fix it, Lucy.*

"Listen, Matt," I began, not entirely sure what I was about

to say was a great idea. "Do you want to get a drink later? Like, after work?"

He stared at me, hope brightening his face temporarily. But then it was gone as quickly as it came. "Lucy, I would love to. But I can't."

"Oh. Okay." I blushed, feeling foolish for even suggesting it. "I shouldn't even have… No problem. Maybe another time." I waved my hand in between us as if to erase the suggestion. What right did I have to ask so much of him? I would have turned me down, too, after everything.

He reached out to touch my arm. "No, I *want* to," he said. "But I have to put in a long night at the bank. Rain check?"

"Of course," I said. "Rain check."

"Hope you have a good day," he said, watching me as I walked backward a few steps, avoiding bumping into him for a third time.

"You, too." I waved and ducked into the meeting room, just as Brooke finished setting up the room.

"I'd say that went perfectly fine," she said, noting my pained expression.

I sat at the table and, with a groan, laid my head in my arms.

34

"How's your first week going?" Daniel asked.

We were walking, take-out coffees in hand, through the University of Toronto's campus. Spring had finally arrived; the trees sprouted leafy green, and the crocuses, daffodils and tulips pushed impatiently through the garden beds flanking the stone buildings. It was after work and Jenny was going to be late getting home and so I had nowhere to be, no one waiting on me. When I got Daniel's text asking if I wanted to join him for some fresh air, I considered ignoring it—I was still confused about how I felt toward him—but ultimately I had some questions I wanted answered. Mainly about what happened between us, and why I ended our engagement four years earlier. I was done speculating and it was time to know the truth only he could give.

"It's going okay," I replied, shrugging my shoulders and tucking my chin into my soft turtleneck sweater. The sun had lost some of its daytime steam and the temperature was still cool as evening approached. I was distracted by the questions swirling in my mind and nervous being with Daniel, even though there was no reason to be. Matt and I were…not together right now. My feelings on that relationship were even more confusing than the ones I had about Daniel.

My workweek *had* been good—I remembered my colleagues, I

was on top of my workload thanks to Brooke's help and everyone seemed genuinely happy to have me back. Sure, I wasn't as fast or efficient as I used to be, taking longer with tasks like writing memos and PR blasts I used to be able to do in my sleep.

But then I'd delivered a wrong—and time-sensitive—press release this morning to one of the senior partners, Greg Harlow. I had no clue how it happened, as I had triple-checked the file before I emailed it. But when Brooke told me Greg had called her (I was writing an urgent memo for one of the consultants and Brooke said she'd take my calls for the hour), wondering why the release was about one of our previous oil and gas clients rather than the new one we'd acquired, I'd been shocked to realize my mistake. *At least it went to Greg first*, Brooke had said, and I tried to hide how badly the whole mess had shaken my confidence.

I didn't *think* it had anything to do with my memory issues, but I knew both Brooke and I were worried. "Don't stress. I've got your back," Brooke had said, a big smile on her face as she quickly found the correct release—the one I remembered writing but somehow had mixed up with the old release before hitting Send. "But maybe you should take a break for the afternoon, Lucy. It's a lot, coming back and boarding a train already going full speed. I'm happy to cover things."

"Thanks, but I'm good. I shouldn't have switched to decaf this morning." I had laughed to cover my anxiety and Brooke had kindly laughed with me, later bringing me a double shot of espresso with a smile.

"Lucy?" Daniel's voice broke through my thoughts.

"Yeah? Sorry, what did you say?"

"What's up?" Daniel asked, putting a hand on my arm and slowing us down. "I've mostly been talking to myself for the past five minutes. You okay?"

"Am I okay?" I punctuated each word, then sighed. And a moment later, inexplicably, started to laugh. Daniel watched me, the smile growing on his face mingling with confusion as he tried to catch up to what was so funny. Soon I was laughing so hard tears poured from my eyes and I had to cross my legs so I wouldn't pee.

"Here, let's sit." Daniel led me over to a bench while I tried to catch my breath. "You know, you always did have the best laugh."

"I don't know about that," I replied. "I snort in an incredibly unflattering way when I get going. It's not my best feature."

"Nah, I love it." Daniel nudged his shoulder into mine and smiled. "It's adorable."

I smiled in response, then looked down at my hands, cupped around the take-out coffee cup. I felt awkward, Daniel having invoked our past while I struggled—still—to accept it wasn't also my present.

Now or never. "Can I ask you a question?"

"Anything," Daniel said.

"Why did we break up?" I asked, glancing his way. I wanted to watch his expression as he took in my question.

"Just going to jump right in, huh?" His face darkened briefly, but then he smiled to cover it.

I nodded but didn't say anything else.

He sighed, turned toward me on the bench. "You don't remember?"

I shook my head. "It's locked away somewhere, but I have no idea if I'm ever going to remember. And I need to know, Daniel. I think…it might help with everything if I know what happened with us."

"Okay, Lucy," he said, nodding. "You dumped me."

It felt so abrupt, his disclosure of the truth, that my heartbeat accelerated to the point I was certain he'd be able to hear it pounding in my chest. I wanted to blame the late-day caffeine for my jackrabbit heart rate, but I knew that had little to do with it. "What? But *why*? All I remember is being happy."

"We *were* happy."

"So what went wrong?" I asked.

His jaw clenched. "We wanted different things."

"What does that even mean?" I said quietly, more to myself than him. I dug deeply into my mind, trying to pull up anything resembling a memory of that time. Tried to recall what these "different things" might have been, but there was nothing there to hang on to.

"It was a long time ago, Lucy." I couldn't read the expression on his face. "And look, here we are. Having coffee and reminiscing about your snort-laugh. So why does it even matter now?"

"I guess it doesn't." I felt dejected. If Daniel couldn't give me the magic bullet answer, who could? But his words kept running through my mind. *We wanted different things...*

What had I wanted that was different from Daniel?

"You know, it's been nice. Spending time with you again," Daniel said. He went to say something else but then shook his head.

"What? What is it?" I asked.

"I've missed you." He gave me a smile and a surge of warmth moved through me. "I *miss* you."

"I miss you, too," I replied, the confession sitting heavy between us. But as soon as I said it I wanted to pull back because it wasn't right for us to be talking like this. He was married; I had a boyfriend. This wasn't a fair game to be playing.

"I can't believe it's still light outside," I said when I could no longer handle the silence. "Must be spring, after all." But Daniel wasn't interested in my attempt to turn the conversation in a less charged direction.

"I haven't said anything to Margot, about us hanging out," he said. I tried to cover how discomfiting it was to hear her name. Not loving that now I had to consider her, admit my guilt her husband told me he missed me—present tense. "You know, we were always better suited, I think. You and me."

At first I wasn't sure what he meant. And then once the words settled over me, along with the meaning, I wasn't sure what to do with them. *Better suited than him and Margot? But if that was true, Daniel, why aren't we together anymore?*

"Don't get me wrong," he added quickly. "I love her. I do. And we have a great life together." I nodded as if this wasn't being disputed, feeling sick to my stomach. Why was I subjecting myself to this? "But, well, I miss you."

Sometimes the things that used to make sense don't make sense anymore.

I was more confused than ever. I didn't know what to do with his admission, or how much importance to assign it. "Thanks," I replied, knowing it wasn't the right response but unable to think of anything more fitting.

"Thanks?" he said, chuckling. "That's all you've got for me?"

I started laughing, too, and soon was snorting away. "Sorry," I finally managed. "I didn't know what else to say."

"It's cool. I get it," Daniel said. "I probably shouldn't have said anything. Not fair to you."

"It's okay. I'm glad you did."

"You are?" He turned to me, closer this time, and for a moment I thought he might kiss me. He was so close now…it would have been easy. But he didn't, then shifted to lean back against the bench, which moved his body farther from mine. I was both glad and disappointed.

"I'm having a hard time getting the truth out of people these days," I said, stretching back, as well. My muscles in my shoulders and lower back screamed, unaccustomed to spending so much time in a chair hunched over a desk. "So it's refreshing when someone offers it without me having to ask."

"Happy to be of service," he said.

"But, Daniel," I added, "you can't 'miss' me. We can't keep doing this, talking about all this stuff. I know it's on me today because I asked the question, but still. We need to…stop."

"Why?" he asked, his mouth turning down into a frown. He hunched forward so his forearms rested on his knees, and furrowed his brow. "We're friends, right?"

Friends. My stomach recoiled and I stood to toss my nearly empty cup into a nearby trash can. I had definitely had too much coffee. "Of course we are." I tried to keep my tone nonchalant but knew I had failed by the look on his face.

He watched me for a beat longer, then stood, as well. "I never wanted to make you uncomfortable, Lucy. I shouldn't have said anything. Forget about it, okay?"

I nodded and gave him the best "don't worry about it" smile I could. Then he walked me to the subway as we chatted about things we had no emotional connection to—his classes, and Jenny's most recent film project. Weekend plans, and a great book he'd recently read. But while I forced myself to stay engaged, my mind was split. Half of it with my newly resurrected "friend" Daniel, who had told me he missed me, and the other half with the Daniel I used to know, who I still felt connected to in a deeply meaningful, yet dangerous, way.

I had to stop seeing him. Had to shut down whatever this was because it wasn't good for me, and by what he'd admitted tonight it wasn't helping him, either. I might have been overthinking it, assigning meaning to his words that wasn't there: missing me, his snort-laughing friend, and missing me, the woman he once proposed to, were not necessarily the same things, and I wasn't sure which version he had been referring to.

Yet, no matter how convinced I was I had to let Daniel go, tonight he had given me a much-needed hit of a powerful drug— hope. *You have the right to change your present if it doesn't fit with the future you envision,* Dr. Kay had told me. But did I also have the right to change someone else's future, too?

35

I was at the office early again the next morning, catching up on email and some communication requests that had come through overnight. After seeing Daniel, I'd been unable to sleep, tossed and turned most of the night on Jenny's futon. In reality his confession changed nothing, because he was still married, and not to me. Yet...

What if things could be different? If Daniel still had feelings for me (wasn't that what he had said yesterday, though not in so many words?), what could that mean for us? Would I want to be with Daniel again? Yes and no. Yes, because it continued to feel like I'd been ripped against my will out of our relationship. No, because I could see the carnage such a decision would leave in its path, and everyone who would get hurt. Also, not knowing *exactly* why we broke up cast a dark fog over everything. There had to be a reason why I'd ended things, and a good one.

We wanted different things.

My mind was elsewhere and so I jumped when Greg Harlow popped his head into my office. "Morning, Lucy," he said in a deep baritone. Greg was a large man, and his voice was no exception.

"Oh, hi," I said, unconsciously putting a hand to my chest to still my heart rate. "I didn't see you there."

"Sorry," Greg said. He smiled, but it didn't reach his eyes. It worried me—both the look on his face and the fact he was at my office door before nine. I had worked more closely with Greg over the years than any other partner, so I knew how to read his expressions. *This has to be about the press release.* I sighed imperceptibly, smiling to hide my growing concern. Already crafting assurances in my mind for Greg that it had been a "one and done" error.

"No problem," I replied. "Come on in."

It was then I saw Greg wasn't alone. Susan Chong—Jameson Porter's head of human resources—was right behind him. An intense prickle of anxiety moved through me, and I shivered. Susan also came into my office and then shut the door behind her. It felt crowded with the three of us in there, and I took a shaky sip from the glass of water on my desk.

Greg and Susan each took one of the chairs across from me, and I noticed a file in Susan's hands. Saw *Sparks, Lucy* typed on a sticker on its tab. My stomach dropped.

"How are things going, Lucy?" Greg asked, while Susan fiddled with her gold lariat necklace with one hand and kept the other on the closed folder. I tried to avert my eyes from the folder and to concentrate on Greg.

"Things are great, Greg." My voice was high, definitely not relaxed. "Everyone has been fantastic, and I think things are going well."

Greg looked at me sympathetically, and Susan kept on fiddling, smiling. *Am I being fired?* The press release fiasco didn't seem serious enough to warrant me losing my job. After all, it had only gone to Greg before the mistake was realized. We hadn't yet pushed it to the media outlets, so it was an easy fix with zero fallout. But then I had a disconcerting moment of panic when I considered maybe I'd screwed something else up, something much worse for the firm. Maybe my memory had failed me again, and I hadn't even realized it.

"Good, good," Greg said, shifting to cross his other leg over his knee. The chair was small for his large frame and he looked squished and uncomfortable. "I've asked Susan to join me today so we can talk about something that's been brought to my attention."

My heart beat furiously in my chest and my mind raced as I tried to sort out what else it could be. I ran through the communications I worked on during the week, coming back to the press release. My mouth went dry. "What is it?"

"There's been some concern about the, uh, repercussions of your accident," Greg said, the corners of his mouth turning down.

"Oh?" I crossed my arms over my chest. I quickly uncrossed them, not wanting to appear defensive. Maybe I hadn't been ready to come back to work. I should have given myself a bit longer to recover, to get back to who I was before. The Lucy we could all count on. "What 'repercussions' exactly?"

Now it was Susan's turn, and she was more direct. "Brooke Ingram expressed some concern about your memory issues."

"She's worried about you, Lucy," Greg added, setting his chin on steepled fingers. "We all are, of course."

I stared at the two of them, unable to keep my mouth from falling open in surprise. *This was Brooke's doing?* The same Brooke who told me only yesterday she had my back? The worry morphed into something else...a sense of disbelief, and then one of betrayal.

Susan opened the folder, pulled out a piece of paper and set it on the desk and I recognized it immediately. The incorrect press release. "Yes, I made a mistake," I said, my voice not as strong as I'd intended. "But honestly, it has nothing to do with my accident or my memory. I'm not sure exactly what happened, but I had two files on my desktop with the same client name. The old client name." I shrugged. "I attached the wrong release to the email I sent you, Greg. But luckily we caught it before it went out to the media."

"Lucy, this is the *second* release you sent Greg. Not the first one." She gently pushed the paper across my desk. I turned it around so I could read it properly, and saw the date stamp and the client's name in the top line. It was the same press release, they were right—but I also could see it was the supposedly corrected one because at the top of the page was my email conversation with Greg. Please trash the other release, I'd written. This is the correct one. Sorry about the error.

I looked up, confused. "I don't understand." Then I looked back down at it again, read the date again. How did I screw it up twice?

"But it only went to you, right?" I stammered. Greg shook his head. "Unfortunately, you sent this to me as an FYI note. You had already sent the release to the media outlets." He saw the look on my face. "But don't worry, Lucy. Brooke retracted it before they turned it around and pushed it out. We got lucky."

"Brooke told me it was handled," I said. I pressed my lips together and thought back to our conversation, after I'd realized the first release was incorrect. Yes, Brooke had told me not to worry. It hadn't gone beyond Greg. She had sat in my chair as I fretted, found the correct release and then attached it to the email I'd drafted for Greg. She'd hit Send. Then I'd gone to the washroom to splash some water on my face and...

Damn it.

A cold realization settled over me. Brooke had done this on purpose. But I still had no idea why.

"I'm sorry," I said, the weight of what had happened pressing me into my chair. "I'm not sure how this happened, but I can assure you it won't happen again." I thought I might cry and took a deep breath. "I promise it has nothing to do with my memory. A miscommunication between me and Brooke." I barked out a laugh, which surprised both Greg and Susan. "Which is sort of funny, considering I'm the head of the communications department."

Greg looked at Susan and then at me with some concern. "I assure you it won't happen again," I repeated, more firmly this time.

"Well, glad to hear it," Greg said. Susan seemed to have something else to say but took her cue from Greg, who was now standing. "But if you need anything, Lucy—even if it means taking some time off—you say the word, okay?"

Susan nodded. I held up the printed email and release. "Do you mind if I keep this?" I asked.

"Sure," Susan said. "Let me know if I can help you in any way, Lucy. That's what I'm here for."

I smiled at her, did my best to look appreciative. "I will. Thanks, Susan."

"Okay, good chat," Greg said, now at the door. "See you at the one o'clock?"

I nodded. "Looking forward to it."

And then I was alone. My hands shook as I held the printout, angry and unsure what I wanted to do next.

Brooke walked by, stopped in front of my door and did her best to look concerned. I set the email on my desk, upside down so she couldn't read it. "Did I see Greg and Susan leave your office?" she said, her voice an exaggerated whisper. "What's going on? Is this about yesterday?"

"No. Something else," I replied, keeping my tone even. "Everything's fine."

She looked momentarily surprised but recovered quickly. "Oh, good." She leaned against the door frame and tucked her hands into her pockets. "Can I help you with anything for the one o'clock?" Normally I would have been grateful for her offer, would probably have delegated some of the work on my desk.

"I've got it handled," I said. "I came in early today."

"Okay, well, let me know if you need anything."

"Will do," I replied, only dropping my smile after she left my office.

Then I got up and closed my door before settling myself in front of my computer and going through all my folders. In only thirty minutes I found three duplicate press releases, including the one I'd sent to Greg—all dated this week and all with old client names in the place of new business mentions. For a moment I considered it was my mistake, a simple copy and paste error. But I'd cut and pasted only small bits of text and had written mostly new copy for all three releases.

After dragging the duplicate, incorrect releases to the trashcan icon—emptying it to be sure they were gone—I clicked through my email archives during the time I was in the hospital and recovering at home, when Brooke had had access to my inbox. I found a number of outgoing messages she'd obviously handled but nothing that gave me any idea about why she seemed to be trying to sabotage me. Then I logged in to my personal email account and did the same search, putting "Brooke Ingram" into the query box. One email caught my eye, in my drafts folder. It was addressed to HR, but I obviously hadn't sent it yet.

Brooke—to discuss

Why was this in my personal account? It was dated the week before my accident. I quickly opened it and scanned the contents, which turned out to be a list of grievances. Like her lateness (there was a note beside it she had agreed to be on time after I brought it to her attention) and an important conference deadline she had missed because she didn't get the application in on time. Some of the items I'd highlighted to discuss went back a full six months.

I sat back and looked at the list, realized my memory *did* have something to do with this, after all.

Brooke Ingram was not who I thought she was. But somehow

all of these issues had been lost in the shuffle of my mind resetting itself. I had believed my work memory had stayed intact, yet here was proof that wasn't true. Now I had to admit maybe Brooke wasn't the only hole at Jameson Porter. What else had I missed? Cold fingers of fear wormed through me.

It was clear by the email I was organizing to have Brooke fired. Had been getting my ducks in a row, including a notation at the bottom of the email where I had written down a couple of other people on our team who might be good candidates to move into Brooke's position. I had probably kept it in my personal email because I didn't want Brooke to be able to access it. I hadn't trusted her then, and I couldn't trust her now.

And then it hit me. Brooke *had* apparently been displeased when I was hired—Susan had confessed that when we discussed the team I would be taking over, feeling it relevant to my leadership strategies. Brooke believed my job should have been hers, and if everything was as it had looked on paper—Brooke was loyal and hardworking and knew the communications department inside and out—she was right. It should have gone to her.

But there had been concerns about her ability to handle the leadership aspects of the job. Susan had further confided Brooke was a valuable employee, but she was a bit of a "lone wolf." She wasn't as skilled as she needed to be at delegation, had a hard time trusting others with the work. And that was a critical aspect of the director position—if you couldn't delegate, you couldn't lead a team.

So Brooke had seen her opportunity with my accident. Was trying to erode my position within the company, clearly positioning herself to take over the role and using my memory challenges as ammunition. I felt weak as I thought about everything I'd shared with her recently—especially the personal stuff, like the part about forgetting Matt and remembering someone else as my husband. That certainly didn't sound like someone who should be trusted with my workload and responsibilities.

I suspected Brooke had divulged this conversation to Greg and

Susan. That, coupled with the release flubs that I now understood were Brooke's doing and quite purposeful, meant a worrisome picture of my fitness for this job was being painted. And it had been only one week. What if I hadn't figured this out now? How much damage could she have done?

No. This wasn't going to happen. I was not going to let Brooke Ingram destroy my career. With the rest of my life in shambles, Jameson Porter mattered more than ever.

36

When I called Daniel to tell him I needed help, I ignored my promise to put some distance between us after the whole "I miss you" conversation. I asked if we could meet the next morning for breakfast because I needed to pick his lawyer brain.

"My lawyer brain is on permanent hiatus," Daniel had said with a laugh. "But it's all yours if you're willing to put up with the cobwebs."

We met late morning at Aroma, a restaurant chain with an all-day breakfast option that served a square of chocolate with every coffee order. Daniel tucked into his croissant and egg sandwich while mine sat untouched on my plate. "Not hungry?" he asked, his mouth half-full, glancing at my food.

I shook my head, picked up my latte instead.

"So what's up?" He was focused on his sandwich, dragging the croissant through a splash of hot sauce on his plate. "How can this ex-lawyer help?"

I filled him in on the Brooke situation.

"So you never sent the email?" he asked.

I shook my head. "It doesn't appear so."

"And are you sure you didn't talk about this with anyone else?"

"I don't think so," I replied. I picked at my sandwich, tearing off a small piece of the croissant.

"Not even Matt?" he asked. I felt nauseated, hearing Daniel say Matt's name, and dropped the piece of croissant without eating it.

"No one. Or not that I can remember."

"Which is why I asked." Daniel cleared his throat. "You said before your memory has been a bit unreliable?" The implication in his words was obvious.

I sighed with frustration. "Trust me, you're not suggesting anything I haven't already considered. But let's assume this is what it looks like, which is Brooke trying to steal my job," I said, and Daniel nodded. "I need to know how much trouble I'm in and what I can do about it. About her."

He wiped his hands on a napkin. "Look, this is sort of out of my wheelhouse. Employment law was not my area," he said, his tone measured. "But you're positive you didn't send that email, right? From your work account, maybe?"

"It wasn't in any of my work inboxes. Just my drafts folder, in my personal email."

Daniel frowned and leaned forward on his elbows. "So you have this whole list of things Brooke had been falling behind on. Things that would have given you cause for firing her." I nodded. "But you wrote that list preaccident and never shared it with anyone."

"And?" I had a feeling I knew where this was going and I wasn't going to like it.

"And so it's going to look like you wrote that email *after* she started messing with your work."

"But…but I have everything written down! Can't I use it to prove she's the one who's incompetent, and is clearly trying to set me up for a fall?"

He watched me for a moment. "Don't take this the wrong way, because I promise you it's coming from a good place, but… *are you* well enough to be back at work?" At my exasperated groan he held up his hands. "I know. You seem fine. I trust you when you say it hasn't affected your work. But an unsent email in your drafts folder—in your personal account—isn't much better than you writing all that stuff down on a sticky note. It's not officially date stamped until you send it."

"But it is date stamped, sort of. From when I created the draft. Which was a week *before* my accident."

"True, it will show you started an email on that date, but the contents could have been rewritten at any time," he said. "She could easily argue you wrote that list of grievances yesterday, not the week before your accident."

Of course. I felt like an idiot for not realizing that draft was of no use because I could never prove I hadn't written my complaints *after* Brooke went to Greg and Susan. Naturally Brooke knew the truth, but it would be her word against mine, and based on these past couple of months, she would undoubtedly come out ahead.

I felt sick. The one thing I'd been clinging to—my job, my career—might not be as secure as I'd believed. Maybe they wouldn't fire me, but they could force me on long-term disability. Which would leave me with nothing but time to contemplate how unrecognizable my life had become.

Daniel's voice was gentle as he dipped his head to look into my eyes. "With my lawyer hat on I would tell you to document everything that's happened, and without question don't let Brooke near your computer or files again." I nodded, swallowed hard. "With my friend hat on? It's time for a pep talk. Don't let her get to you, because you're giving her way too much control here. And that's not the Lucy I remember."

Alex's warning from when I was thirteen rushed back, that I would one day regret giving Nancy McPherson so much power over me. The situations were obviously not the same, but the feeling inside my gut certainly felt familiar.

"Hey, come on, Luce. You can do this. You're stronger than you think."

"Am I?" I sighed. "Maybe I used to be, but I don't feel strong these days. I'm barely keeping my head above water."

"Want to get out of here?" Daniel asked, and I nodded. I still hadn't taken a bite of my sandwich, but my appetite was long gone.

"So what can I do to distract you?" Daniel took my hand and pulled me along the sidewalk once we got outside Aroma. My insides jolted at his touch, which was too intimate for who we were to each other. *Friends.* But I didn't let my hand drop from his and, instead, squeezed a little tighter.

"I don't know if you can," I said. "I'm fairly committed to this bad-attitude-Betty thing right now."

He smiled, then picked up the pace. "I know just the thing."

Our hands separated out of necessity as we moved through the throngs of people shopping along Bloor Street. It was probably for the best, as I was starting to worry about how long was too long for Daniel to be holding my hand. A short walk later we stood on a residential street near the university, everything starting to green up with buds and blossoms now that spring had arrived. It was relatively quiet here this time of day, everyone out and about doing what you do on errand-filled Saturdays, and the students who lived in the area were probably still sleeping after being out late the night before. I looked at the big house we'd stopped in front of, the green awning and red sign so familiar after many nights here while I was at U of T, and grinned. "What's this? A pint and a cheerful trip down memory lane?"

"Don't you think you could use both?" he asked, and I laughed.

"That's fair," I said as we walked up the front steps and into the Madison Avenue Pub—the "Maddy" as it was fondly known by the locals—and settled into a red velvet banquet booth on the second floor.

"I know we just ate—well, at least I did—but I should have suggested this instead. A lot of happy memories, right?"

I nodded, looking around. Taking in the decor that hadn't

changed much over the years. It was comforting to be in a place that both felt familiar and, as Daniel said, was filled with good memories. My stomach growled and I pressed my hand to it. "I could use a grilled cheese. They make the best one."

"I hate to tell you this, but it's not on the menu anymore," Daniel said, and I gave a small grunt of disappointment. "But the Voodoo Chicken Fingers are amazing. And you can't go wrong with the stuffed burger."

An hour later I was full of chicken fingers and two pints of the Maddy's Mad Blonde Lager and felt better than I had in weeks. We'd laughed a lot—reminiscing about our many messy Maddy nights, and how they should probably have named bar stools after us for all the money we'd spent there. We waxed poetic while we drank our pints about how carefree life had been back then, before we had to start "adulting."

A touch light-headed from the beer and not paying enough attention to where my feet were planted, I missed a step as we walked out of the pub. Luckily Daniel was right behind me and caught me before I landed on my ass, though it wouldn't have hurt much on the carpet-covered stairs. It also wouldn't have been the first time I stumbled down these steps, but definitely the first time in the middle of the day.

"Thanks for bringing me here," I said, leaning back into Daniel so he could stretch around me to reach the handle and open the door for us to leave. "You were right. This was a great distraction." My voice was boozy and relaxed, and I wished we could go back upstairs and keep this thing going. Order another pint and reminisce a little longer. But by the time I thought to suggest it we were outside already on the pub's small front porch, under the shadow of the awning, and I knew the moment had passed. He had to get home, to study, to Margot. And I had to figure out what I was going to do about Brooke.

I turned around to look at Daniel, still behind me, to thank him again for knowing exactly what I'd needed, and as I did he leaned down and touched his lips to mine. But it wasn't a quick kiss this time—it was one that lingered.

He held his lips to mine long enough for me to reciprocate. His hand moved to my lower back, his fingers clutching my jacket, and he pressed me closer. I closed my eyes, the feel of him against me reassuring and exciting. I didn't even worry we were making out in broad daylight, where anyone could see us. I didn't care about that—only about how fierce my need for him was, and how well we fit together (unlike with Matt, I had enough height on Daniel that my arms could go easily around his neck and rest on his shoulders) all these years later. His mouth was warm, all-consuming, on mine and I got lost in what we were doing. Lost in him, and the memory of us.

It was incredible and exactly as I remembered how it felt to be with Daniel. At least at first.

Then something strange happened. Like the magnetic pull of our lips reversed, and I could no longer keep my mouth against his. The taste of him was all wrong, too, even if I couldn't sort out exactly why. But even though I pulled away from the kiss, our bodies remained in contact and the energy between us continued to buzz. His breath was heavy in my ear and his heart beat fast against my chest. I rested my head into the crook of his neck and grabbed my bottom lip, pulling slightly, feeling the lingering tingle. I wished I could go back to kissing him, in nearly the same place we shared our very first kiss. But the sensation of being repelled increased in intensity with every passing second and soon I couldn't bear to be near him.

"What's wrong?" Daniel whispered, his lips brushing my ear. I shivered and he pulled me closer despite my slight resistance. I wanted him so badly, in a way that made me feel weak and pathetic. But while my mind shouted for me to stay, my body was retreating.

"We can't do this," I whispered back. But why was I the one saying this? Daniel was married. I was instantly furious with myself for letting things get to this point. But, my God, kissing him… For the first time since I learned what had happened to me I felt normal. Like all the puzzle pieces were finally back in their proper places. Except they weren't.

For a moment Daniel didn't respond, kept his arms around me and his lips near my ear, his breath slowing as the intensity between us lessened. "I know," he finally said. He rested his forehead against mine, closed his eyes, looking pained. "I'm sorry. I should never have—"

I pulled back, waited for him to open his eyes and look at me. "No, it wasn't you. I wanted to. But it has to end here. It's not fair for anyone." He nodded and I knew he was thinking of Margot, like I was thinking of Matt.

"I don't know what happened, Lucy." He scraped a hand through his hair and smiled sadly at me. "I got caught up. Being here again, with you."

I extricated myself from his arms and stepped back, nearly tumbling down the last few stairs. He reached out for me, but I managed to hold myself up on the metal railing. Now that we were a few steps apart and I was no longer in his arms, he seemed unsure about what to do with his hands. He tucked them into his pockets and gave me a long, miserable look.

"We can't be friends," I said.

He nodded, his chin dropping as he stared at his feet. His jaw tensed and released a few times, and I nearly started crying as I watched the turmoil move through him. It was as though we were breaking up all over again, and I wondered what it had been like the first time.

"Are you going to be okay?" he asked.

"Yes," I said, wondering if it was true. I longed for things to be different, already regretting my words even though this was the only thing that made sense. "Well, bye, Daniel."

"Take care of yourself, Lucy."

I walked away, keeping my head high and not glancing back to see if he was still standing on the porch, watching me and wishing, like I did, we could have another chance.

But even if Daniel had told me he still had real feelings for me, wanted to leave Margot, I wasn't sure what I wanted anymore. When I first woke up and learned Daniel was not my husband, the moment we had just shared was what I fantasized about—where he would tell me he wouldn't let me get away a second time, and the confabulation I'd created would become a reality. We would be married. "Better late than never," I would say before I kissed him and we exchanged long-overdue vows.

But the moment I'd imagined, hoped for, hadn't been real. Instead, it had felt like something inside me was opposing Daniel. I couldn't explain why, or how, but it was undeniable—the sense we were not matched, after all. We were not supposed to be together. Otherwise, we never would have been apart in the first place and it would have been Daniel I woke up to in the hospital. He was not, I was beginning to understand, the missing piece I'd been looking for.

37

I wasn't up to going out, but Jenny was relentless and told me she wouldn't leave me home alone and *there was no way I would make her miss the best party of the year.* So because she was letting me crash on her futon, but mostly because she was right that being alone probably wasn't the best idea, I agreed. With Jenny's nudging and most of a bottle of wine while we got ready, by the time we arrived—at a swanky downtown restaurant that had been closed for the night to accommodate the who's who of the city's film and television industry—I felt good, ready for anything. The afternoon with Daniel now thankfully buried under my buzz.

"Lucy, I want you to meet someone," Jenny shouted in my ear. It was loud in the restaurant, all the voices mingling to create one giant hum. I let her drag me around for about thirty minutes while she introduced me to colleagues and friends, smiled and shook hands and asked appropriately social questions about what they were working on, nodded and turned my face into a mask of curious interest at their responses. There was an endless stream of drinks moving in and out of my hands. I *was* having a great night, and for a while I simply forgot. About my accident, and Daniel, and Matt. Then Jenny was beside me again, squealing and clawing at my arm and whispering about how she'd met some hotshot director who claimed to know who she was, and she had to leave me for a few minutes to go mingle. She kissed me on the cheek before practically running through the crowd to get back to this director and his entourage.

With so many drinks consumed it was time for a bathroom break, so I made my way downstairs—carefully, the high heels (I'd changed out of my flats at the last minute and into a pair of Jenny's shoes) and alcohol and steep stairs a dangerous mix. The washroom was empty, which was surprising for the number of people at the party. I came out of the stall and clumsily readjusted my short skirt so the zipper was at the back again, and then leaned heavily against the sink ledge as I evaluated myself in the mirror. Jenny had curled my hair into big, glossy waves, my lips were still colored, thanks to a lip stain that lived up to its marketed staying power, and I looked like a girl without problems. If only I could have frozen time. The door opened, the sounds of the party seeping back in, and I turned from the mirror to see Jenny.

"You okay?" she asked, holding two drinks in her hands. Something clear, in short glasses with one giant ice cube sitting in the middle of each.

"Better than ever," I said as I washed my hands. The water splashed over the edge of the basin and I reached for some paper towels, losing my balance in the process. "Oops!" I laughed and stood with my feet a bit farther apart to stabilize my body. Then I wiped up the excess water and took the drink Jenny handed me.

"Maybe I should have grabbed you a water, too," Jenny said, watching me try to stand without swaying.

"No. No water." I shook my head. "I can drink water tomorrow." And to prove it, I downed my glass (gin and soda) in three gulps. Jenny cheered, then we tried to high-five, but it didn't go well because we had both had too much to drink, and we giggled as we walked back upstairs, arm in arm.

I should have stopped drinking then, but I had moved past the point of no return—my ability to be rational about my level of drunkenness gone with that last gin and soda. So I happily accepted a glass of prosecco from a passing tray once we got back to the party. I turned to tell Jenny how much I appreciated her making me come out tonight, but she was no longer beside me. Standing on my tiptoes, I peered over the few heads blocking my eye line to see if Jenny was nearby when someone touched my shoulder and I turned around.

"Lucy! I thought that was you." She smiled, and though she looked different from how she used to, I recognized her instantly.

The half-full glass of prosecco dropped from my hand, shattering near our feet. "Oh! Are you okay?" Margot asked, holding on to my upper arm with her hand and moving us away from the broken glass. I nodded dumbly, staring at her.

Still holding my arm, Margot looked around quickly and made eye contact with a server working the room. She waved her over, and we moved another few feet away as someone else brought out a small dustpan and sweeper.

"Here," Margot said, handing me another glass of bubbling booze. Then she leaned in and hugged me deeply, and I finally found my voice.

"Margot, it's so great t-to see you," I stammered, my words slow and ill-formed. *Pull it together, Lucy*, I thought. Embarrassingly I hiccuped right then, my hand quickly coming up to cover my mouth. "Sorry about that. So, how have you been?" Racing through my mind were a million questions. About Daniel, about whether she knew what had happened between us these past few weeks, what he may have told her about me. Then it occurred to me Daniel might be here with her, and my chest clenched. My eyes darted around the nearby milling crowds, but I couldn't see him.

"I've been well," she said, smiling. She seemed not to notice how much I'd had to drink. Maybe I was hiding it better than I thought. Or maybe she was being kind. "It has been such a long time, Lucy. You look gorgeous as ever."

"Thanks. So do you." Daniel hadn't been kidding when he said Margot was different now. The Margot I had known in school was beautiful, but her edges weren't smooth—she never wore makeup or anything that could be called "dressed up" and her short, choppy bob was often pulled back with elastic headbands. But this Margot…she was stunning. Her dark hair fell to her shoulders, sleek and straight. Her makeup was flawless, as was her outfit—a black pantsuit that billowed at the top and was tight through the leg—and glossy red nails perfectly matched to the large beaded choker around her neck.

"So what brings you here?" she asked, resting a hand and those red nails again on my arm. "I didn't realize you were in the industry." Her smile was warm and friendly—she seemed delighted to have run into me—and then I realized she had no clue Daniel and I had been spending time together recently. Probably had no idea we had run into each other at Jake's party, or that we'd been texting and meeting up from time to time. Then I thought back to today, Daniel and me at the Maddy, drinking beer and kissing under the awning… I swayed again but managed to keep my balance.

"Oh, I'm not," I said, wishing I hadn't tossed back the last gin and soda so quickly—or the three (four?) drinks that preceded it. "I'm here with Jenny."

Margot let out a happy squeal that made me jump, and started glancing about. "Jenny's here? I haven't seen her in ages. Not since I styled a set for her, maybe a year ago now? I would love to say hi."

Jenny and Margot had worked together a year ago? Jenny told me she hadn't seen Margot in years. *Years*, as in multiple. The heavy truth that Jenny had lied to me about Margot settled across my shoulders, and tried to push me to the ground, though I managed to resist the desire to lie down on the sticky bar floor and close my eyes.

"You know what? I'll tell her you're here," I said, though I had no intention of telling Jenny any such thing. I had a new plan: hightail it out of this party as soon as I could extricate myself from this conversation with Margot. "Listen, I need to head out. I, uh, have a big work project to attack tomorrow."

"I get it," Margot said, leaning in with a smile. "I'm only here to make an appearance." She held up her glass. "Water, sadly," she said. Then she winked and turned ever so slightly sideways, flattening the billowy part of her outfit by running her hand down her stomach. And that was when I saw it. The tiny bump of her abdomen, which could mean only one thing because Margot was too thin everywhere else for it to be anything but. "We haven't told a lot of people yet. But it won't be long until I can't hide it, you know?"

I nodded, though I didn't know at all. Margot was pregnant. Daniel was going to be a dad, and he hadn't said anything to me about it. A ball of shock hit me square in my center, and I knew I had to leave the party immediately or things were going to go bad, quick.

"Wow! Congratulations," I said, trying to shift my face into a look that was more delighted versus distraught. "Wow, how exciting. Daniel must be…thrilled."

"He is. We are!" she said, a grin on her pretty face. "It was nice to see you, Lucy. I'm glad we were able to, you know, have such a nice conversation. I know it's been a long time, but, well…" She looked uncomfortable for a moment, glanced at her glass of water before looking back up at me and taking a deep breath. "Anyway, I'm glad we ran into one another."

My mind whirred, but I couldn't hang on to a single thought. Then Margot leaned in and hugged me tightly. "Please say hi to Jenny for me if I don't see her later."

"I will," I said, smiling as best I could, the gin perilously close to the back of my throat. "Okay, well, I should get out of here while I can." I took a step back from her so she couldn't hug me again. "Great to see you, too, Margot."

"Same. Good luck with your project tomorrow."

"Thanks," I said, already half-turned away from her. "Bye." I waved one last time before pushing my way frantically through the tightly knit crowd, beelining for the front door and praying I got out of there before I decorated the party with all those drinks. I made it outside and around the corner of the restaurant's building before I threw up, my hand clutching the brick for stability as the heaves moved through me and my stomach emptied. Then I wiped my mouth with the sleeve of my blouse, shivered violently as I realized my coat was still inside—no way was I going back in there—before stumbling into the first taxi I could find.

38

After leaving the party, I had to ask the driver to pull over once so I could throw up again, then promised a large tip for him to make a stop at Jenny's. As quickly as I could, I retrieved my overnight bag and left Jenny a note apologizing for bailing early on her. Alex had called, I jotted down, begging me to house-sit for a few days. I suspected Jenny wouldn't believe my excuse—the most expensive thing Alex owned, the only thing of value, really, was her camera and it was always with her—but I no longer cared. I wanted to be alone. Somewhere I couldn't disappoint people...or where they couldn't disappoint me.

I texted Alex once I got back into the cab, asking if I could crash at her place for a couple of nights. As long as you want, she responded right away. She'd decided to extend the trip she was on by a few days (something about another photographer with an all-access pass and killer legs) so wouldn't be back until Thursday, Friday at the latest. Relieved for the buffer time, I figured by then I'd be able to come up with another plan for where to stay.

It was hard to believe only a couple of months ago my life looked completely different—I'd had a boyfriend whom I adored, a great job, a best friend I could count on and zero desire to have anything to do with Daniel London. Using Alex's extra key on my chain, I let myself into her place and chugged a large glass of water before crashing into bed.

When I woke Sunday morning, I was expectedly hungover. A disheveled, sick and sweaty mess on Alex's bed—which was directly in front of a floor-to-ceiling window that let in far too much light so early in the morning. She lived in a converted loft in Parkdale, half a block from a strip club Alex liked for the "gritty realness" it brought to her neighborhood. Though with a new Starbucks and a trendy bakery that made only incredibly expensive (but delicious) doughnuts across the road, signs of gentrification were popping up, which Alex hated. She loved the neighborhood as it was, said there was endless inspiration for her photography living in such an eclectic part of town.

Once I was certain moving wasn't going to make me throw up, I padded into the kitchen, which was only five steps from the small ladder that led to the platform and bed. Opening the fridge, I found a couple of past-their-prime oranges, a small bag of apples, a can of coconut whipped cream, a few take-out containers I didn't dare open and a half wheel of Brie cheese. Grabbing the cheese and a knife, I unearthed a box of crackers at the very back of a narrow cupboard by the sink, and a jar of strawberry jam, and sat on the bed eating over my lap while I watched the flow of both human and automobile traffic outside the front window. After polishing off half the cheese, I brushed the cracker crumbs from my lap and stood, stretching my arms high over my head. My muscles contracted and complained, and I realized how out of shape I was. I had a sudden urge to go for a run, and after digging around Alex's clothes, I pulled together a pair of black leggings that could work as running tights, a long-sleeved cotton T-shirt over which I threw on a too-large sweatshirt. Luckily Alex and I wore the same-size shoes, so I shoved my feet into a pair of her running shoes and went outside.

It was still early and the sun wasn't at full strength yet, so my

ears and fingertips were somewhat chilly. But the wind invigo-
rated me as I ran, and I started to sweat as I pushed back against
the effects of my hangover. My body seemed to know what to
do, and my legs pumped harder and faster as I turned down a
side street full of dilapidated gingerbread-roofed houses, all lined
up in a row. They had probably been pristine and beautiful in
their prime, and I felt a sense of solidarity as I ran past them. I
think I used to be like those houses—once new and fresh and
holding great promise—but was now much more like the current versions. Run-down and imperfect but somehow still func-
tioning if not sagging a little to the left.

I knew I had been a runner, before the accident. Both Matt
and Jenny had told me how I always, regardless of weather or
schedule, squeezed in a seven-miler on Sundays. But despite
my memory telling me I hadn't jogged a lap since high school
gym class, as I turned down another side street, the houses on
this one in much better shape than the last, I noted I wasn't out
of breath. My legs, which I had expected to cramp up not long
after I started running, felt strong. My gait was surprisingly
smooth as I ran one street, then another, then another. Even
if my mind didn't remember me being a runner, my feet and
muscles and lungs sure did.

It was around the forty-minute mark of the run when it happened. There was no explanation for why it came back to me
so clearly—Dr. Kay had explained when memories returned it
was often because of a trigger, like a person or place or experience, and this had none of those hallmarks—but regardless,
there it was. A memory about Matt I knew was real without
even having to question it.

It stopped me like a brick wall, sucked all the breath out of
my lungs so dramatically I doubled over to try to keep from
falling to the ground.

*There were candles on the mantel, remnants of a mostly eaten steak
dinner littering the kitchen table and two bottles of wine open and*

empty. A regular Saturday night for us. We were in bed, postsex, and Matt had me spooned against him. I was too hot, a bit woozy from the wine, but didn't want to move because the moment was perfection. I was warm and safe and loved. "I wish we could stay here, like this, forever and ever," I said, sighing with contentment and snuggling against the heat of his body.

I may have been relaxed, but Matt was restless. Shifting his body every few seconds like he had an itch he couldn't quite reach. "I'm seconds from sleep here," I murmured, eyes closed. "But not if you keep twitching." I was used to Matt's inability to stay still—he was always doing something active, like cycling or swimming laps, or doing pushups on our living room floor. But generally some wine and sex calmed the restlessness—allowed him an uncommon stillness.

"Sorry," he replied, his lips and breath brushing my earlobe. I shivered and snuggled a bit closer. "Lucy, can I ask you something?"

"Mmm-hmm," I said, eyes still closed, thinking nothing of the question. Wishing he would hurry up and ask whatever it was so we could go to sleep. "You have about a minute before I pass out."

He cleared his throat, shifted away from me so a draft of cool air painted my back and turned on the bedside lamp. With a grunt of unhappiness I turned my head to look at him, squinting with the sudden brightness. "What are you doing?"

He jumped out of bed, throwing on a pair of plaid pajama bottoms. The ones I had given him for Christmas. "Just a sec," he said, lunging into the closet and fumbling with something in its depths. I sat up, watched the muscles in his back contracting and releasing as he moved stuff around. "Matt, what are you doing?" A prickle of irritation moved through me because now I was fully awake and didn't want to be.

When he didn't immediately answer, I lay back and pulled the duvet up to my chin, sinking my body into our memory foam mattress. Contented and comfortable, I started to drift off again, but then Matt was on the bed, sitting cross-legged beside me. He looked nervous.

I raised an eyebrow, waited for him to explain the grin on his face, along with his forage through our closet and why he looked like he was hiding the best secret ever. "What if we could stay here, forever and ever?" he asked.

"Here? Like, in bed?" I yawned. "Yes, please."

He tapped at his knees like his thumbs were mini drumsticks. "Right. Definitely. Here, in bed. You. Me. Us," he said, a slightly manic look in his eyes as he stumbled over his words. That part was definitely out of character—he was masterful with words, always getting his point across succinctly. It was a skill he'd honed as a consultant and one that had made him successful with the firm and his clients. "But that's not exactly what I meant."

I came up on my elbow and rested my head in my palm, giving him a quizzical look. "What's wrong with you?"

He pulled something out from behind him, a small box, which he held in his hands. I glanced at the box, recognized it immediately. It held the mocha-flavored energy gels Matt consumed regularly during his training rides, which I thought were disgusting. "Nothing's wrong. I'm okay. More than okay," he said, lifting the box's lid.

"Are we about to do something requiring extra stamina?" I asked, gesturing to the box, not seeing what he was looking at inside it because the opened lid was blocking my view.

But before I could ask again what he was doing, he pulled a small black box out of the energy gel box and settled it onto his knees. A moment later he opened the black box and held something out toward me. It happened so fast I didn't immediately register the magnitude of the moment—was shocked by the ring he extended, slow on the uptake.

My eyes moved from his face to the ring. "Where did all your gels go?"

He laughed hard then, tilted his head back as he did, and a nervous giggle bubbled out of me. I was on my knees now, too, facing him, naked. "Lucy Ann Sparks," Matt said. "Will you do me the absolute honor of spending every night for the rest of our lives, forever and ever, in bed with me?"

I was laughing and crying, mumbling something about how I couldn't believe he proposed to me while I was naked.

"You're sort of leaving me hanging here." He chuckled nervously, his face bright and hopeful.

"Yes! Yes! Yes! I love this bed. I love you!" I let him slide the diamond band on my finger and marveled at how perfectly it settled there. Like my finger had been waiting for this exact ring. "Of course I'll marry you. Yes!"

He grabbed me then, wrapped me in his arms and kissed me, our teeth gnashing together as we kept kissing through our grins.

Doubled over on a side street nearly back at Alex's place, I tried to catch my breath while the memory cascaded over me. Matt had proposed. I had accepted. I pulled my left hand up to my face and stared at my ring finger. It was bare, like it had been ever since I woke up in the hospital, no indentation in the skin to prove a ring ever circled it.

The ring I had thought graced that finger when I woke up from the coma was a diamond solitaire—from Daniel—not a diamond band. Now I wondered if the heaviness I had felt on my finger wasn't because of the imagined jewelry from my nonexistent wedding to Daniel, but because that finger knew a different ring all along.

"You okay, lady?" A young guy with a backpack and a tight-fitting beanie cap came up beside me and bent over, peering at my face as he removed his headphones.

"I'm fine," I said, righting myself and taking a breath. "Ran a bit too hard today."

He looked dubious but then shrugged, said, "If you say so," and carried on.

"Thanks for asking," I called out after him, though he didn't glance back, likely because his headphones were now back on.

I'm not sure how long I stood on the sidewalk, replaying the memory over and over. And each time I did I felt it again—a shot of absolute conviction this was real. Matt had proposed; I had said yes.

But with each replay the questions grew. Why hadn't Matt

said anything about this? And why had no one else mentioned the engagement? Despite the memory of the proposal so clearly formed, I couldn't grasp on to anything else—had no idea what had happened next. There was no memory of telling my parents our happy news. I recalled nothing about a wedding at all—except, of course, the confabulated one I had with Daniel.

I held my hand up again, stared in disbelief as I pictured the diamond band. If Matt had put a ring on my finger, where was it now?

39

Back at Alex's place after the run and memory of Matt's proposal, I dug through the few drawers in her kitchen until I found an old take-out menu and pen—in my haste I'd forgotten my notebook at Jenny's—then sat on the bed and, with a quivering hand, wrote out the questions I needed answers to.

Did Matt propose?
Where is the ring?
Why has no one told me about this, especially Matt?
What am I going to do about it?

I nervously chewed the end of the pen while I glanced at the four questions. *I should call Matt and ask him outright*, I thought, regardless of how messed up things were right now between us. But then what? Where did that leave us? Something had happened between the proposal I remembered and my accident, and I wanted to arm myself with more information if at all possible before I talked with Matt. So I called Jenny instead.

"Lucy! Thank God! I've been calling you nonstop. Why was your phone off? What happened to you last night? Why did you disappear? Are you okay?" Her words came out in a rush, and I waited a few seconds to make sure she was done before I spoke. "Lucy? Are you there?"

"Yes, I'm here," I said. I had decided not to bring up anything about Margot, needing to focus on one thing and one thing only: my engagement to Matt. But once I heard her voice, I struggled against a rush of anger, thinking of my conversation with Margot, her pregnancy, the fact she had worked with Jenny not so long ago. With a sigh I tamped it down, would save it for another time. "Why didn't you tell me Matt and I were engaged?"

Silence. Then, "What the hell are you talking about?"

I was exasperated. "Jenny, I know Matt proposed. I *remember* it. But what I can't figure out is where the ring went, and why no one—no one at all—has said anything about it."

She drew in a deep breath and spoke slowly, yet with conviction. "Lucy, I swear to you I don't know anything about Matt proposing."

Now I was silent. *I never told Jenny Matt proposed? I was thrilled to be engaged.* I remembered the joy of it, the way it felt when he put the ring on my finger—like the world made sense in a way I hadn't before thought possible. Jenny would have been my first call, I was sure of it.

"Matt proposed? Seriously. I had no idea." She sounded like she meant it. "Maybe…maybe it's another false memory?"

"But I remember it *so clearly*." All the bubbling, joyful energy that had filled me since the memory came back disappeared, leaving my limbs heavy and my stomach churning. "It felt so real," I added weakly.

Jenny spoke carefully, gently. "I'm sure it did, Luce," she said. "But haven't all the memories felt real? You were convinced Daniel was your husband."

I frowned as I listened to her. She was right, but I wasn't ready to toss the memory of Matt's proposal in the same box with my confabulations. "I know," I replied, my tone carrying more of an edge than I intended.

"It doesn't mean it isn't real," she said. "But for sure you didn't tell me. Sorry, hon. I wish I could make all this easier for you."

"Trust me, so do I." I closed my eyes and leaned back against the pillows, my hamstrings protesting from my lack of proper cooldown after my run.

"Do you want me to come over?" she asked. Then I heard a voice—distinctly male—in the background and I realized Jenny wasn't alone.

"Sounds like you're busy. Who's there?"

She lowered her voice to nearly a whisper. "Thomas. The actor," she said. "Wait, you probably don't remember him. I'll text you the details, and a picture." She raised her voice back up to a normal level. "Are you sure you're going to be okay, Lucy?"

"Like you said, it's probably another false memory. I'm going to lock it up with the others and move on."

"Right. Sounds good," Jenny said, obviously distracted. There was a muffled whisper as she tried to continue our conversation and also speak with Thomas the actor.

"Maybe we can meet up later?" Jenny didn't respond, and I realized her focus had fully shifted to Thomas, and whatever was currently happening between them. "Listen, I'm going to go, okay?"

"Oh, sure. But I can chat more if you want. Just a lazy Sunday over here."

"Go enjoy your *lazy* Sunday," I said pointedly, which made her laugh. I was jealous of Jenny, with her overnight guest and undamaged memory. What I wouldn't give to switch places, even if only for one afternoon.

"Call me later?" she said, and then we said our goodbyes and I hung up.

I sat for a few moments, stretching my screaming hamstrings while I worked out what I wanted to do. I scrolled through my recent calls, found Matt's number and let my finger hover over the call button until the screen went black again. I tried to imagine how that conversation might go. If I'd been braver,

I would have called and asked him. If it was a false memory, it would be an awkward exchange, but then I would know, and we could go back to whatever this current state of things was. But if it *was* real...

So what if it is real? What then?

My breath came faster, because getting confirmation Matt had proposed was almost more terrifying than not knowing if I could trust the memory. We were not in a good place at the moment, and I didn't know how to fix things between us. And no matter how many ways I rolled the memory around in my mind, I kept coming back to the fact Matt had said nothing about being engaged. There had been no diamond band in the personal items bag from the hospital. No evidence anywhere of his proposal. It was almost like it had never happened.

Exactly, Lucy. Exactly.

Paralyzing depression soon crawled its way through me, replacing the antsy, breathless feeling, and in the end I called no one and asked no questions—even if Matt and I had gotten engaged, I was not the same person I had been back then. The moments that had brought us together were no longer shared. You would think the memory of his proposal would have unearthed all the right feelings, too. And to some degree it had—I loved Matt for the dependable and devoted boyfriend he was, for everything he'd done for me, for being there when I needed him, for sticking by me...but I wasn't *in love* with him. God, I wanted to be, but the truth was it was hard to be in love with two people at once. And Daniel—regardless of what I'd told him the day before, of Margot's shattering news, of the mystery that continued to surround the end of our relationship—was still inside me, taking up precious space I wished I could have given to Matt instead.

Sadly there was no list of experiences I could memorize to put Matt and me back to where we had been and send Daniel packing, no data chip I could load into my brain to reboot what had been lost. I wanted to shed the old Lucy, like a tissue-paper-thin snakeskin that would blow away with a stiff breeze. The life I used to know was gone.

Then I remembered Matt was in California for the weekend, visiting his parents and sister, and so realized our place was empty. Two hours later I had looked through every drawer and closet and cupboard, twice, but didn't find the ring. But what I did find, tucked behind a shoebox full of old receipts on a shelf in our bedroom closet, was a stack of save-the-date postcards that took my breath away, proving, once again, I had no idea who I was.

40

"We were engaged." My tone was matter-of-fact so it was clear I wasn't asking a question. It was late Sunday night and Matt had, moments earlier, walked in the door from his trip to California, back from visiting his family. I wondered what he told them about me, about us. I hoped it helped him, seeing them, having people to talk to who would always look out for him first.

Still in his coat, his overnight bag strap slung across his chest, Matt stood in the front hallway looking stunned to see me there as my words hung between us in the room.

"You're here," he finally said. Then with a sigh he took his bag from his shoulder and set it down against the wall, but he left his coat on. I was impatient for him to respond to my statement and repeated myself. Matt was silent for another long moment as he watched my face. I wondered what he saw there. "Yes, we were engaged."

"Why didn't you tell me?" I asked. It was like I was swimming and drowning all at once. I now knew for sure my memory hadn't completely failed me. Matt had put a ring on my finger and I had been happy about it. All that was good head-above-water kind of stuff. But what I didn't know was why we had kept it a secret? Why hadn't Matt said anything about it after

I came out of the coma? That was the part dragging me down below the depths.

He shrugged, his face haggard. "At first I didn't want to overwhelm you. You were having such a hard time keeping things straight and obviously didn't realize we were…engaged." He didn't need to mention Daniel; we were both thinking about him and I hated how he was still right here between us. "But then everything happened, and I wasn't sure if you would ever…" He paused, cleared his throat and looked away. "I didn't know what would happen with us, so I decided not to make things harder for you."

Then he looked at me, surprise registering on his face. "Wait…how did you find out?" When I didn't answer immediately, he kept talking. "You remember." He said it quietly, reverently. "No one else knows, so you must have remembered on your own."

I nodded, my arms tightly crossed over my chest. One of the save-the-date engagement party cards I'd found was in hand, tucked up under my armpit.

In a rush he was in the living room and standing in front of me, the space between us gone. "Oh, my God, Lucy, it's finally happening. I thought maybe, *maybe* if we went back to the beginning, started over, it might help you… Luce, this is exactly what I've been waiting for—"

I took a small, but telling, step back and his face registered confusion and then hurt. "Wait. Matt, I need to explain something. I *do* remember the proposal, everything about that night. But that's where it ends."

He tilted his head slightly, his confusion deepening. I hated what I had to say next, but it needed to be said.

"It's hard to explain, because I know how important it is that I had this memory," I began, stalling. He nodded for me to continue. "And I do remember it happening and I remember how happy I was in the moment, but my feelings for…" I paused and looked away, unable to hold his gaze.

He knew what I was trying to say; I could tell from how his face changed when I looked up at him again. Hardened against the hurt I was inflicting. I wasn't trying to be cruel, but I needed him to fully understand that while getting my memory back was significant, it was still complicated. "You remembered it, but not me, right? Not how you felt about me?"

"I know in that moment I was the happiest I'd ever been, Matt. But the person who said yes to you, well, I don't know her anymore. I only remember the versions of her that came... before. Am I making any sense?" I was trying to be gentle, but I didn't want to give him the wrong impression.

"I see," he continued, grasping the full picture now. "Do you love Daniel, Lucy?" His words were blunt and he was frowning, any joy at hearing I remembered his proposal long gone now.

"I'm still...confused about how I feel," I replied, being as honest as I could. Matt deserved more, but it was all I could offer. "Yes, my memories of Daniel haven't disappeared. But I don't want to have those feelings, Matt. Believe me."

"So you feel something for him you don't feel for me. Is that it?"

"I never wanted to hurt you." It was answer enough, and he acknowledged it as such. "I'm trying to figure things out, I am."

He seemed to be sorting out his response but then pressed his lips together and sat down hard on a kitchen table chair. "But Daniel's married, Lucy. So tell me. How does that work? You know, with this whole *figuring things out* piece."

I didn't want to talk about Daniel anymore. It was a conversation that would get us nowhere, and Matt was too hurt and angry to have a rational discussion about things—rightfully so, even if I'd never meant to hurt him, that was exactly what I had done.

I uncrossed my arms and held out the card. "I found this." He looked at it but didn't say anything.

"The date is only four weeks after my accident," I said. "So I have to ask. Why hasn't anyone said anything? Not my parents, or Alex, or Jenny, who told me she had no idea we were even engaged." I expected him to say this was yet another case of them trying to protect my now-delicate nature, not wanting to overwhelm me with details of a life I no longer recognized.

"It wasn't an engagement party, Lucy," he said, his voice low and slow, as though the effort to speak was too much.

With a frown I looked at the card, which clearly stated it was, in fact, an engagement party. Then I looked at the wording more carefully. *We're getting engaged!* Not *We got engaged!*

He shook his head. "I know that's what it says, but we were…" He stopped, lowered his face into his hands and rubbed at his cheeks and forehead. "We were going to get married."

Still I stared, frown in place. "I know. I remember the proposal."

"No," Matt said, looking up at me. "We were getting married *that* day." He gestured to the card. "It wasn't a party to celebrate our engagement. It was our wedding day."

My legs started to tingle and I had to sit down, too, worried I would collapse if I didn't. Now we faced one another at the table. "What?"

"The reason no one knows we were engaged is because we didn't tell anyone. Your mom had started dating Carl and your dad was struggling a bit, and Alex was still fairly anti-wedding after what happened with Paolo, and Jenny was frustrated by her single status, and you said you didn't want to 'rub our perfect happiness' in their faces." He used air quotes and smiled, but it wasn't on his face for long.

"Plus, having done the whole engagement thing before, you said you wanted to skip the year of fussing and fawning before the wedding. You didn't even want the white dress. You were going to wear the same dress from my parents' anniversary party." *The canary yellow A-line I had looked so cheerful in.*

I glanced at the card, which was now crumpled on one side from me squeezing it too hard. I released it onto the table, where it unfurled.

"It was your idea, and it was superspontaneous. Like, you came up with it the morning after I proposed before we had the chance to tell anyone. But I loved it. The plan was for me to mail these cards out with a note saying the party was a surprise—I was going to tell you it was an anniversary dinner or something to get you there—and I would propose in front of all our friends and family."

I tried to wrap my head around the idea that if everything had continued on as expected, Matt and I would now be married. We would be newlyweds, and ecstatic about it—in stark contrast to how we felt right now, both of us with sagging shoulders and long faces.

No matter how hard I tried I couldn't see the line leading from where Matt and I were now back to the couple we had been. Too much was different, even if much had stayed the same: Matt loving me, Matt wanting to marry me, Matt believing we could make it work if we tried hard enough. My accident broke us right down the middle, with no apparent way to stitch the frayed ends back together.

"But of course you were in on it, though no one else would know that. And then when everyone showed up for the 'Matt is popping the question' party, we were instead going to exchange vows." He sighed deeply, leaned back in his chair. "That was the plan."

"We were so, so close," I whispered.

"We were."

Sadness engulfed me as my fingers smoothed the creases on the save-the-date card's crumpled edge. "And then I hit my head."

"And then you hit your head," he said.

41

"Are you feeling better?" Dr. Kay asked. "It's a bad bug going around."

I had canceled my appointment the week before, begged off sick even though I wasn't. I couldn't face talking about Brooke or Daniel or Matt and my goddamn memory confidence, so tired of the drama and sorrow that surrounded all of it.

"I am. Thanks," I replied.

"So, Lucy, tell me—how have the past two weeks been?" she asked, settling deeper into her chair. My intention today had been to tell her everything. I needed an opinion from someone who had no stakes in this game. It was all in my notebook— carefully documented day by day so I could know for sure what was real and what wasn't, in case my memory went haywire again. But for whatever reason I couldn't pull my notebook out, wanting to keep it tucked away so I didn't have to deal with the fallout of recent events.

I knew at the very least I should mention the proposal—it was, after all, the game changer, wasn't it?—but it stayed stuck in the back of my throat. I didn't want to share it quite yet, to analyze how I was feeling about knowing Matt and I would have been married already if I hadn't slipped. Of all the memories that could have flooded back, this one felt the cruelest, because it was both critically important *and* useless. If I wasn't in love with Matt in the present, what difference did it make that I remembered saying yes to his proposal in the past?

I opted to focus on the work issue instead. "It was…interesting," I said.

She raised her eyebrows behind her tortoiseshell eyeglasses, finely tuned into my tone. "Care to elaborate?"

"Well, work was going well, until it wasn't," I began, sighing deeply as I told her about Brooke and what had happened with the press release. How I was sure she was trying to undermine my position at the firm by using my memory against me. And finally I admitted, for the first time out loud, how I was most worried Brooke wasn't completely off base.

"How so?" Dr. Kay asked.

"I thought my work life was secure. My recollection of it, I mean, because I remembered everything correctly. But it turns out I was planning to let Brooke go. The same week I had my accident. And I didn't remember a single thing about it." I rubbed my temples, pressed my fingertips in deeply.

"Would you like a glass of water, Lucy?"

I let my hands drop. "No, thanks. Just thinking things through."

"I'm not at all surprised there are a few gaps with work," Dr. Kay said. "We would expect that in a case like yours, where large chunks of your memory have been wiped out or altered."

"But it all seems so random. What I remember and what I don't," I said. "Like, I know I don't like wearing wool because it itches—I remember my grandmother knitting me a sweater when I was a kid and my mom making me wear it when we visited her despite the rash I would get. I remember all my passwords, and how to write a press release, and the names of every one of my colleagues. I also remembered why I don't like slices of lime in my drinks, but forgot I never stopped eating meat."

I was ramped up now, my words spilling out. "And apparently my body remembers I'm a runner, because I went for this unplanned jog on the weekend and it was like my feet knew exactly what to do, you know?" Dr. Kay nodded. "But I would swear on my life I had never run farther than half a block." Now I held up three fingers. "Matt told me I've run three half-marathons. Three!"

"I'm impressed," Dr. Kay said. "I once signed up for a Couch to 5k program and never made it off the couch." She smiled.

"Well, I can't remember a thing about any of the races, so did I do them?" I shook my head. "Am I a runner if I don't re-member running, even if my feet do? Am I good at my job if I can't remember the very valid reasons I was going to fire my coworker? Am I a meat eater or a vegetarian, because my brain can't seem to make up its mind? Oh, and apparently I like eggs again, after hating them for years because of a food poisoning incident I can't remember. So, which is it? Do I like eggs, or don't I?"

My questions came out quickly, my voice rising with each one. I tried to breathe into my belly but was too hopped-up to bother with the simple relaxation technique Dr. Ted had taught me in the hospital months ago. Dr. Kay watched me, stayed quiet as I took another ragged breath.

"Can I have a boyfriend if I don't remember being his girl-friend? Can I feel married even if I'm not? Who am I now if I can't remember who I was? The life I used to have doesn't exist anymore, and I have no idea how to get past that."

Dr. Kay allowed a few moments of silence to fill the room, giving me time to catch my breath, before she spoke again. "Those are tough questions, Lucy. Not because there aren't an-swers to them," she said. "But because it's not for me to say."

Tell me what to do! I wanted to shout at Dr. Kay. *Your job is to help me figure out who to be.* She shifted forward on her chair, leaning toward me. "Look, Lucy, you've made fantastic prog-ress in the short time we've been seeing each other. And I do understand it feels like you have little control over your life at the moment," she said. "You've mentioned before feeling like you're a passenger in a car, versus the driver."

I nodded. That was exactly how it felt many days.

"So what happens if you step back from everything? Stop holding yourself responsible for everyone else's happiness so you can focus on your own? Put your memory confidence list away, and think about what you want. Not what preaccident-Lucy wants, but what you want, right now. Today." She put her hand up, stopping my inevitable argument that I *obviously* had no idea. "Don't think too hard about it. What's the first thing that popped into your mind when I asked the question? What is the one thing you want, right now, more than anything else?"

The answer came to me fully and completely, no hesitation, and I quaked with the force of it. "I want to remember being in love with Matt."

"Okay. Good. And now the harder question," she said. "What if that memory is locked away forever? Then what will you do?"

I considered the question for a moment. "Then I figure out how to fall in love with him all over again."

It had seemed so obvious, what I wanted to do about Matt, when Dr. Kay asked me during our session. But once I got outside her building and had a moment to think it through, I felt paralyzed. Matt and I had tried—really tried—hadn't we? There were the photo albums, the reminiscence therapy, the play-by-play re-creation of our first date. So much effort for such little return. Shouldn't I feel *something* more by now, even if my memory wasn't back?

And then, in a flash, I realized the problem. Matt had really tried, that was true. But what about me? Could I say the same?

No, I couldn't. While Matt did everything he could think of to jog my memory, all the while accepting it might never work but sticking by me nonetheless, I played along but kept one foot outside the circle. I had allowed myself to stay distracted—mostly by Daniel—and that had hurt all of us, but Matt especially.

Dr. Kay's office was beside a parkette, and I had a sudden urge to take off my shoes and walk barefoot in the grass. Jenny was working on a documentary on something called "earthing"—walking barefoot on dirt, or sand, or grass, or some other natural surface—to eke out electrons from the earth. It sounded a bit (a lot) out-there, but its proponents swore to a host of benefits: everything from generating feelings of happiness to reducing anxiety to helping with insomnia, and Jenny had been pretty psyched about the whole thing. Told me she'd been doing it every day for fifteen minutes at the park near her work, and felt ridiculously joyful afterward; she suggested maybe it could help with my memory. "But if not, trust me, you'll still feel fantastic."

And for whatever reason, it seemed like exactly the right thing to do at this moment. So I sat on the bench, took off my shoes and rolled up my pant legs into wide cuffs. Then I started walking, the soles of my feet initially ticklish as they settled into the grass. Soon I was walking in a large circle around the grassy parkette, furiously typing a message to Matt on my phone as I did.

My ten minutes of earthing didn't jog my memory or change my life, but as I slipped grass-stained feet back into my shoes I reread my message to Matt. Then with a grin, I hit Send.

42

After sending Matt the text, I walked back to the office while I waited for him to respond (what was taking him so long?), and with every block closer, the more my anxiety ramped up. Because while I had made a decision about Matt—which I couldn't do anything about until I heard back from him—I'd also made one about the Brooke situation.

All weekend I had been running scenarios through my mind, everything from backing off and biding my time until I could build up examples showcasing Brooke's incompetency, to going into HR today with a printout of my grievances and a plan to replace her. But none had sat quite right with me. I didn't want to work indefinitely with someone who was gunning for my job, and willing to use my accident and aftereffects to get it. Nor did I want to end my time at the firm by marching into HR and ruining all the goodwill I'd built up. Unless I had hard proof, going in and accusing Brooke of such a thing would be the equivalent of career suicide.

It was Dr. Kay, again, who helped me figure out what to do in the end. The whole "it's time to get back in the driver's seat" thing had been effective, and I appreciated how right she was. I had been waiting—for someone else to sort out my mess, for my memory to reboot, for an obvious answer to every difficult

question to be revealed, to get back to the Lucy I had been before the slip and fall. And by letting everyone else—my parents,
Jenny, Alex, Brooke, Daniel and Matt—drive the car for me,
things had gotten seriously off track.

"Even though I know nothing about cars," Dr. Kay had said
with a laugh at the end of our session. "Let's stick with this
analogy for a moment. You, Lucy Sparks, have the map. You
always have—it's been inside you all along, even if you can't
remember every street name, or shortcut, or which route is
free of construction delays. So when you're feeling confused,
or angry, or lost, remember—*you have the map.*"

It was time to make my own choices, and good or bad I would
deal with them. Finally back at the office, I answered outstanding messages and emails, shared a quick coffee with Mary in the
break room, then typed out the letter I'd been writing in my
head for the past couple of hours.

"Lucy, hello," Greg said when I knocked on his door later
that afternoon. "Come on in." He gestured at the chairs in the
sitting nook in his office and got up from his desk to join me
as I sat down.

"How are you doing?" he asked, his brow crinkling.

"Well. Thanks for asking," I replied. Then I got right to it,
didn't want to spend time on idle chitchat knowing what had
to come next. "This isn't easy for me, Greg, because I've loved
working here. And I wanted to tell you directly because you've
been a great mentor to me over the years." Without another
word I handed him the envelope, which he opened, unfolding
the letter inside. I watched his face as he read the short note,
which I had signed only minutes earlier, hoping I was doing
the right thing.

"I have another copy for HR, which I'll drop off to Susan
after we're done here," I said. Greg folded the letter and nodded.
"I also wanted you to know I'm not leaving Jameson Porter for

another firm. This isn't about me being unhappy with my job, or this place."

"And I don't suppose I can change your mind?" he asked.

I shook my head. "I appreciate you'd even try," I said. "I know it's been difficult, having me out for so long and then only back for a couple of weeks."

"Is there anything we could have done differently, Lucy?" I suspected a similar question would come from Susan, but the tone would be different. From Greg it was meant as an almost-apology—the timing of my resignation so close to my return, he was concerned they had let me down by reintegrating me too quickly. But Susan would be worried I had already had an informal conversation with an employment attorney.

"Nothing at all. You've all been wonderful," I said. "And not just recently. For the past four years, too." I stood and held out my hand, which Greg shook warmly. "Thank you for the opportunity."

"Thank you, Lucy. We're going to miss you around here. Especially me. No one writes up a report quite like you do." He smiled.

"Well, you still have me for two weeks, so it's not goodbye yet." I returned his smile. "I do have a couple of suggestions for who might be a great fit for the job. And Brooke will be a fantastic resource for whomever you choose. You'll definitely want to keep her where she is. I would have been lost without her help these past couple of months."

"That's good to hear," Greg said, and if he sensed anything other than my absolute support for Brooke, he didn't show it. "And I agree. Why don't you put some thoughts together and let's have lunch later this week to discuss. Sound like a plan?"

"It does," I said, thanking him again before leaving his office and heading to Susan's. After I gave her the other copy of my resignation letter—Susan *was* glad to hear I didn't have any formal grievances to file—I went back to my office, smiling at Brooke when I stopped by her door.

"Hey, Brooke, thanks again for handling that release for Greg the other day. Glad we caught it before the outlets turned it around." I cringed for effect. "It would have been a nightmare."

"No problem at all," she said. "Happy to help."

Then I frowned, gave her a confused look. "But the strangest thing about that. It was a duplicate. For some reason a few of my recent releases all had old client names in them, and I found two versions of each. Any idea what happened there? I mean, you *were* the one who sent it to Greg for me, so I thought maybe you might know."

"I have no idea," she said, her frown matching mine. I could tell she knew I was onto her, but was working hard to hide it. "That is strange. Maybe it was a program bug?"

"Maybe." I waved my hand, as if shelving my concern. "But no worries. I figured it out and fixed them, and explained everything to Greg and Susan. I'm sure it won't happen again."

"Oh, let's hope not." She looked somewhat stunned, which, I have to say, made it even easier to smile.

"See you for the meeting at three?" I said, and she nodded mutely, realizing she was being dismissed. I felt great as I settled back into my office—I was liking this new, in-control Lucy and considered maybe it was some sort of electron magic from my mini earthing experiment—and then my phone buzzed in my pocket.

Excited (and nervous) that Matt had finally gotten back to me, I grabbed for my phone and read the message. But it wasn't from Matt; it was from Daniel.

I need to talk to you. Please come over tonight—9:00 p.m. I'm here alone.

He had written his address and closed the message with two simple words.

Please come.

And though I knew I shouldn't have gone, I found myself standing outside Daniel London's house and ringing the doorbell at 8:58 p.m.

43

As soon as the front door opened I knew I'd made a mistake.

"Hi again, Lucy."

At first I was too shocked to say anything. Stood statue-still on Daniel's front porch—a swing full of nautical-themed striped outdoor pillows (nicer than the ones on my couch at home) to my left, a large urn filled with winter greenery and white sparkling orbs on the right. It was a small house but gorgeous—the kind you'd find in a *House & Home* magazine, the clear touches of a skilled designer visible everywhere.

"Margot. Oh. Hi." My mind raced for a way to explain why I was here, on Daniel and Margot's front porch, late on a Monday night. I came up blank. Margot stared at me, unsmiling, and I wondered if I should turn around and walk away. But then she smiled and seemed to come out of the trancelike state from a moment earlier. "Come in, come in," she said, ushering me inside.

If I thought the house was beautiful from the outside, I was in awe of its interior. Sweeping ceilings, intricate crown molding, beautiful art, everything in its place. Definitely magazine-spread-worthy. "Your home is stunning."

"Aw, thank you," Margot replied, glancing over her shoulder as she hung my coat up on one of five antique brass hangers by the door. "Daniel and I did almost everything ourselves." I hadn't meant to give her my coat—had no intentions of staying—but was still in shock from finding Margot on the other side of the door, and my reaction times were off. "I baked some buttermilk blueberry muffins. Cravings." She smiled again and rubbed her stomach, then gestured for me to follow her into the kitchen.

For a moment I stood by the front door, unsure what to do, but then I quickly unzipped my boots and followed her. The kitchen was clearly the central spot of their home—a large square island of white marble right in the middle, reclaimed wood stools lining one side. Two dozen muffins—striped and spotted where deep purple blueberry juice had oozed out during baking—sat on cooling racks on the island, and the sink was full of neatly stacked dishes yet to be washed. Margot took two plates from the cupboard and set a muffin on each one, handing me a plate even though I didn't say I wanted a muffin and was pretty sure I wouldn't be able to eat it.

Where was Daniel?

She sat on one of the stools and took a big bite of muffin, blueberry juice staining her fingers and a corner of her mouth. "These are so much better with fresh blueberries, but frozen will do in a pinch." She took another bite, then stopped chewing. "Sit. Eat," she said. "Are you going to make a pregnant woman enjoy her muffin alone?"

"Sorry, no. Thanks." I sat down awkwardly two stools over and broke off a small piece of muffin, which was still warm. I ate it, despite my nerves making it nearly impossible to swallow anything but my own saliva, and told her how delicious it was. "Maybe I can get the recipe," I said, trying to break the icy tension hovering between us. Margot seemed happy I asked, and smiled wide as she wiped a crumb from her lip.

"Totally. I'll email it to you." Then she put her muffin down. "Better still, I'll text it to you right now." And she pulled her phone out of her back pocket.

"Do you need my number?" I asked, but she shook her head.

"Already have it," she replied, which was odd. I wondered how—did I give it to her at the party the other night?

I was about to tell her there was no rush, but she seemed determined to send the recipe immediately and so I stayed quiet and nibbled another piece of muffin while she tapped out the message. She paused only once to stare up to the ceiling as she mumbled about whether it was one teaspoon or one tablespoon of baking soda. "And...done." She put her phone down and I felt mine buzz in my sweater's pocket.

She raised her eyebrows. "Aren't you going to check that? Make sure it came through okay?" It didn't seem like she was asking—more like demanding I do it—so I pulled my phone out and was quite certain all the blood in my face drained when I saw what was on the screen. A message from Daniel.

Margot's Buttermilk Blueberry Muffins

I quickly looked up at Margot, my heart beating so fast it was all I could do not to press both hands to my chest to keep it from exploding from my chest.

She popped the last bite of muffin in her mouth and held up the phone, the one she'd used to send me the text with the recipe. For a moment I stared while she chewed and swallowed, then with her next words everything fell into place.

"Daniel's phone," she said, pulling another muffin from the cooking rack. "Want a second one?" I shook my head slowly and she shrugged, placing the muffin on her own plate.

"I know what you're thinking," Margot said, carefully tugging the parchment paper wrapper from the muffin. "Why did I send you a message about meeting me—or Daniel, I guess—here?" She licked her fingers of the blueberry juice.

"I know what happened on Saturday, at the Maddy," she said. Then she sighed. "Danny told me yesterday." *Danny?* "When I mentioned seeing you at the party and that I'd told you about the baby, well, he sort of broke down then. He felt terrible about the whole thing." Her elbow knocked a few muffins off the cooling rack. "What a mess," she muttered, using a nearby cloth to clean up the purple smudges before they ruined the white marble. I wasn't sure if she was referring to the muffin splatter, or the entire situation.

"Margot, I don't know—" My mind couldn't move quickly enough, and even if it could, what would I have said? *I don't know what happened. I didn't mean to. It's complicated.*

"Stop. It's fine," she said, which confused me even more. "Of course, I'm not happy about it." Her lips moved into a frown to prove her words. "But there's been no real harm done." And back to her muffin she went.

I swallowed hard and coughed when some of the muffin crumbs got caught in my throat. Margot took a glass off the open shelf by the sink, then turned on the faucet and let the water run. She held one finger in the stream and, when she was satisfied with the temperature, filled the glass and handed it to me.

"Thanks," I said. I took a big sip and the cold water moved the muffin bit along.

"Look, I'm not blaming you," she said, back on her stool. "You know how Danny is," she said. *How he is?*

"Sorry, I'm not sure…what you mean." *Thump, thump, thump* went my heart. I took another sip of water, trying to calm down.

"Ah, that's right. The whole memory thing. Yeah, Danny told me about that, too. I'm sorry you're going through this, Lucy. It sounds terrible." She paused then, gave me a knowing look. "What I meant is it's not like either of us should be surprised you and Daniel *reconnected.* He's always been a flirt. He got caught up." She shrugged, continuing on with her second muffin, and I thought back to Alex's comment about the pretty bartender at our engagement party. The fact Daniel had been engaged when I met him. The picture grew clearer…

"Margot, do you know why Daniel and I broke up?" My voice quavered, but I held her gaze.

Her face stayed still for a moment, and then…a nod. "I take it you don't remember?"

"I do not," I said. "Are…are *you* the reason we broke up?" This last part came out quietly and I held my breath. Waiting for the answer no one had yet been able—or willing—to give me.

I expected her to say, *Yes. I'm sorry, yes.* To tell me Daniel had been unfaithful, the two of them hooking up behind my back a couple of months before our wedding, and I steeled myself for her response. When she finally answered, I detected a hint of pity in her tone. "No."

"No…?"

"You've got it backward," she added softly. "It wasn't because of me, Lucy. I swear to you."

I nodded, because I needed her to go on but couldn't trust my voice.

"Danny and I started dating about six months after you guys broke up. I had been in Ecuador, volunteering as a translator with an entomologist friend of mine, so I was pretty off the grid." I thought back to the wedding I remembered, tried to picture Margot there but couldn't. Of course, the wedding hadn't been real, but I understood now why I couldn't place her in any of my memories around that time—she hadn't even been in the country.

"I ended up with malaria, came back earlier than expected and ran into Danny at an art exhibit a couple of months later. We started dating, I went to design school and he left his father's firm and then we got married and, well, here we are."

At her explanation a sense of calm settled over me. There was no malicious story here, at least not when it came to Margot. But then I remembered something. "Wait…you said I got it backward. What did you mean?"

"Lucy, I'm not sure it's my place to tell you this." Margot seemed uncomfortable, and I moved to the edge of my stool, wanting to get closer to her. To the truth. "I know you don't remember, because of your accident, but, well, maybe it's better that way?"

My body quivered with the adrenaline, the pent-up tension from being on edge. "*Please*, Margot. I have to know what happened."

She pushed her second half-eaten muffin away, fiddled with the wedding rings on her finger. Sighed deeply before speaking. "I said you had it backward, Lucy, because Daniel didn't cheat on you. You cheated on him."

I gasped, nearly fell off the stool as the shock moved through me.

I cheated on Daniel? I would never have done something like that. "You're lying." My words shook along with my body. Of course Margot was angry about what happened between Daniel and me, but this was taking things too far.

But she shook her head, and the look on her face told me this was the absolute truth. "What reason do I have to lie, Lucy? We used to be friends. I wouldn't do that to you. Especially not now, with everything you're dealing with.

"I appreciate how difficult this must be to hear, and I'm sorry to have to be the one to tell you. But *you're* the reason you and Daniel broke up." She looked sad, whether for me to be hearing the truth this way or because of what I'd done to her husband I couldn't be sure.

"Do you—" I gulped back the rest of the sentence, then tried again. "Do you know who it was, uh, with?"

"I don't, and I don't think Daniel did, either. Or at least he never mentioned a name. Just some guy."

Just some guy. I had cheated on my fiancé with "some guy." Who does that?

"Danny was devastated, though to be fair to you he wasn't the easiest to be with. Especially back then. He was pretty unhappy with work, and his dad wouldn't let up on him. It wasn't the best time of his life."

"He told you all this?" I was breathless, trying to catch up.

Tried to accept I had known this all along—that it still lived inside my memory even if it couldn't be recalled. I was also incredibly embarrassed for how I'd acted with Daniel, for confusing him with my kisses and affections. It amazed me he'd even spoken to me that first night, when we'd run into each other outside Jake's party.

"When things started getting more serious with us, he told me what happened. And so you know, he did feel partly responsible. Like I said, he was a flirt. He drank too much. He wasn't always kind with his words." She gave an apologetic smile. "He's put the work in, has come a long way. He's a good husband, Lucy."

I saw in her face then how much she loved Daniel. Had already forgiven him for what happened on Saturday, accepted his apology and explanation because they had both history and a future to focus on.

"I'm so sorry," I said, welling up. "I…I had no idea. I don't remember any of that." My breath caught and this time I did press a hand to my chest. She reached out and held my arm gently.

"Can I ask you something?"

"Okay." I nodded, still trembling a little with the aftereffects of shock.

"Do you love him? Like, love him again?"

I answered quickly so she wouldn't read anything into my hesitation. "No. I don't think I do."

It was a lie, but it was the right thing to say.

"Good," she said, letting go of my arm. She swiped a few crumbs off the counter with her napkin and then folded it onto her plate. "I hope you understand, and I wish things could be different, but we probably shouldn't do this again." She laid a hand on her belly and I understood how hard this must have been for her, asking me here tonight. Margot needed to move forward with Daniel as much as I needed to move farther away from him.

"Of course." I stood on shaky legs, grateful to have the counter's edge for support.

At the door I thought she might hug me, but instead she offered her hand. The formality felt strange, yet it was the right choice for the moment as we were essentially strangers now. At one time we had been friends, but that was a long time ago. I shook her outstretched hand, my palm clammy against hers. "Good luck, Lucy."

"You, too, Margot." And then she shut the door and I stood on her front porch, realizing I had better sit down for a minute before I passed out. So I was on the swing, leaning against the multitude of pillows and trying not to hyperventilate, when I felt another buzz in my pocket. With shaking hands I pulled out my phone. It was the message I'd been waiting for from Matt, and my heart sank with his three simple words.

I'll be there.

44

I didn't sleep all night after I got back to Alex's from my visit with Margot. Didn't even try, just sat in the one chair in her place and watched the sky transform from dark to dawn. I contemplated canceling on Matt. Almost did many times before it was seven in the morning and, by then, far too late.

Things had been so clear before Daniel's message—or rather, before Margot lured me to her place under the guise of an invitation from Daniel. What might have happened if I'd ignored it? Texted back a curt and definitive I can't. Please don't ask me again. If I had done that, I'd be filled with excitement this morning versus exhaustion and dread, but I also would never have learned the truth. And it was significant, as hard as it had been to hear, that I had been the one to end my engagement. I had been the one to hurt Daniel when I changed our course, not the other way around.

By 7:15 a.m. I was sitting on the curb outside the capybara pen in the High Park Zoo, a take-out tray with two coffees (black for Matt, sugar and cream for me) and two egg and bacon sandwiches greasing up the paper bag beside me. The sun was finally out, and the park was quiet except for the odd early-morning jogger. I anxiously tapped my feet, my arms wrapped around my knees as I waited. It wasn't warm this early in the morning quite yet, and so I blew into my bare hands to counteract their chilliness. I saw Matt then, riding his bike through the zoo's path and heading toward me. I jumped to my feet, nearly upsetting the tray of coffees balanced on the curb's edge, and waved, shouting his name, though it was unnecessary to do so—Matt and I were the only ones here.

He got off his bike a few feet from me, the grin on his face tightening the knots in my stomach. "Hey, Luce," he said. "Fancy meeting you here." Unclipping his helmet, he hung it on the handlebar of his bike, which he leaned against a nearby bench.

"Here. Breakfast," I said, smiling as I handed him the coffee and one of the wrapped sandwiches. "Bacon and egg from the Grenadier. I'm having the same."

He looked surprised. "You're eating an egg?"

"Oh, right. I didn't tell you. Turns out I don't remember the whole food-poisoning thing." I shrugged. "So I like eggs. Again."

"No kidding," he murmured, opening the sandwich and taking a bite. "Thanks. This is exactly what I needed." But as he said it he gave me a look that told me he wasn't talking about breakfast.

"I'm glad," I said.

Matt set his coffee down so he could take off his messenger bag. "Listen, I'm not sure exactly why we're here at the capybaras at seven in the morning, and I have no idea if I'm going to leave here glad I came or wishing I hadn't." He bent down to balance his partially eaten sandwich on the lid of his coffee cup, then stood again. "But can I say something first?"

I nodded, wrapped my arms around my body and did a few little jumps to warm up.

"Cold?" he asked.

"A bit," I replied, and then there was a moment of silence as he watched me and I watched him, the couple of feet between us like a giant chasm. But then I felt it—the distinct magnetic pull between us, as strong as the one that had repelled me from Daniel's lips under the Maddy's awning. I took a step toward him, said, "What did you want to say?"

"Okay, first? I love you." He closed the gap between us, held my chilled hands. I wasn't prepared for him to open with this, for how intensely his words would pierce me, and my knees started to shake. "It's both that simple and that complicated. Nothing has changed for me, but I know *everything* is different for you.

"But while you don't remember us, we do have history, Lucy. I know things about you no one else does. Like how you cry every single time an animal rescue meme hits your Facebook stream. Or that you wear your underwear inside out on days when you need a bit of good luck, because once you did it by accident and something great happened and so you decided it had to be the underwear thing."

I smiled, pulled one hand out from his to wipe my tears. *Oh, I don't deserve you, Matt.*

"I know when you're sick you like to be left alone. 'Throw a Gatorade in here, some ibuprofen, and then go—I'm disgusting and you don't need to see disgusting,' you said the last time you had a stomach bug. I *remember* you take your coffee with cream and sugar, that you prefer red over white wine, that you hate hockey but watch the games with me because you know how much I love it, that you have a surprisingly large collection of scarves for someone who doesn't like wearing them because they make you claustrophobic. You love your work but sometimes wish you'd gone the creative route with your writing instead."

The tears were hot against my cheeks and I didn't bother to wipe them away. How could I possibly tell him what I needed to after this?

"I remember all these things, Luce, even if you don't. So maybe right now we only have my memories to count on, but that's okay." He clutched my fingers tightly and pulled me closer, only inches apart now. His voice dropped to a near-whisper, but it didn't lose any of its intensity. "I don't care if you remember being married to Daniel. I honestly don't care... I love you. And I believe you love me, too." He laid one palm flat against my chest and pressed gently. "I know I'm still in here, Lucy. I know it."

I wondered if he could feel how quickly my heart was beating. I took a deep breath. "I quit my job."

He gave me a confused look, pulled back a little and shook his head. "What? When?"

"Yesterday. And I cheated on Daniel."

Now a full step back. His hand dropped from my chest. "What the hell are you talking about?"

"Matt, that Lucy you remember? The one who cried at dog rescue memes and wore her underwear inside out and hated eggs and said yes when you asked her to marry you?" I shook my head, pulled in a ragged breath. "You don't know her the way you think you do. She cheated on her fiancé, apparently with some random guy. She is not the person you think she is."

Matt's jaw clenched and he took a deep breath through his nose. I wasn't sure if he was going to cry, or yell at me. "Why are you telling me this?"

"Because you are kind and decent and the best boyfriend, and you deserve more than this shit show, Matt. You deserve better than me—both past *and* present."

His mouth dropped open. "You brought me here to break up with me?" His face reddened and he scrubbed a hand through his hair. "What the hell, Lucy? Why did you even bother?"

I stepped right up to him and brought his hands to my chest again, held them tightly in my own. "No, when I sent that message, my plan was to propose we start over. Like, at the beginning. And not re-creating our first dates but to make new memories together. To see what might happen if we did."

"Okay, yes! Let's do that. That's what I want, too."

I shook my head. "But then I found out about what I'd done to Daniel, and I knew—" My breath caught and, oh, the way he looked at me. So full of hurt and anger I wanted to take it all back, to erase everything I said that made him look at me this way. "I knew it wasn't fair to you. I have no idea if I'm ever going to remember us the way you do, and even if I do, I won't be the same person I was before. The person you wanted to spend the rest of your life with.

"I know you miss her," I whispered. He wouldn't look at me now. "I miss her, too, Matt. I wish she would come back. But there's a good chance she's gone for good. And you deserve better."

"You keep saying that, but what if that's not what I want?" Matt said, his voice gruff. "Why do you get to choose what I deserve, or don't?" He looked depressed, and lost, having been forced into a holding pattern all this time. Matt hadn't yet mourned the loss of our relationship, and even if we had found our way back somehow, it would never be the same as it had been.

"There's nothing connecting us except for our past, Matt. And no matter how much I wish it weren't true, only one of us remembers that." I pressed his knuckles to my lips and held them there for a long moment, then let go, already walking backward, away from him.

"I'm sorry. For everything. Please don't hate me," I said, then turned my back to him and broke into a run.

45

It rained the day I became Mrs. Lucy Sparks Newman.

I had hoped for sunshine, a positive sign of what lay ahead. But the rain was better, I realized as we huddled under the wide, clear umbrella Matt held while we exchanged vows as planned. The minister stood dry under her own umbrella, its see-through surface speckled with the fat raindrops, while our guests gathered in rows under the Old Mill's awning to watch the ceremony from afar. The rain was better than sun because it meant Matt and I didn't have to share the moment with anyone—even the minister couldn't hear the words we uttered, for the deep dome of our umbrella created a bubble just for us.

Matt made me sweet promises as he slipped the plain gold ring onto my finger, where it nestled against the diamond engagement band I'd started wearing nearly a year earlier. Then it was my turn, and I cried when I slid the matching band over his knuckle—blubbered actually, though later Matt would say I'd shed only one gorgeous tear when I'd said my vows. I laughed at that, teasingly said, "I thought we were done with making stuff up?" and he smiled. Told me if I got to have false memories, then it was only fair for him to have a couple, as well.

I love you, Lucy Sparks Newman, he'd said, after we shared our first kiss as husband and wife.

I love you more, Matt Newman. And no one would convince me otherwise.

Soon after, Matt was twirling me around a packed dance floor, full of our family and friends. I'd never felt so completely alive, or happy or certain about anything. To think of how close I came to missing out on all of it…

I had tried to walk, or rather run, away from Matt that day in High Park. To give him a chance to start over and make new memories with someone else, rather than be forced to try to puzzle back together a relationship that died the moment I hit my head. But I only got as far as the zoo's entrance before he caught up to me, his legs much longer and faster than mine. Told me he didn't care about what I'd done with Daniel, or who that Lucy was. He knew me and loved me and believed in us more than he'd believed in anything else. *I have enough faith for the both of us, Luce,* he had said. *Do you trust me?* I did. So I decided to follow Dr. Kay's advice about choosing the future I wanted, even if it didn't seem to fit with what was happening in my present. And so, with that, I chose Matt.

I never got all my memories back. I still don't remember what happened the day I slipped and fell, and the gaping holes in the years preceding it remain, though I have since memorized critical details of that time. Can talk about them as though they are memories versus facts I've learned and, well, committed to memory. The reminiscence therapy Matt started, and Dr. Kay and I continued, did help me recover somewhat. But even with therapy I realized I wasn't remembering the original experience—I was recollecting a construct of it. And, in fact, a construct of someone else's construct, because like Dr. Kay explained during our first visit, no one's memory was one hundred percent accurate. We all confabulate to some degree. And so I've accepted that my memories—all our memories, actually—are little more than fiction. The present is far more reliable than the past.

After resigning from Jameson Porter, I started my own communications business—Sparks + Co—doing freelance public relations work for anyone who would hire me. So far I was founder, president and the only employee of my company, but I did have a virtual assistant for when projects started to stack up. And if things kept going as well as they were, I'd have the money to hire an associate in the next year. It was nice, starting over. None of my clients knew about the accident, or what I had lost because of it, and it was a relief not to worry about what I might have forgotten. I was all about the new memories now.

But while starting over was great, it hadn't completely eliminated the anxiety about my memories. Especially the fragile ones I had only recently gotten back. I worried about going to bed one night and waking up with blank holes again. The pliancy of my memory only affording me so much stretch, like a vacuum cord that seemed to unwind longer than possible until the moment it snapped, ripping the plug out of the wall. The doctors assured me it was unlikely to happen now, losing more memories, unless I was to hit my head again. So I took precautions, just in case. I wore grippy-soled winter books at the first sign of cold and kept a log of the best part of every day in a notebook in case anything were to happen my history would still exist in my own words.

Some days were harder than others, accepting what had transpired over the past year. But most days were better.

Interestingly enough I still had guilt when eating meat and had seriously flirted with vegetarianism a few times over the past couple of months. Jenny told me there's an eighty-eight percent chance I'll be vegan by Christmas, and she might be right even if I would desperately miss bacon. I still cannot recall my parents telling me the first time they'd split up, or that I had been ready to fire Brooke the week I had my accident, or how I cheated on Daniel with a random guy who ended having no place in my future but was quite important to ending ours. But none of it mattered anymore because of what I *did* remember.

I may not be able to recollect falling in love with Matt the first time, but I remember everything about the second time it happened. I can't explain why the memory of Matt's proposal sneaked back into what I'm calling my "lost years," but I'm grateful it did. Because while little else of our relationship was retrievable, that became enough. It was the pivot point, and the foundation onto which we would build. It was the memory that single-handedly brought us to the moment under the rain-splattered umbrella on our wedding day, when a huge gust of wind nearly turned it inside out and Matt whooped as he grabbed for the umbrella, saying the weather was obviously sending us a sign.

This is our real Gone with the Wind moment, he added. To which I whispered back, because I didn't want the minister to know we were talking when we were supposed to be listening, preparing for our vows, *Like, the movie?* He laughed then, kissed me even though the minister hadn't yet told us we could, and a few guests clapped enthusiastically, thinking it was *the* kiss.

No, not the movie. The Halloween costume that started it all. Remember?

I didn't remember. It was lost along with so much else. But I knew it had happened—could practically picture every detail because it was one of Matt's favorite stories to tell—and that was enough.

★ ★ ★ ★ ★

ACKNOWLEDGMENTS

Thanks to everyone, for everything.

This was almost the shortest acknowledgments section in history! However, I would be remiss not to mention some folks who have made this book possible. So like Lucy's memory confidence list, here is my Thank You For Making This Novel Better list:

Michelle Meade, who always gives my words, and my confidence, a boost.

Carolyn Forde, my sidekick from the beginning of this adventure.

Shara Alexander (and team), who tirelessly promote me and my novels, and who introduced me to Moscow Mules—Dark and Stormy's cousin.

Randy Chan (and team), for the creative and inspired ways my books get into readers' hands.

Erika Imranyi, whose Tweet about a twenty-nine-year-old North London man who after a bike accident woke up from a coma with fantastical, yet false, memories left me asking "what if?"—the question that starts every one of my stories.

Rohit Bhapkar, who kindly gave me his valuable time and insights, making this story, and its setting, more authentic.

Jennifer Robson, Marissa Stapley, Kate Hilton, Liz Renzetti,

Chantel Guertin, my strong and talented author friends who make it possible to survive—and thrive—in this business.

Amy E. Reichert and Colleen Oakley, who always read my early words and tell me "You've got this!"—even when we all know I don't.

The Tall Poppies, the most supportive group of women an author could ask for.

Harlequin and HarperCollins, whose combined vision, talents and enthusiasm for my books mean I can continue doing this thing I love.

In researching this book, I found *The Memory Illusion* by Dr. Julia Shaw to be particularly enlightening in explaining exactly how our memory does—and doesn't—work. However, this story, its characters and their experiences are entirely fictional and fabricated, and so any errors in wording or description are mine alone.

To my readers, author pals and the tireless book bloggers, your continued support and engagement make getting up at 5:00 a.m. to write the easiest decision of my day.

Finally, to my friends and family, especially the ones who put up with my writing schedule and at-times-frenetic author brain (Adam, Addison), I could thank you with every book (and I will), but it will never be enough.

There is always the fear of forgetting to thank someone, and writing a memory-themed novel—whose research taught me our memories are surprisingly unreliable—has only increased that worry...so if I forgot to thank you, I'm sorry, and, well, thank you!

THE LIFE
LUCY KNEW

KARMA BROWN

Reader's Guide

PARK
ROW
BOOKS

1. As fantastical as Lucy's situation seems, the truth is that our memories are unreliable and not as secure as we'd like to believe. If you were in a similar situation to Lucy's, how do you think you would cope? How much value do you place on the strength of your memory?

2. Lucy's family and friends keep a few big secrets from her in hopes that it will make her recovery easier. Do you think this was the right approach? Would the full truth have made things easier or harder for Lucy?

3. Even though Lucy's memories of her marriage to Daniel aren't real, it's easy to understand why she is so confused about her feelings toward him. Were you ever rooting for her and Daniel to end up together? How did you feel when they eventually kissed?

4. Were you surprised by the reason behind Daniel and Lucy's real breakup? Did it change your opinion of Lucy—or of Daniel?

5. Matt is incredibly patient with Lucy after her accident and with her false memories. Did you ever feel Lucy was taking advantage of his loyalty?

6. If you were in Matt's position, do you think you would handle the situation the same or differently?

7. Did you agree with Lucy's decision to find happiness in the end with Matt?

8. What is one of the most significant memories of your life? Have you ever wondered if you've embellished this memory over time, or how accurate it is? And does it even matter?

9. If you had to create a memory confidence list, what would be on it? What specific details would it be important for you to remember about yourself in a situation like Lucy's?

Lucy's experience with confabulated memory disorder is a unique take on the familiar theme of amnesia in fiction. What was the inspiration for her story? Is memory confabulation real?

I read a Boston Globe article about a twenty-nine-year-old North London man who had a bike accident, and after waking from his medically induced coma, he had all these fantastical made-up memories. Like many people I've told about this story, I had no idea this was a real condition! Or just how complex and unreliable our memories really are. As I read the piece I thought, "What if this happened to me?" and almost instantly Lucy's character started to take shape...

The relationships Lucy has with Daniel and Matt are both very complicated—she remembers intimate details of her life with Daniel that never really happened while forgetting the truth about her deep connection with Matt. As you were shaping the story, did you find yourself rooting for one relationship over the other, and did you ever consider giving her the happily-ever-after she initially craves with Daniel?

It was an interesting love triangle to write, not only because of the false memories that produced it but also because it allowed me to explore the idea of choice, and creating our own happiness—like how Lucy's therapist tells her, "You have the right to change your present if it doesn't fit with the future you envision." As for who got the happy ending with Lucy, it was always going to be Matt. But I wasn't going to make it easy for her to realize that!

You finished *The Life Lucy Knew* **by doing something very different from your previous novels: including an epilogue with a happy ending! Can you tell us about your decision to finish the story this way?**

I have, so far, finished my novels with what my editor and I like to call "satisfying" endings. Meaning by that last page, readers will probably have cried (in some books, quite a lot) but will also see a glimmer of hope for the characters despite what they've endured. However, I knew from the beginning this book had to be different in how it ended—a glimmer wasn't going to cut it for Lucy. Because while I'm (mostly) the driver when it comes to my characters' decisions, sometimes they take the wheel and we veer in another direction. This is a perfect example of that phenomenon.

What was your greatest challenge in writing *The Life Lucy Knew*? **What about your greatest pleasure?**

One of the greatest challenges was how to write authentically from inside Lucy's head when she wasn't sure which memories were real and which ones she had confabulated. Also, keeping the interactions between the characters from feeling contrived. I told my editor early on to keep an eye out for overtly cheesy moments, but a couple may have slipped in because, well, I've learned a little cheese isn't the worst thing. The greatest pleasure? Writing Lucy her happily-ever-after ending.

Tell us about your writing process.

I am always knee-deep in story ideas, often inspired by people in unique and mind-boggling situations, like the man with the false memories. And once I have an idea I can't stop thinking about—and usually the beginnings of a character who won't stop chattering to me—I write down a formal pitch for the story, always starting with a "what if?" question. If I can't answer that question, I know the story *doesn't (yet) have legs. Then I craft a full synopsis and outline for the idea, including its main players, and only then do I get to work on the actual writing. It's a long process that involves much coffee and staring off into space and endless internet searches and loads of self-doubt and plenty of evenings where I ask (force) my husband to brainstorm scenarios. It's a lot of work, but I'd be lying if I didn't also say it was a lot of fun.*